BRINLEY'S SAVIOR

A No Surrender Novel # 2

C.M. YOUNGREN

Enjoy ♥
C. M. Youngren

Cover Design by
AVERY KINGSTON
Edited by
ANGEL NYX

DEDICATION

This book goes out to my mom. If you have kids then you know as well as I do that parenting is no walk in the park. I am lucky to have brought up my girls in a two parent household.

My mother, however, was a single mother who raised me on her own. Sure, she had a wonderful family support system, but she worked her behind off to love, protect, and provide for me the very best she could.

The sacrifices—a word she never once used—that she made along the way because I know there were some, make me feel cherished.

She did a fabulous job. I mean I think I turned out okay. Wink. Wink.

Love you mom.

And thank you from the bottom of my heart for loving me so much.

PLAYLIST

It's So Hard To Say Goodbye - Boyz II Men
Fix You - Coldplay
Let Her Go - Passenger
If I Knew What Was Good for Me - Chris Young
True Colors - Cyndi Lauper
Baby Come Back to Me - Kane Brown
Listen To Your Heart - Roxette
Whatever It Takes - Lifehouse
What Ifs - Kane Brown & Lauren Alaina
Open Arms - Journey
I Won't Give Up - Jason Mraz
When You Love Someone - Bryan Adams
You Are The Reason - Calum Scott
From this Moment On - Shania Twain & Bryan White
Valentine - Jim Brickman & Martina McBride

PROLOGUE

Brinley

I WAS SICK TO MY STOMACH.

When people said no news was good news, they were dead wrong.

The phone had been silent for a couple of days and when my eyes landed on the military vehicle that pulled into my driveway, I squeezed them shut and tried to wash away the image. But when the repeated raps at my door echoed through the house, my heart plummeted to the ground.

He's gone.

It was impossible to hope that it was all a bad dream. One that had been playing on repeat in my mind during those days of utter silence. If I opened the door I couldn't pretend any longer that things would be okay.

The knock came again and my pulse raced with an abundance of dread, fear, and sorrow. And I hadn't even heard the words yet.

I couldn't imagine our lives without Luke.

Zander let out a whimper from his bassinet that I'd set up in the living room so he was close by when he napped. He was just a baby and wouldn't understand anything. For that, I was thankful because I didn't want him to feel an ounce of pain or sadness.

The soul-gripping kind I was feeling right then.

My gaze landed on the window, the sun setting, darkness slowly creeping in and a shiver ran through me as more knocks had come. On autopilot, my bare feet slowly shuffled across the hardwood floor toward the door and I reached for the knob with a trembling hand.

Pausing, I vowed that no matter what Zander would know what a remarkable man Luke was, as well as how much he loved him.

God, how the hell am I going to do this?

Luke always took care of me and was there for me since the day we met when I was just sixteen. He also promised that he would take care of Zander too.

He was the only man I'd ever been able to count on. Luke was selfless, honorable, and the nicest person in the whole world.

Even when he knew I wasn't in love with him.

So many times I'd wished I could've been. But we don't get to pick the way we feel deep down. Guilt was an awful feeling and that was what I felt knowing I'd never been able to be the woman Luke needed.

Someone else had held my heart back then and had never given it back.

My husband was my best friend. And while he had another best friend already at the time I showed up in town, he never faltered to make room for me in his life. But thinking about the other part of our trio brought more emotions I couldn't bear to think about.

Shutting my thoughts down, I took a deep breath and pulled open the door. I tried to tell myself to be strong. That I had a baby to take care of and I needed to keep it together for him. But the moment my eyes landed on the military officer and the chaplain, all that flew out the window.

And my knees hit the ground with a hard thud, as a life-altering howl broke from my lips.

Chapter One

BRINLEY

WHAT HAD I BEEN THINKING?

I should have never come. At a desperate moment, I hadn't thought things through. Who in their right mind grabs their four-year-old, jumps in a car, and drives to another state on a whim with no plan in place?

Oh, that would be me.

But in all fairness, I didn't know that I would walk into a party and I also never in my life had imagined that I would encounter the one man I didn't want to see there. And yet, he was hanging out with Gyth, who I *had* come to see. He clearly knew him well too. A pang of sadness jolted my heart as I took in the whole group of friends who looked to be enjoying themselves.

Until I walked in.

After exchanging a few words, I panicked. I turned on my heel and took back off the way I'd come, headed toward my car as fast as my feet would take me.

"Mommy, you're going too fast," my sweet boy said from beside me as we hurried toward my car.

Feeling like I'd just failed my son yet again, I slowed

down right before we reached the passenger side door and I squatted down so I was eye level with him. But as I did, suddenly a large man loomed over us causing my pulse to pick up and race frantically through my entire body.

"Brin," Rowan said in a deep voice.

That's it, just Brin? Hearing him call me by the nickname he always had in the past in that alluring voice of his caused a shiver to race down my spine. I was pissed and confused at the way my body was responding to him after all the years that had passed.

I kept hold of my son's hand and stood, Rowan, towering over me by many inches. He was way too close for my liking and I needed to get out of there.

"Mommy," my son started as he tugged on my hand. "Who is that?" He pointed in Rowan's direction with his free hand and I saw the big man wince. But if the question bothered him, that was on him.

For me the inquiry was like dumping a bucket of cold water over my head and had reality hitting me hard. Rowan didn't know my son and sweet Zander didn't know him.

"Nobody, baby," I said looking down at my little guy. But as soon as the words left my mouth, guilt plagued me, and the lie that had rolled off my lips hurt me to the core.

"That has never been true and you know it," he said, causing my head to snap back up and my eyes to meet his. Eyes that looked guilty, sad, and determined. It was the determination that scared me most because Rowan was good at getting what he wanted. But he was also good at running away.

I lifted my chin in defiance. "It has been now for many years," I told him. "Our friendship or anything else walked right out the door with you the last time you did."

The air around us intensified and was charged with so

many emotions, some of them unwanted. Anger and sadness took center stage, but I couldn't deny the third that was still ever-present even after all those years.

Desire.

That was the one I didn't want to exist and sadness right behind it. It seemed to me that with our history and the time that had passed, that anger was the only thing I should be feeling as he stood in front of me.

But as I stared into his intense, dark, almost black eyes, which reminded me of a smooth Onyx rock, I knew he wasn't the only one to blame for how things turned out and the way I felt. I didn't have time to deal with that right then, I had to take care of my son.

"We have to go." I picked Zander up and opened the back door to put him in the car.

"Where are we going, Mommy? We don't have a house no more." The almost worried and sad tone in his voice made me want to cry. It was my job now to take care of him.

Alone.

"Brin, what is he talking about?"

I frantically tried to get my son buckled up while avoiding the question that Rowan had fired off at me, his tone demanding an answer. But I didn't owe him anything. Not when he'd ghosted us and hadn't bothered to care before. I'd come to see Gyth, not him.

Now I had nobody or nowhere to go.

Then before I could stop him, my son blurted out more classified information. Meaning, it wasn't meant for the man that was standing at my back, an intensity that was hard to ignore, rolling off him in waves.

"Our house burned to the ground and my Mommy's work too. Poof, it is all gone," Zander said dramatically, both his hands making a motion like something had exploded and was instantly gone. Which it was, but I hated that he could describe it so well.

We hadn't been there at the time of the fire which was a blessing because as sad as my son was to lose all his toys and stuff, he hadn't had to experience the actual event.

The one that took *everything* from us.

I finished securing Zander, then shut the door and turned around intent on getting to the car to the driver's side so we could leave, but I froze when Rowan spoke.

"Brin, please. Let me help you."

My stomach tightened at his request and I wondered how it was possible to dislike someone so immensely and be attracted to them at the same time. Because why would he want to help now? And why did he have to be so damn good looking?

Everything about Rowan was mysterious and sexy, from his midnight-black hair on his head and face, and dark skin, to his rippling muscles that bulged from his short-sleeved white t-shirt. Looking at him made my belly flutter.

It had always been that way. My husband was my best friend and my world for so many years, but the man standing mere inches from me had always been the one I had been in love with since the day my eyes took him in.

He'd never been available though.

Rowan didn't do relationships, he didn't invest emotionally, and he obviously never cared for me the same way I had him. One time I thought maybe things had changed but he'd squashed that notion come morning.

The closest he got was his friendship with my husband and me at one time. He and Luke had been best friends before I came into the picture. And I wish I could have chosen which man to be in love with.

If only it could have been Luke.

As that thought crossed my mind my traitorous body, in the vicinity of my lower region, tingled with lust as Rowan stepped closer to me. And that had only ever happened with him.

Close enough to touch me, he reached out his hand and touched the side of my cheek. I should have moved, but just for a second, I was lost in the touch. I'd even leaned into the warmth of his palm as I remembered what it had felt like to be on the receiving end of Rowan's caress.

"Mommy, I have to go pee," my son said through the half-open window.

I pulled back, ashamed of myself for letting my guard down with the man that had stood in front of me and turned back to Zander needing to find him a bathroom. Opening the door, my little man was squirming in his seat with his hand covering his privates as if he could hold it in if it suddenly decided to spring a leak.

"Take him in the house and let him go to the bathroom," Rowan said.

I unbuckled Zander and picked him up, swiveling around toward the house. When I glanced at Rowan his eyes were on my son, an odd look in his gaze that I couldn't quite decipher.

"Mommy," my little guy whined.

Shit, I was not rocking this mom thing at all right then.

Just then I saw Gyth headed right toward us, a beautiful blonde woman at his side. She'd been in the backyard when I first arrived looking for Gyth. But once I spotted Rowan, I turned around and ran. I couldn't deal with him and yet he had followed me to the car where we'd stood, caught up in the first conversation we'd had in years.

I had mixed feelings about the couple approaching. On one hand, I was glad they were going to interrupt Rowan and me, but I also was nervous because we'd caused a little scene and it had been clear that they were celebrating something. And I'd interrupted.

Just as they reached us, Zander whined again saying he really had to go. The gorgeous woman's eyes softened and she pulled herself away from Gyth who had a protective arm wrapped around her waist when they walked up.

"Hey Brinley, I'm Summer. Gyth has told me a lot about you."

I stilled for a moment, wondering what Gyth had said, but the radiant and genuinely friendly smile on Summer's face made me relax instantly.

"Please, let me take you inside and show you where the bathroom is," she said sweetly, looking at me and then at Zander. "Then, there are some kids outback playing if you want to join them after. If that's okay with your momma?"

"Can I, Mommy, pretty please?" I looked at Zander and the hope in his eyes was not something I could turn down, especially after everything he'd been through. That face of his melted my heart every time and the little man had me wrapped around his finger.

Turning back to Summer, I said, "That would be great if we are not intruding." I could hear the uncertainty in my voice, but I didn't know all these people except for Gyth and Rowan. Gyth I didn't know well at all but he was so kind to me when he'd come to me after Luke died. And Rowan I didn't want to be around.

At least that was what I had to keep telling myself but everything in me was conflicted with so many emotions at seeing him again.

"You ladies take the little guy to the bathroom and then while he plays Brinley and I can talk," Gyth said.

It was exactly what I had come for even if I didn't know what good it would do. But now that I would be getting the chance I wasn't sure what to say or how he could even help me.

Summer put out her hand toward the house and said, "Follow me."

I started to walk off and glanced over at Rowan one last time. Big mistake. We had witnesses again and I knew the next comment he made would raise more questions.

"We're not done talking, Brin."

If I had anything to say about it we were. I could only handle so much at one time and I was already on overload.

Pushing back the tears that threatened to make a show, I marched after Summer with my world in my arms. My son was what I needed to focus on now.

Especially since someone was threatening to take him from me.

Chapter Two

ROWAN

My heart seized in my chest.

I stood watching Embry corral all the kids, ruling them with the authority of the eldest of the group. At almost seven—a very mature one at that–she was used to taking charge, getting her way, and also wrapping everyone who met her around her little finger as she went. And while she may run the show more times than not, she was also a loving, sensitive, beautiful soul. As well as, funny as heck.

She reminded me of another little girl, in another time and place. A girl who stole my heart the minute she was born and broke it the second we'd laid her to rest. Every time I thought about her I felt broken all over again as if it was thrown back in time to that devastating day.

The day I lost my baby sister.

Lost in my grief, I turned away from the kids playing and tilted my head back as I let the sun wash over me and wished away the despair that always crept in when I thought of the tragedy that took her too soon.

One that was my fault.

It was what always held me back from becoming too close to anyone, never allowing me to invest my heart for fear I would lose someone special again. Or hurt someone innocent. So I kept people at arm's length most of the time. Only a few people had managed to sink themselves a little deeper into my world than any others. And while I always thought I was protecting them while I did myself at the same time, I was sure I'd hurt us all.

I was lost in the past when a tingle raced down my spine and the hairs on the back of my neck stood up. My instincts screamed at me to turn around and my breath caught in my throat when I did.

At first glance, I thought my eyes must have been playing tricks on me when they landed on the woman who'd just walked into the party. But Brinley was there in the flesh. I always noticed her since the first time I laid eyes on her and could feel her presence whenever she was around. Even when I worked my ass off to push away the feelings she provoked in me.

I craved to be close to her.

Which was why I should stay far away.

My gaze took in every one of her features and my pulse raced. Brinley was beautiful, always had been, but seeing her all grown up with her son felt different and made me long for something I could never have.

While I may not have been around the little guy growing up, I knew it was Zander the moment I saw them together because of his age and the fact he was the splitting image of his mother.

My feet moved without thought, even after I had just reasoned with myself to not go near her. However, when I reached her, the exchange didn't go so well. I'd soon found myself racing after Brinley and her son toward the front of the house, desperately hoping she would talk to me.

Brinley was stubborn and she wasn't giving up much. The few things she chose to say felt like a knife had plunged through my chest. Though, the little guy had no problem rambling on about things his mother was trying to keep from me.

But she had sought out Gyth?

When she'd headed into the house with her son and Summer, leaving me standing there with the man in question, I knew he was going to drill me for answers. I could handle the scowl or worried look on his face, but it was the protective tone when he spoke that got me fired up.

"Mind explaining to me what is going on between you and Brinley?"

Mind? Yes, I minded. Because even though I didn't know how to answer that question, what I realized at that moment was that I wanted to be the one to protect her, not anyone else, and it pissed me off that Gyth was trying to do it.

I also realized Brin didn't want me to protect her or most likely even be around.

When Luke died I thought she and her son were better off without me. I'd been absent for multiple years, hiding from my feelings. It was what I did. I ran.

I never stayed around and I made every attempt not to risk my heart.

Besides, I felt guilty for not being there for my friends. Not just after my best friend died, but before too. The two people I'd allowed to get closer to me than anyone except my mother, I avoided most of the time once I had left for the military.

Two of the best people I knew, who deserved to be happy, and therefore deserved one another.

But that didn't mean it didn't kill me deep down that it actually had happened.

At one time I'd broken down and just once I had let myself believe I could have more. That I could even give more. Then I did what I always had and turned tail and ran. Before I had got my head on straight, it was too late.

Running into Brinley had brought a lot of old wounds to the surface. I may not have known the story yet behind how Gyth knew Luke, but the fact remained he obviously had been in Luke's life and Brinley's too.

And I hadn't.

Having not answered Gyth's question, he growled like the big bear of a man he was and when I looked at him, his scowl grew.

"I don't want to talk about it!" I snapped. "I think that's between Brin and me," I added through gritted teeth. I knew I was acting like an ass but the truth of it was, I didn't know anything right then except I had a thousand feelings whirling inside me.

"Well I promised Luke I would watch out for Brinley and Zander so you are going to have to talk about it," he fired back sternly.

My stomach bottomed out and I felt sick hearing that Luke had to ask Gyth to watch over Brin and Zander. He'd asked me multiple times to come see Zander when he was first born, but I hadn't been able to bring myself to do it.

As much as I wanted them to be happy, I knew seeing the life and family they built together with my own eyes might just kill me. I'd made up excuses as I always did, well aware that my best friend was not buying them, but he let it slide like he'd had all our lives.

But he'd figured out he couldn't count on me. Especially for something as important as taking care of his family.

Gyth must have seen something in my expression because his demeanor changed and I found myself standing in front of the flip side of the angry bear. The guy who cared and would do anything to help a friend. That was when I'd spilled my guts to him right there out on his front lawn.

When I got done, we both stood there in silence for a bit. I mean I had word-vomited all over the place, which wasn't like me at all. I never talked about my past, my feelings, or admitted to the things I just had.

I could see wheels turning as Gyth took in everything I had laid before him. He was assessing thoroughly–it was his nature–to determine the best course of action.

Me, well I had been standing there wishing I could take it all back. My heart felt ripped to shreds while my body vibrated with nervous energy and my mind was telling me to run. Get as far away as I could so I didn't have to think about everything that was wrong with my life, including what I had lost, and the things I never could have.

I couldn't believe I told him the story about how I lost my sister and how it had been my fault. I didn't talk about her and I hadn't told anyone about how she died since I was a teenager. But as I went on it was clear how my silence had shaped my life. Then I spoke of Luke and Brinley, my two friends who were always there for me, but I could never manage to do the same for them.

"That is some big stuff, man. I knew you were dealing with some heavy shit, but I didn't know it amounted to all that." Gyth let out a high-pitched, drawn-out whistle before going on. "I'm so sorry about you sister. I'm not going to sit and tell you to stop blaming yourself because I know that saying the words doesn't make it happen. Every time I think of the day Luke died I have to fight down some of the blame I feel."

Gyth looked stricken with grief and it messed with my head. I knew the day was coming when I would have him tell me exactly what happened, but right then I wasn't ready and I told him so. He hadn't pushed and said to let him know whenever I was. I got the feeling it would be just as hard on him to recount that grave situation in detail.

"Luke told me about his best friend he'd grown up with and would tell stories of the two of you, but he never said your name. He always called you Casanova." Gyth let out a chuckle at the same time I groaned. "He'd told me you were quite the ladies' man and all the girls flocked to you so he had deemed you with that nickname, but you despised it. Because, while they may adore you and fall at your feet, you didn't care or partake in all that was offered." Gyth looked at me strangely with a gleam in his eye as if a lightbulb had just gone off in his head. "Maybe the women in the backyard were on to something," he mumbled.

"What?" I asked him, confused.

"Oh nothing," he said and then carried on. "Anyway, without him using your name, when Braxton brought you onboard with *No Surrender* and us not knowing Luke was the friend you lost, I had no way of knowing you two knew each other and had been that close."

I was surprised Luke had even mentioned me after what a shit friend I had been for so many years once we had both left home and joined the military. While he'd joined the Marines, I had joined the Army and that took us in two different directions. But I was the one who'd put an even bigger gap in our friendship when I just let myself drift further away from him and Brinley.

And I regretted so many of my decisions.

It was too late to change things for Luke and me which would forever eat at my soul, but Brinley was here, and seeing her made me think maybe I needed to pull my head out of my ass and make amends with her. Besides she needed help, and while she came looking for Gyth and I knew the big guy would want to do what he could, I wanted to be there for her and Zander too.

But would she let me?

The thought of Zander brought a pang to my chest. My friends had a child and the little guy didn't have a clue who I was. That was another thought for another day though because right then I could only handle so much and I realized Gyth was staring at me expectantly.

"Did I miss something?" I asked him.

"I asked you if we were going to have problems if Summer and I helped those two in there?" He pointed toward his house. "Because I don't plan on breaking my promise to Luke."

How could I be mad that Brinley and Zander would get Gyth's help and with that would get a whole group of truly wonderful people? Something told me that was exactly what they needed. But I still was fighting down the urge to try and stake a claim where it didn't belong and I hadn't earned in doing so. I shoved down my feelings and answered him.

"No, no problem. You are a far better man than I have been over the years and they could use all of you." As the words left my mouth, guilt plagued me again for the distance I had put between me and the only true friends I had growing up.

Because that was all I had allowed.

Though over the last few months, the guys, their women and even the kids had put a small stamp on my life in a way nobody had since I met Luke and then Brinley bounced into ours in high school. So while I was standing there thinking I left a little bit out of the things I had told Gyth, I couldn't bring myself to do it for fear they would think I was a total shit and not want me around.

"Rowan, man, I am sure she could use you too. You're part of our group and you are part of her past, so let's all help them, yeah?"

Just as I was about to answer, I heard the screen door shut and turned at the sound. Summer was walking toward us. I glanced at Gyth and saw his facial expression change the moment his eyes landed on his wife.

And I was jealous.

What they had, and the other guys I worked with too, was something to envy. Their relationships were right out of a romance novel. They were so on point and amazing. In fact, Alley wrote the smutty books herself from what I had heard. I wouldn't be surprised if she got phenomenal material for her stories from the world and the lives of her friends around her.

Summer walked right up to Gyth and plastered herself against his side. He hugged her close to him and she smiled up at her husband before looking back at me. It was like looking at Beauty and the Beast. They seemed to have a fairytale life too.

"I introduced Brinley to the other ladies and Zander is playing with the other kids," Summer said with a smile on her face. "That boy is a charmer and sweet as sugar."

That didn't surprise me, look who his mother was. Brinley was the nicest person and had always been sweet. She put up with me for many years so that said something. She even seemed to like me most of the time. But at times she confused me and once had truly thrown me for a loop. I shook my head to stop myself from thinking of the past.

"I do have to say, something big is going on with them and they need help. That was clear when she walked in and came searching for you," Summer said, looking back up at her husband. "But the poor woman was a bigger mess when I took her into the house." With the last comment, she looked back at me with a question in her eyes as she assessed me and I felt like I was a bug under a microscope.

Silence stretched on as I debated if I should tell them what Zander had said, but they needed to know so they could be helped.

"Zander blurted out that they had a fire and lost Brinley's bookstore, along with their house."

Summer sucked in a breath and Gyth looked shocked.

"I knew when I had talked to Brinley after Luke died, that even though she thanked me for coming and letting her know she could always ask for my help with anything that she and her son needed, that she wasn't going to." Gyth let out a huff of air. "I could see the stubbornness in her, so she fits right in with all the ladies around here."

Summer slugged him in the stomach and Gyth just chuckled and carried on.

"What I am saying is when she showed up unannounced, I knew she was desperate and that worries me."

A knot formed in my gut at his words. I felt the same way. I just hoped that my being here didn't send her packing as fast as she had come in. But the fact that she was still here and in the back with everyone else was a good sign. Once those women back there knew she needed help, my bet was on them. And Brin and Zander were in good hands.

"She and Zander can stay with us," Summer announced. "Right, Big Guy?" she asked, turning her eyes toward her man.

It was great she asked, but funny as hell. Her husband wouldn't deny her anything unless it was harmful to her. His immediate reply confirmed it.

"Of course, Sunshine."

Summer's megawatt smile lit up her face just as the sun did on the bright summer's day. The woman was truly beautiful and Gyth was a lucky guy, but she didn't hold a candle to the woman who had walked back into my life moments ago.

Nobody ever had.

Chapter Three

BRINLEY

I'D LOST MY MIND YET AGAIN.

Once Zander had gone to the bathroom I should have declined Summer's offer to let him play with the kids and grab some food. I didn't want to intrude on their gathering and I also didn't want to run into Rowan again. Seeing and talking to him had me twisted in knots enough as it was. But the longer I stayed the more likely it was I wouldn't be able to avoid another encounter with him.

It was just too hard to tell Zander no when his eyes lit up at Summer's words and his body vibrated with excitement. So I'd relented and time slipped away from me while I watched him happily play. The children were all adorable and there was one little girl that seemed to be the ringleader of them all. My assessment was abundantly clear as she approached a short time later.

I'd just been introduced to a group of women who seemed very nice, but I was a little uncomfortable and feeling out of my element around them all. I didn't have a lot of girlfriends through my teen years. I spent a lot of time with my mother since it was just the two of us. Then, later after I had Zander,

I was busy with him and my business. There was also the fact that my husband and Rowan had been my best friends in high school, so I understood guys a lot better than I seemed to other women.

The semi-awkward moment for me was interrupted when Embry, who I learned was Braxton and Jurnee's daughter—*please let me keep all these names straight*—marched over to us, cocked one leg, and placed both hands on her hips. "What did I tell you already about being outnumbered by the boys when the last one was born? Now there is another one!"

The attitude that rolled off her was adorable, not rude, and you could tell she was being half-silly even while being serious too.

"Zander is fun though so you guys can stay. You need us," she continued, her voice changing to a more sincere, mature tone.

I realized that Embry was wise beyond her years and was a little flabbergasted at how much she took in and picked up on. Then she looked around the group until her eyes landed on Summer and her sass returned.

"You—" she pointed at Summer "—get on it, Gyth said he could help with this situation."

All the women laughed wildly and I sat there confused as Embry turned and scrambled off, yelling for all the kids to sit in a circle so they could play a game. When my eyes looked toward Summer, she was still laughing, but I could see something else going on behind them too. I'd gotten that there were more little boys than girls but I didn't know why Embry had said that about Gyth or singled out Summer.

I wasn't going to ask either.

It was clear all the ladies were good friends and although they graciously invited me to stay awhile, that didn't give me a pass to barge into their lives and get all personal. However, as their giggle calmed, it seemed Summer was going to explain anyway, but she didn't get much out.

Just as she began to talk, the sliding door opened and my stare darted in that direction as Rowan walked out right behind Gyth. When his intense stare landed on mine, I sucked in a huge gulp of air and diverted my gaze quickly. The only problem was I brought my eyes back to the group and they were all looking at me with an odd look on their faces.

"Umm, I am just going to c-check on Zander, we should probably g-get going," I stammered.

When I stood I wasn't sure what else to say to everyone but I needed to get out of there because what I couldn't do was talk to Rowan again. He made me a wreck. I wanted to slap him and hug the asshole at the same time. I spent many years being mad at the man and missing him immensely at the same time.

"Brinley," Summer's sweet voice started. "Let your son play while we go around the front and talk for a few minutes. Gyth and I would like to help."

Help? I wasn't sure what she was talking about. I mean I'd come for help, but I hadn't told Summer anything and even if I had, letting them help Zander and me wasn't possible now that I'd found out Rowan was around.

I also didn't want to be rude so I told her okay and followed her around the house, the same way I had run a short time before that when I'd been trying to flee from the man I knew was staring at my retreat as I took off a second time.

I could feel Rowan's eyes on me.

Trying to ignore the feeling that it provoked in me, I searched to think of something else. I let the sun's warmth sink in and took in the beautiful home that Gyth and his family had, which was also in the perfect neighborhood with well-manicured lawns, colorful flowers, shiny cars in the driveways, and a peace that washed over me just being there.

All that brought on a new thought.

This was what I wanted. I could only dream of a perfect life like this with Zander, his father, and an amazing home. I had it pretty good for a while thanks to Luke, but we both knew there was something big missing. Now I had nothing and was just missing him, along with what could never be.

I followed Summer to the white wooden porch swing with cute yellow pillows on it and sat down, folding my hands in my lap, gaze cast downward, unsure what was going to come next. I may not have thought things through before coming, but I never expected all this.

Pushing against the floor with one foot nervously, the swing swayed back and forth. "Oh sorry," I muttered, trying to stop the motion.

"No worries, I love to sit here and sway. It is so peaceful," the gorgeous woman next to me said.

Summer could be a model, she was absolutely breathtaking, but also so down to earth. While I felt plain next to her, she didn't treat me like that or any of the other women either. Friends like them would be wonderful, but they were Rowan's friends, not mine. And he and my time together had ended so I would have to go somewhere else.

Somewhere *they* couldn't find me.

Summer's voice cut in and I pulled my gaze from the wood decking.

"I was going to offer for you and Zander to stay with Gyth and me, but then I thought of an idea you would maybe like more."

My heart sank a little at the fact she changed her mind for some reason about us staying here, even if I could have never taken her up on it.

"Don't get me wrong, we would love for you to stay with us if that is what you want to do, but we do have another option I hadn't thought of when I talked to Gyth earlier." The excitement in her voice was infectious and I found myself smiling along with her.

"We still have Gyth's old condo for people to use when needed if they come in town for business or work with *No Surrender,* the company the guys own or work for. Anyway, you guys could use it and have your own place if that would be more suitable for you?"

My eyes widened in shock and my heart perked up at the sincerity in her tone when she stated she would be fine either way, even if we were invading her space. But I couldn't do either. I didn't realize I was slowly shaking my head side to side in a motion that told her no.

"Brinley, let me be honest," she started, as she placed her small hand on mine. "I may not know what is going on, but all of us ladies have had our fair share of problems and one day we'd be more than happy to tell you about them. But what I can tell you is that we will help you if you need it and something is telling me you do. Let us be there for you, please?"

I gnawed on my bottom lip, furiously.

I wanted to grab onto what she was offering. Maybe I could do it and just avoid Rowan. I didn't have to see him, right?

"Are you sure we wouldn't be imposing if we stayed there?" A slight taste of blood hit my tongue as I bit down on my lip hard, worrying about what I was thinking of doing. "Not that I would mind your place," I hurried to add. "But I don't want to take your personal space. Besides, Zander and I are used to being alone, so maybe it would be better at the condo. I have money and can pay you for the time we are there too."

Summer frowned and I wasn't sure what I had said that brought that look to her once sparkling face.

"Girlfriend, you are not paying a cent for staying there. It's why it is there and what we do. Teal was using it, but she and Kace bought a house recently so it is yours now as long as you need it."

That didn't feel right and I could argue later, but she now looked hopeful and I was feeling a sense of relief that we didn't have to get in the car and drive off with no destination in mind.

"Okay, thank you."

The smile was back, beaming so bright and I mirrored her without thought. The damn look on her face was contagious. Gyth never stood a chance against his wife because any time she flashed him one of her smiles I knew he must cave in a split second and grant her any of her wishes.

What would that be like?

Luke was the most amazing guy and he would have done anything for me. He had gone above and beyond as it was. But what he and I had was not like what you saw with these couples when you looked around. My heart ached that my best friend was gone, but it hurt even more knowing that because of me, he never got to experience what I'd seen when I showed up at Gyth and Summer's home.

My throat was clogged with emotion and tears pooled in my eyes. I reached up with my free hand and frantically brushed them away. I had to be strong even if sometimes it was really damn hard.

For my son, I'd been doing my best.

"I'm here whenever you need to talk," Summer said with her hand still laying on top of mine.

"Thank-k you," I told her, emotionally. "I better check on Zander." I stood, causing her hand to drop from mine. "He probably is wondering where I'm at."

She stood too and we started to head off the porch. "Sure, then we can talk to Gyth and tell him the plan and we will take you over to the place you'll be staying in a little while."

As we walked back toward the backyard, I felt awful once again and second-guessed my decision. They had company, they couldn't just leave and tend to Zander and me.

"Maybe we should go to a hotel and wait until tomorrow. You guys have company right now."

"Nonsense, it will all work out and why go to a hotel when the condo is already ready for you to use?"

I didn't reply because we had already made it back to where the party was in full swing and my gaze immediately searched for my son, whom I found hooting and hollering as he chased the other kids. Looked like they were playing tag.

"Looks like he didn't even notice I was gone," I mumbled.

Summer giggled and I turned her way.

"The kids all have a blast together, despite what Embry said. She loves every single one of them, even if they are mostly boys, and the only girl is too little still to help her gang up on them."

I watched as Summer looked back at the kids, so much love on her face. "Maybe we will give Dexter a sibling soon," she said wistfully.

Again, I didn't want to pry so I stood there silently as we looked on and watched them play. Then the vibrant, outspoken woman named Alley started over, the full lady posse all close behind.

"Where have you two been? It's time to beat the guys at a game of volleyball and we need you."

I was surprised she was including me in this, but it felt nice too.

"Maybe I should sit out and watch, keep an eye on the kids," I blurted out.

"The grandparents can watch the kids, we need all the help we can get. There is no way I'm losing," Alley added and strutted off toward the net. "Time to kick some butt."

The other ladies laughed and followed her.

"She is a force," Summer said, beside me. "You will get used to her."

I wasn't sure about that. I'd probably be gone before that happened, but Alley was funny and it was interesting to watch the different personalities and dynamics of all the women. And it was kind of cool that they all got along so well.

"You heard her, let's go kick some butt." Summer grabbed my hand and started dragging me toward the group that was gearing up for the game.

"That is completely unfair," I heard a deep familiar voice shout out.

Everyone turned to look at Rowan and I found myself doing the same. When my eyes clicked with his, I knew the game, the condo, and everything in between that may come with it was a bad idea.

"What?" Alley goaded. "You afraid of us or something?" she asked, looking straight at Rowan, who's eyes were trained only on mine.

I knew what Rowan was going on about. Volleyball had been my game since I was young and it was the one thing I stuck with even when I started at his and Luke's school. I finished out my senior year with our school as state champs, but it had been a long time since I had played so I didn't believe anyone had to worry.

"You might want to prepare boys, that one," he said, motioning in my direction. "She is a beast when it comes to this game."

The guy's eyes registered with surprise and Alley pumped her fist in the air. "Hell yeah, that's what I like to hear! Let the game begin."

I couldn't stop staring at Rowan as memories of him and Luke at all my games, cheering me on my junior year before they left for the military came rushing forth in my mind. Then, I thought about my senior year when they were gone and how lonely I was without them. Suddenly, I just wanted to flee, but Rowan's gaze stayed on mine and a challenge glistened in his eyes that I didn't want to walk away from.

That was when I found my feet moving and I was getting into position.

I was going to stomp his fine ass.

When I realized his ass had crossed my mind, my cheeks turned warm and I stumbled a little as I brought the ball up to serve. Getting my bearings, I closed my eyes and pictured the old days. I knew this game and I hoped it was like riding a bike. Because when I opened them and saw the smirk on Rowan's face, I knew exactly where my target was.

He was going down.

Chapter Four

ROWAN

SHE WAS FUCKING MAGNIFICENT.

Even if she had handed me my ass.

On the first serve, the ball slammed over the net right in front of me. I dove and I missed.

Every woman screamed with glee and the men chuckled when I landed with a big oof as I hit the ground.

"Damn I wish I'd been recording that," Kace said from beside me.

"You got schooled, man," Lyric added.

My head came up and I glared at the guys. Then, I looked at Brinley who was wearing a triumphant expression on her stunningly beautiful face.

I was in deep shit.

And so was she because I had no intention of letting her hide from me.

We had a lot to talk about.

Chapter Five

BRINLEY

OH SHIT.

I knew that stubborn look on Rowan's face. I may be sticking around, but I had to put an ocean of space between us. He lost his chance at reconciliation a long time ago. I was still pissed, but also very hurt. Friends didn't leave each other the way he had. And it wasn't just me he left, it was Luke too.

He would never know what else he'd left behind.

All I wanted to do was start a new life, but it didn't look like that could happen where I'd thought because this was where Rowan's life was. Disappointment settled in the pit of my stomach. The ladies, Gyth, and even the other guys seemed to be nice people, and there were kids Zander's age around too, but it wasn't possible.

I'd almost forgotten we were playing a game while I was thinking until I heard Zander yell out to me and the other kids cheering.

"Go, Mommy, you can do it!"

I smiled over at my special little guy and then my head snapped to Rowan who was getting ready to serve. He had a devious smile on his face. I glared at him as my body vibrated with the need to show him a thing or two.

If I still had it in me.

I held my breath as he threw the ball up in the air with his left hand. Then his right arm came up, muscles bulging, and he served with no mercy. The ball came flying straight for me and I jumped up as it skimmed the net putting everything I had into the spike that had the ball barreling right back at him.

It hit him right in the head. A stunned look flashed across his handsome face as the guys roared with laughter and the women came running at me. All of a sudden I had multiple sets of arms thrown around me and they were jumping up and down.

The kids yelled with glee and Zander screamed, "That's my mommy!"

"Girl, you showed him!" Alley yelled.

When I glanced back at Rowan the look on his face had too many emotions racing through me. He looked proud, just like he had at all my games back in high school. Rowan hadn't missed any of them. My heart cracked when I thought about the past and the fact that he clearly hadn't missed me when he left either.

"I have to go," I blurted and took off, cupping Zander's hand in mine as I went by and headed toward the house, taking us both inside, straight to the bathroom where I could hide for a few minutes.

Surely the group must have thought I was losing it, leaving in the middle of a game, but I couldn't stay there any longer and pretend like things were fine, smiling, and playing around when I felt like my heart was cracking wide open.

"Mommy, are you upset?"

Zander was very in tuned to my feelings and that was why

I always worked hard to shove them down. It didn't always work.

"Don't be sad, Mommy." He wrapped his small arms around my legs and squeezed them tight. I kneeled on the tile floor and hugged him close to me.

"I'm okay," I said, trying to reassure him.

"Did my snuggles help?" he asked in my ear.

My heart warmed and I thought to myself, *This is all I need.*

I may have thoughts of wanting more at times, but having Zander was the best thing in the world, so if it was just him and I, then it was a damn good life. It just killed me that I may not be enough for him one day. He'd recently been asking more questions about his daddy.

A very sensitive subject that brought a pang to my chest.

"They sure did. Your snuggles always make everything better."

Gently pulling back, I looked into my son's eyes that were so much like his father's and another pang hit me square in my chest. But his radiant smile pulled my attention away and it was enough to wash away my worries for the time being. Then, I went on to ask him how he felt about staying in Gyth and Summer's old place.

"If it's old, does it smell bad?" he asked, pinching two fingers to the bridge of his nose and scrunching up his face like he smelled something sour.

I couldn't contain the laughter that he brought on sometimes. He was not only sweet but he was animated and the two qualities together melted my heart.

"When I said old I meant they used to live there but now live here in their new home. I am sure it will be great, honey."

After being around the couple for the day, I figured even

if it was originally Gyth's and people had since stayed there, it was probably perfectly fine. Besides, they were doing us a favor and so anything would be wonderful.

"Okay. Will I get to play with the kids again?"

"We can ask the other parents but I am sure they won't mind or we can work something else out."

"Yay!" he squealed. "Let's go ask them now, Mommy."

I wasn't quite ready to go back out into the group of people, especially if I ran into Rowan. I ran like a coward and left the game. I was feeling silly about it now but at the time I couldn't think.

All I could do was feel.

IT LOOKED as if my hiding had come to an end.

When the knock on the door came, I frantically looked around the small bathroom searching for a secret doorway to appear and Zander and I could just use it to escape reality. But there was nowhere else to go and my little guy didn't waste a second. He pulled away from me and rushed to the door, flinging it open.

While I hadn't wanted to see anyone quite yet after making a spectacle of myself, I was glad it wasn't Rowan standing on the other side.

"Hey," the adorable woman named Teal said. "Summer wanted me to tell you that it's time for dessert and the kids are looking for Zander here," she added, patting his head as he bounced on the balls of his feet.

"Can I go, pretty please, Mommy?"

My son's twinkling eyes pleaded with me.

"Sure, go ahead," I told him. He started out the door,

squeezing past the woman standing there with a smile on her face. Before he got too far I added, "Use your manners and don't forget your—"

Before I could finish he cut in.

"Please and thank yous. I know, I know, you tell me every time."

Then he was gone.

Teal chuckled. "He sure is cute. How do you ever say no?"

I laughed. "It's not easy."

Getting up off the ground where I had been kneeling, Teal and I stood in silence for a moment. Her eyes assessed me and I wasn't sure what she saw, but I found myself hoping it wasn't all bad. That was a new revelation for me because for so long I hadn't cared what people thought, but for the first time, I wanted her and the other women to like me.

And then I wondered why it would matter.

When I left I would never see them again.

Uncomfortable with the quiet, I searched for anything to say. "Congrats on the new baby and getting married."

Her sparkling eyes fitting her name perfectly twinkled with happiness. "Thank you." She looked away and seemed to be thinking before she glanced back at me and spoke again. "It is all very new to me and things were far from perfect not so long ago. Maybe sometime I can share my story with you if you'd like?"

I felt my brow scrunch up in confusion. Why would she want to do that? I found myself blurting out the question.

"Why would you want to?"

"Because although our lives or situations may not be the same, maybe just one thing I say can help you or someone in some way. I haven't known all those people downstairs for very long and I certainly didn't come here trusting anyone, but they saved me. I think we could be there for you too."

Now I was more than a little curious about her story and I still didn't understand why everyone was being so nice to me.

But it felt good.

"That would be nice," I told her.

"Let's go have some dessert. After, Summer said she was taking you to the condo. You will love it." She graced me with a huge smile, then chuckled a little and the sound came up a little devious.

What is that about?

"The security on your floor is amazing," she added as she walked off.

I followed behind her and down the stairs more than puzzled at what was going on. As we reached the kitchen where a big group seemed to be gathered I heard Gyth telling Rowan they were taking me to the condo.

His dark eyes landed on mine as they widened in surprise, but a slight smile lifted the corners of his mouth.

"Is that right?" I heard him say to Gyth, his gaze never leaving mine. "Interesting."

I turned toward Teal, pulling my gaze from Rowan's, and realized all the ladies were now gathered around us.

"Why is going to the condo so interesting?" I asked the whole group.

I felt a little nervous now and wasn't sure if I wanted to go. Something was going on and I was out of the loop and didn't have the slightest clue what was happening.

"I have a feeling things will change for you there just as they did me," Teal said.

"Amen, sister!" Alley shouted and the ladies giggled.

My eyes strayed back to Rowan's and I noticed the sexy

smirk he had on his face then. Something was seriously up with everyone and I felt like I had shifted into an alternate universe.

I also had a feeling I was in deep doo-doo.

Chapter Six

ROWAN

SHE WAS GOING TO BE RIGHT WHERE I WANTED HER.

Operation Forgiveness had just been launched.

I would have to grovel and Brinley would have to find a way to let me back into her life.

Her and Zander had lost a lot and something told me there was more I didn't know yet. It was time I stopped running from everything that made me feel anything.

She needed me.

Or was it the other way around?

Chapter Seven

BRINLEY

MY EYES WIDENED AT THE SIGHT OF THE CONDO.

"Whoopie!" Zander shouted as he raced around in circles in the front room.

As soon as we crossed the threshold a homey feeling washed through me. The vibe was a cool mix of casual, earthy tones with slight feminine touches that trickled throughout the spacious area. It was better than I ever imagined when Summer made the offer. And it was also nicer than the apartment Zander and I had over my bookstore before we lost it.

After Luke died I couldn't stay in the house we'd had together. The place just made me think of losing him even though he was away so much. It had been his idea to buy it and make it our home, so it felt wrong without him. Besides, it was just Zander and I, so using the apartment over my store was easier in the long run. Although, it still never felt like I was making the two of us a real home. Yes, I loved the bookstore and the loss of it and our things was devastating, but I wanted the two of us to have roots and carve out our own life.

Without the input of others.

Luke's overbearing mom never seemed to ease up on reminding me what Luke gave me or how much he provided me with, and she thought it was her duty now to oversee everything when it came to Zander. She had even been making noise that suggested taking things to a new level. So when the fire happened and there was nothing keeping us there any longer, I ran.

And while this temporary place was a stepping stone to hopefully find out what Zander and I needed, it also wasn't home. But it was a damn sweet gesture from people who didn't even know me and would be a comfortable place to stay while we figured things out.

"It's perfect. Are you sure it is okay if we stay here for a bit and it's not inconveniencing you?" I turned to face both Summer and Gyth who were standing behind me. Their son had stayed at the house with the rest of the group and their adorable dog. It was a little difficult prying Zander away from the kids and I knew he would be asking for a dog night and day now that he'd played with theirs. Summer had stepped in and promised a playdate soon so that seemed to satisfy him enough to get him moving.

So there we were.

"Remember what I told you when I came to your house?" Gyth was looking right at me. "Anything. I said if there was anything you ever needed I would do everything in my power to help."

I watched Summer lay her palm on her husband's arm in a soothing gesture. You could hear the emotion clogged in his throat as he spoke and she sensed it.

"I promised Luke." Gyth looked away for a minute. A far-off look crossed his features and then sadness as if those last moments with my husband had been playing in his mind.

A shiver ran through me.

Gyth was the only one right there that knew everything that happened and when he had come to me, I made him tell me the whole horrid story. I'd felt so bad for asking him to do it, but I needed to know. And now that I did there were times when I wished I hadn't asked. It was hard enough for me to know the details, but I would never know what it was like to be there in that moment like the big, amazing man who stood in front of me, vowing to uphold his friend's last wishes, did.

He looked back at me as Summer leaned in closer and wrapped both arms around her husband.

"As far as I am concerned, you're family. Remember that and lean on us."

Tears formed in my eyes as Summer nodded at Gyth's words and added, "He's right, sweetie."

"Mommy," Zander said, tugging on my hand. "Where am I going to sleep?"

Pushing back my emotions and willing the tears not to fall, I turned to my son who had broken up the emotionally charged exchange.

"Let's go check out the rooms and we can see what you want to do. How does that sound?" Summer asked him, reaching out her hand.

Zander took it and they headed down the hall, Gyth and me following behind. I was glad for the reprieve from the talk we'd been having. I felt too raw after everything back at home and then seeing Rowan again. We just needed to settle in and then I could figure out what the heck my son and I did next.

After looking at the rooms, Zander had declared that while the picture painted on the wall was cool, it was meant for a baby and he was a big boy, so he would sleep in the other room with the large bed. It was bigger than he was used to, but I knew he would be fine.

The group had the baby room made for Teal previously and it was sweet as heck. They also hadn't had time to change it but Summer said they could work on that or the other room for Zander so he felt like he had his own space that matched what he liked.

"Oh, that's not necessary. I don't know how long we will be here and I don't want any of you going to any more trouble."

That remark earned me a stern look from the beast of a man who was telling me with his eyes, that he'd already put me on notice with that shit I was sputtering out.

A giggle escaped me that I wasn't able to hold back.

Gyth was sweet as pie and big as a Grizzly bear. Something with the whole mix had made me laugh and I lost it.

"Do you find something funny?" he asked.

When I told him I thought his bark was a lot worse than his bite, Summer started cracking up and Gyth rolled his eyes. The total girl move had us both rolling more. The laughter had released some of the anxiety that had me in knots.

"You girls are pure trouble. It was bad enough, but now your posse is growing. All of us guys better watch out for the load of S.H.I.T to come." His spelling out the word shit was nice of him since Zander was right beside me and his little ears picked up everything.

However, I didn't think he or the guys always remembered because at the party I had caught wind of Embry collecting money for the swear jar she had whenever their potty mouths, as she liked to call it, got the best of them. It was rather hilarious.

"Alley is the troublemaker, we just follow along," Summer told him, leaning up and giving him a quick kiss on the cheek.

"I can't argue with that, but you all feed off her and each other. You all have innocent little Teal corrupted, for heaven's sakes."

"Oh poor baby. Stop whining and go start grabbing their stuff out of the car, Big Guy," Summer told him.

At her words, I froze. I was a tad embarrassed about the fact we barely had anything to bring in. In my mind, I knew I couldn't help it. The fire had been set by a faulty wire in the kitchen upstairs and spread to the shop downstairs wiping everything out. But I was a mother and grown woman so I felt like I should have my shit together better.

Another thing Luke's mom tried blaming me for. She insisted I hadn't kept the place up or had it checked out better when we had moved in there. But it was no fault of mine and thankfully once it was ruled an accident, my insurance company came through. That was not good enough still and there was no hiding her dislike of me. It had been that way since the first day we met. I was the daughter of the hired help and not someone her son should be hanging around.

If I could bottle the look on her face when Luke had said he was going to marry me, it would be enough to scare the scariest of villains everywhere. That woman was worse than the stepmother from Cinderella and I had her for a mother-in-law. But there were many reasons I had married Luke and he was nothing like the evil lady.

Maybe I was overreacting a bit, but after some of her last comments to me, I wasn't sure. Even knowing the truth, she was still trying to control our lives. I just hoped the distance away from her would help. Luke would never want his mother acting like she was and he wouldn't have put up with it, but he wasn't here any longer to intervene.

God, I miss you so much.

I spoke to him sometimes. He was my best friend and he

was gone. I wasn't sure even after four years how to live without him. He'd been my sounding board, my rock, and my biggest cheerleader. He always believed in me and was there for me before and after my mom had died.

He had also supported my dream of opening a bookstore. I could rebuild, but the problem was I didn't want to rebuild in the same place.

"Can I go with him to get my stuff?" Zander asked, pulling me from the chaos swirling through my mind.

"Umm, we don't have much," I told the couple, quietly.

"Yeah, all our stuff burned to the ground," Zander added. Why was it little kids had no filter especially when you wanted them to?

A look of horror must have crossed my face because Summer went into her natural soothing mode again.

"Honey, we already heard and nobody would have expected you to have a house full of things in your car when traveling or after what you have been through. Now let Gyth and Zander go grab your things."

When Gyth headed out with my son, who was talking a mile a minute as if he'd known the man all his life, Summer ushered me over to the couch. Zander had taken to the whole group, but who could blame him they were a great bunch.

All except maybe one.

The scary part was that Zander seemed to like Rowan too.

"We can go get the two of you anything else you guys need. The girls and I love any excuse for shopping."

Summer had carried on, no clue to the turmoil going on inside me, but how could she? Nobody knew that story and I was keeping it to myself.

Forever.

I was about to reply when my gaze landed on the huge bookshelf on the other side of the room. I couldn't believe I hadn't noticed it. Books were my thing. I must have seriously been losing it. Standing, I rushed over to take a peek.

"Oh my gosh, you have so many books," I told Summer.

She had got up and came to stand beside me. "Oh, those are not mine. That's Gyth's collection."

I gasped and she snickered.

"You're teasing." When I looked at her, she shook her head.

"Nope, Gyth loves to read. And he reads a bit of everything. He has a ton of books at our place too but left a shelf here with a mix so whoever was staying could have their pick if they wanted to give something a try."

I picked up a book that had a hot, muscled fireman on the cover and gulped. "Every Moment With You by J.E. Parker," I read aloud. "Gyth read this?" I asked her with a raise of my brows.

"Well, that one was mine originally. Alley is friends with the author and made us all read her books, including Gyth. You should give it a try."

I loved finding new authors and I would definitely be borrowing this one while I was staying at the condo. How cool was it that Alley knew an author?

"That is awesome. I've owned a bookstore and don't know a single author."

A huge smile spread across Summer's face. "You do now," she stated.

My brows crinkled in confusion. Then, Summer picked up another book off the shelf and handed it to me. I dropped my gaze to the cover. It had a couple on it. They were in a bedroom, the gorgeous man had the woman pushed up against the wall, her legs wrapped around him and they were locked in a passionate kiss. It was damn sexy too. Then my eyes dropped to the bottom and I saw the author's name.

"Holy shit." Eyes wide, they turned back to Summer. "Alley?" My mouth gaped open and closed like a fish.

"Yup. Our girl is a romance novelist. And she's good too. Wait until you read that one." The pride in Summer's tone was as clear as day. "You are going to have so much fun talking about books with her."

This group of friends got more interesting, amazing, and sweeter by the minute. I had a feeling that if I got to know them and learned about each of them, their stories would blow my mind.

"I can't wait."

"Mommy, look who we found," Zander said, racing back into the condo.

When I twirled around to see who got him so excited, I sucked in a quick breath. It was not who I'd been expecting at all and I was stunned speechless.

What the hell is he doing here?

But my stomach took a nosedive when my gaze moved down to Zander's small hand wrapped in Rowan's. My breathing picked up and I felt lightheaded.

This cannot be happening now.

Gyth walked in behind the two with his arms full of stuff and stopped. Taking in the room, his gaze came to mine and I could tell that he may know more than anyone else. But he must not know everything or I didn't think we'd all be standing there like we were.

"Guess what, Mommy?"

When my eyes roamed back to my son's, I could see him practically dancing in place and he didn't wait for me to answer before he told me exactly what I was supposed to be guessing.

"Rowan lives right down the hall. Isn't that great?"

Gasping, my eyes flashed to Rowan's and I thought I might be sick.

Because nope. Just, nope. This could not be happening.

My mind quickly recalled something that was said at Gyth's and Summer's before we had headed over here. Teal had told me the security on my floor was amazing.

"You're the security," I muttered, not meaning to say it out loud but I had. That was clear by the look on Rowan's face.

"That would be me," he said with a slight smirk on his rugged face.

"What does security mean, Mommy?"

Letting my gaze leave Rowan's, I looked at Zander, but no words came out.

Rowan squatted down so he was eye to eye with Zander and answered for me. "It means I'm right down the hall in case you guys need anything and close by to protect you if you need it."

My little guy had a thoughtful look on his face. "You mean like if the boogeyman comes when we are sleeping or there are monsters under my bed?"

Watching their exchange was killing me but there wasn't a lot I could do and didn't want to make a scene or worry Zander.

"Sure. If any of those things happen, you can call me," Rowan told him.

"But I don't have a phone or your number," Zander told him in a very serious tone.

Rowan chuckled. "I will make sure your mom has it."

"Wait, can we call you if Grandma comes to our house because sometimes she is scary too?"

Rowan's gaze snapped to mine and the look he gave me told me that we would be having a conversation that I truly didn't want to have. My son was killing me with the world of information he kept spitting out. When I looked away, I noticed Gyth with just as serious of a look on his face.

Well shit.

I started for my son so we could finish getting our things and hopefully avoid any more conversation. As I approached I noticed Rowan was studying Zander, his head tilted as he looked directly into his eyes.

Oh no.

Chapter Eight

ROWAN

I'M MISSING SOMETHING.

Before I could figure out what niggled at the back of my brain, Brin grabbed Zander and pulled him away. She rushed them out of the condo to go to the car for more things.

"What was that all about?" Summer asked.

How was I supposed to know? I couldn't even figure out what was bothering me when the little guy looked up at me the way he had.

"Not a clue," I answered honestly.

I may not have known, but I was going to find out.

Brinley didn't want me around and she sure as shit wasn't happy to find out I was right down the hall. But there was one thing she was.

An amazing mother.

I could tell she'd wanted to throw me out and didn't want Zander anywhere near me, but her son's feelings came first above all.

Pure *love.*

I saw it in her eyes every time she looked at her boy that day. I wouldn't have expected anything else from her. If

Brinley accepted you into her world, she did it with her whole heart. She also had a loving, amazing mom who showed her exactly how a mother should be.

That was something else besides being raised by a single parent that we had in common. We both had fabulous mothers, unlike Luke's overbearing one. We'd both also lost them.

Shaking off the thought because I didn't like the feeling that struck me when I thought of the loss, I focused back on Summer. She had a worried expression on her face. Not that I could blame her. Everyone had caught on the second the two newcomers showed up that they needed help. There were no better people than the group they found either. I'd seen how they'd come together to help Teal recently and how they were there for one another anytime someone needed anything.

It was a protective group.

"Maybe the girls and I weren't thinking clearly when our conniving and matchmaking instincts took hold," I heard Summer mumble.

"Lord, woman. I had a feeling you ladies were up to something," Gyth said, shaking his head. "I'm going to put these things in the bedroom." He walked over to his wife first and kissed her quickly on the lips. "Behave while I am gone."

"Funny, Big Guy," she sassed back.

Once he left the room, I couldn't wrap my head around what in the world the girls were thinking. But then again, they didn't know all the history behind Brinley, Luke, and me.

But matchmaking?

I couldn't help myself, I laughed.

"What are you laughing at?" Summer asked.

"I was just thinking all you ladies had lost it if you thought you were going to push Brinley and me together. Besides, I am not relationship material and certainly not with my dead best friend's wife."

I winced as the words left a sour taste in my mouth.

Talking about this kind of shit was not my specialty and I avoided it like the plague. That was one thing that Brinley had always pushed me on. Trying to get me to talk about my feelings. Whereas Luke allowed me to just hide away.

They played the good cop, bad cop routine, as they tried to get me to open up. But I never could. And while Brinley knew the story that had me shutting down my emotions, Luke had been there when the devastation happened and understood me better than anyone.

After a while, I think Brin had realized what a lost cause I was and gave up trying.

Who could blame her after disappearing like a ghost in the night?

I'd done her wrong and I was sure it was me who'd truly lost in the end. I had lost everyone.

Now I had a group of people I trusted and would be happy to call friends, but until the day Brinley showed up and I talked to Gyth, nobody honestly knew me. Even he didn't know everything.

"We may have not thought it all through, but we just want you to be happy. And it was obvious there was history there. Teal noticed right away and once she caught on then everyone jumped on board."

Summer's face had a sheepish look on it. No way would I be mad at her or the other ladies. I knew they meant well.

"We just want you to be happy," she added.

What was it with people when they found their better halves and always wanted to make everyone around them to be as blissfully happy? It was kind of amusing, but also annoying. Well for me it was since it was never going to happen.

Nobody but one person had ever made me feel like it was

even an option. And even then I couldn't commit. Even if I was ready one day, I wouldn't ever be given a second chance.

"Thank you. But if you knew everything about me, you wouldn't be so quick to try and match me with an innocent woman. Especially with sweet Brinley."

I thought once I said my peace, Summer would get it, but a weird gleam entered her eyes as she held my gaze and I wasn't sure what I saw in her stare was her backing down.

"I don't need to know everything but if you ever want to talk to me you can. Or anyone else in the group. You are one of us now and we take care of our own."

My body reacted to her words and a pleasing tingle ran through me as I felt the wall around me crumble a fraction.

"Any woman would be lucky to have you," she added fiercely.

And the wall snapped back into place.

"I don't want any woman."

Shit, I meant to say, women, meaning anyone. Even to my own ears, the way I had said it, made it clear I had one person, and one person only in mind.

"I know. I can see that." A smile played at the corner of her mouth.

What the hell could she see? I was losing my touch if Summer and the others could get a read on me like she was suggesting.

I was about to open my mouth and ask her what she saw but Gyth walked back into the room. He looked at me and then at his wife.

He studied Summer's face. "Lord, it never ends." He chuckled. "What are you up to now, Sunshine?"

Summer didn't have a chance to answer because Zander burst through the door.

"Rowan, Rowan, want to see my G.I. Joes?" he chirped excitedly.

He slammed into my leg, grabbing onto it with one hand while holding a tiny backpack in the other.

"Mommy bought me a whole bunch of new ones after mine melted in the fire."

Everyone in the room was focused on him and it was hard not to notice the sullen faces as they took in what Zander had just said. Kids seemed to be more resilient than adults but losing everything for a child seemed as if it would be devastating. Yet, Zander seemed happy and thankful for what his mother had started to replace.

We could've all taken a page out of his book.

Looking down at the monkey hanging from my legs, I smiled as he started pulling his toys from his backpack. His zest was contagious and once again I found myself bending down to his level almost as eager as him to play with his Army guys.

"Did you know I was in the Army and wore a uniform like this?"

His eyes widened. "Wow, so cool. I want to be in the Army just like you."

I heard someone suck in a breath and looked over to see Brinley's face almost turn pale. I had a feeling it wasn't the first time her son may have mentioned wanting to be like his G.I. Joes, but hearing him say like me, well that was probably in a whole different ballpark. Especially when his dad was a Marine.

Not wanting to rain on the kid's parade, I tried to steer the direction away from me but still acknowledged his eagerness.

"You can be anything you want to be and those are some awesome toys," I told him. "We can play anytime you want, but it has to be okay with your mom."

I never was around kids until I came to Portland and started working with the guys at *No Surrender*. The thought had made me cringe because all I could think about was my sister.

And what if I hurt another innocent child?

However, I hadn't been able to get out of being around the group's kids all the time. They had slowly started to grow on me, but it still wasn't always easy. Memories still crept in and took me for a spin in the land of sorrow.

With Zander, I found myself even more drawn to him and unable to tear myself away, though his mother was probably wishing I would vanish again. I snuck a peek at her one more time and confirmed that was most likely what she was thinking right then.

"Mom, Mom, can Rowan play with me?"

Plastering on a fake smile for her son and the audience we had, she made an excuse and let him down easily.

"Maybe another time, baby. We need to get settled in and put your things away. Then you get to help me go grocery shopping."

I didn't have a clue how grocery shopping trumped playing, but it certainly worked on the little guy. He was jumping up and down like a jackrabbit, dropped his bag, toys forgotten, and ran over to his mom.

"Yay. Can I put everything in the cart and pick out one candy at the end?" he asked her in a pleading tone.

"You bet. That sounds fair for being my helper."

"Yippee! I'm going to put my bag in my room." He ran back toward me, scooping up his stuff, and took off down the hall.

Brinley glanced around the room, an unsure look on her face. Gyth, who'd been silent throughout the exchange, finally spoke up and saved her from finding any words.

"Well, we better get back to the house and let you get settled. You have our numbers so you call us if you need anything at all."

"Thank you," Brinley told him as both he and Summer moved toward her by the door.

When Summer reached her, she gave Brin a quick hug. Then I heard her say, "I'll call you tomorrow but you can call me before if needed."

Brinley whispered another thank you and then the couple left, leaving me there alone with the one woman who wished I was anywhere else but standing in her living room. I stood from where I had been squatting and walked slowly toward her.

A look of alarm crossed her face and I stopped a few inches from her. She shifted on her feet and her scent tickled my nose, weaving its way through my system. Brinley had always loved lavender and that had apparently not changed. Its soft, delicate, floral smell had always soothed my crazy spirit and calmed me.

Just like she had with her sweet personality.

Sucking in a breath and dragging the intoxicating aroma into my system, I closed my eyes for a second to get a grip on how being near to her made me feel.

"Brin," I whispered, eyes still closed.

"You have to go." Her strangled voice had my eyes snapping open.

I'd ask myself where things went wrong between us, but since it was my fault, I knew exactly when it happened.

"Just give me a minute."

She was slowly shaking her head back and forth when Zander came running back into the room.

"Are we going now, Mommy?"

"Yup. Did you go to the bathroom?"

"Mommm." Zander rolled his eyes and drew the word out in exaggeration. "I'm not a baby."

"Nope, you're a big boy. Let's get going then." She pulled the door open wider and I got the hint. But not before her son put her on the spot once again.

"Can Rowan come with us to the store?"

If I thought her eyes were alarmed before, that was nothing compared to the five-alarm fire burning in them after Zander's question. It was my turn to save her.

"Hey, Champ, I can't go to the store right now. I got things to do, but maybe another time okay?"

"Okay," he said, pulling on his mom's hand.

Taking my cue, I started to move past her but paused remembering I'd forgotten something.

"I'm just down the hall. Please call me if you need anything." I held out a piece of paper with my condo and cell number on it.

She hesitated a moment before reaching out to take it from me. Our fingers brushed one another and the contact jolted all my senses as a tingle raced through my entire system. Brinley pulled her hand back as if she'd been bitten by a snake.

My eyes met hers and instead of finding nothing but hate, something else lingered in their crystal blue depths.

Interesting.

"Catch you later, Brin," I said as I walked out the door.

A soft intake of breath caught my ear and a smile broke out across my face.

Maybe there was hope that *Operation Forgiveness* could be a success.

Chapter Nine

BRINLEY

I WOKE UP SERIOUSLY JONESING FOR A CUP OF COFFEE.

Was there such a thing as a coffee fairy?

I'd forgotten to grab it at the store last night when Zander and I went. Something I was contemplating crying about when I woke up after a few hours of sleep, a stiff neck, and a mountain of worry about where our lives were headed.

My brain wouldn't shut off. There simply wasn't an off switch for that and it was a damn shame. Life would be a lot simpler if that was available when one didn't want to think anymore. Which was me all night long.

Being in a new place and not having his own room, my little man didn't want to sleep alone. Who could blame him when he was in a strange place and had also gotten used to sleeping with me since the fire? Then with him tangled all over me, I'd laid awake nervous, frustrated, and scared.

It felt like I'd just dozed off when Zander flopped his arm toward me, smacking me in the face, and waking me to the early morning light filtering through the cracks in the blinds. Glancing at the clock I groaned. Noticing it was still early, I contemplated trying to go back to sleep but my mind had already started racing.

What would the day bring?

Hoping it wasn't a run-in with Rowan, I climbed out of bed and headed to the bathroom. He was what had kept me up half the night. It was a shock to my system finding him at Gyth's, and I felt even more unsettled than I had before I showed up.

I jumped into the shower with a wish that it would wash away the troublesome thoughts in my mind and also allow me to not feel like a zombie so I could function for the day. But I truly didn't know where to begin or what to do. With no home, needing to get away from where I lived, and not having a job, I was in desperate need of some direction. Along with help.

After toweling off, I threw on a pair of yoga pants and a t-shirt that had piles of books on it, with a person peeking out from underneath the stack and it read, '*Get lost in the story.*' I felt marginally better.

Until I looked in the mirror.

Dark circles underlined my eyes, I'd lost weight, and I looked pale. The woman staring back at me looked like someone who'd seen better days. Things had for sure been rough. I ran my hands down my face and sighed. It was time to turn things around. Hopefully coming to Portland would be good for us and not a mistake.

But if we left, where would we go?

The thought crossed my mind as I walked out of the bedroom trying to be quiet and let my kiddo sleep. As I padded down the hallway, a knock sounded at the front door, and although it was quiet, I still jumped out of my skin.

Getting my bearings, I slowly moved toward the door and

went up on my toes to peek through the peephole. I frowned, confused at why someone would knock so early in the morning and walk away. Too curious to let it go, I checked the peephole one more time. When I didn't see anyone, I dropped back to the flats of my feet and opened the door.

Nobody was there.

But an earthy, woodsy scent that had always short-circuited my brain lingered in the air. And I knew then exactly who'd been outside my door. I just didn't know why.

Then my eyes caught sight of a white, paper, handle bag, and cup sitting on the ground. It was a damn good thing I hadn't kicked them. Squatting down, I picked up the paper cup with the plastic lid and my breath caught when I saw the writing on the outside.

'Brin, it's just how you like it.'

It may have been Rowan but how would he know what I liked anymore or even remember anything about me? He only cared about himself.

Yet he brought you coffee.

Wasn't I the one who'd just been resting in bed praying there was such a thing as a coffee fairy? I just never imagined it would be in the form of Rowan.

Grabbing the items, I stood and took one last look both ways down the hall to make sure nobody was watching me. Then because I couldn't help myself, I took one more whiff and inhaled before quickly shutting the door. Rowan's scent was like a drug.

Addicting.

I spun around and headed to the marble kitchen island and set the stuff down. I stepped back and stared at it. What if he didn't know me at all and everything he brought was stuff I hated? How would that make me feel?

Or what if he was right?

Maybe that feeling would be worse.

He made me lose my mind. Always had. Rowan was infuriating, reckless, exhilarating, charismatic, and as much as I hate to say it, he also was sweet. But his free spirit and fear of attachment always outweighed softer feelings.

As one of his best friends, it had been difficult at times but our friendship had been worth it. He watched over me just like Luke had. And he needed me as much as I had him.

But as someone whose heart had been invested differently, it crushed me to the core. I learned to deal with it, live with it, and move on. So how was it that I was right back where I had been before with so many emotions circling my system like a swarm of bees ready to sting?

I wasn't sure but the need to see what was in the cup was calling my name and I reached for it, taking a small sip.

A moan escaped me and a tingle raced up my spine.

He remembered.

The smooth, strong taste of a banana nut, white-mocha latte hit my tongue and warmed my throat. I was crazy for anything banana flavored and that hadn't changed. How did he remember that?

Another gulp made its way to my stomach and swirled like a tornado, twisting my insides with an intensity that was hard to ignore. Trying to shove down my emotions, I looked around the room, but my eyes came back to the bag still sitting there. With shaky fingers, I opened it and peered inside.

A couple of gooey cinnamon rolls laid inside, making my mouth water. It was another one of my vices and I loved them. Next to them was a smaller white bag. I pulled it out and opened the top. Inside sat a kids-sized apple juice.

One lone tear slipped down my cheek before I could stop it.

Not only had Rowan remembered me, but he thought about Zander too.

I couldn't let the sugary sweet treats and thoughtfulness cause me to let down my guard or things to go any further. It was all a weapon for disaster in the making.

If I let the wall down a smidge, then it may keep tumbling down and he'd get closer to finding out—

"Mommy," Zander said sleepily as he approached.

Thank gosh he'd saved me from where my mind was headed.

Looking at my son in his lightweight transformer pajamas, his blonde hair sticking up in all directions, and his innocent face made my heart go pitter-pat.

No matter how hard things had been throughout the years he was the best thing that had ever happened to me and I wouldn't change any heartache in a million years because it brought me the biggest joy in life.

Being a mother.

While I may be doing it on my own, I had a damn good role model. My mother was like the queen of single mothers. Well, she may have shared that position with one other person. Rowan's mama. They had both been spectacular, bless their souls.

A small hand slipped into one of mine that was free of the delicious coffee I held.

"I'm hungry, Mommy."

We didn't normally start the day off with sweets, but it was a different kind of day in a new place and we had been given a gift so I would let him indulge. With a banana added to the mix.

"Go sit down at the table, honey, and I will show you what Rowan brought you."

"He got me something?"

My son sounded amazed. He didn't have many people in his life except for Luke's parents and I did my best to stay clear of them as much as possible. Although they made that very difficult. I could barely handle them and Zander didn't take to them well. So I couldn't see why the group of people we'd found just the day before and the fact Rowan already had given him something was a treat for him.

As much as it scared me that it had been Rowan who Zander seemed to be clinging to, I was happy to see the big smile on my little guy's face.

"He did, wasn't that nice?" Even as painful as it was being around Rowan again, worrisome too, I always would teach my son to be thankful and appreciate what he had.

"Yeah, it was super-duper nice."

He ran to the table and jumped up into the chair while I grabbed the stuff. I took it over to him and set the apple juice, banana, fork, and plate down in front of him. Zander looked up at me with a confused expression and a small frown. I couldn't hold back the little giggle that escaped me at the look on his face. He'd expected it to be good and I was teasing him.

Then I pulled the bag from around my back that I had held hidden and his eyes lit up. "Is that what he brought me?" he asked, touching the bag.

"Yup." I smiled and pulled out the messy, sugary, substance and placed it on the plate.

The darn things were huge. Zander may be on a sugar high the rest of the day after eating it, but he was practically vibrating with excitement.

"Wow." He grabbed the fork and dug in for his first bite.

"This is so good, Mommy," he managed to say with his mouth full of food.

"Manners, Little Man. Don't talk with your mouth full."

Making an exaggerated show of chewing the massive chunk of cinnamon roll he just shoved in his mouth, he finished and then said, "Sorry."

Smiling, I ruffled his hair and went back to grab my treat so I could eat with Zander. When the first bite hit my mouth a moan of appreciation escaped me. It was best not to ask where to find the scrumptious baked goods or I may not be able to talk myself out of going there all the time.

I had enough of that in my life as it was.

THE MORNING HAD GONE by in a blur.

Zander and I had gotten dressed before running out to find a store where we could buy a few more clothing items for the two of us and some things for the room Zander was using so it felt more like his and for a boy his age. I am sure I could have called one of the ladies to ask where to find the stores needed, but I didn't want to bother them. We managed to find a Target and also grabbed some lunch at a Red Robin while out and about.

Just as we walked back in the door from our outing, my phone alerted me to a text from Summer asking if we'd like to come over so the boys could play and have dinner. I knew I'd come to get away from everything back where I'd lived and hoped Gyth could somehow help me if it came down to me needing it, but I wasn't sure I had been thinking clearly.

And now that I found Rowan was in the same place, thinking was even harder.

However, my biggest reason for coming was for my son

and I knew that playing with his new friend would make him happy. That was all I needed to know to give her my answer.

I fired off a quick text to tell Summer yes, ask what time, and check on what I could bring.

My nerves got the best of me as we walked up to her door, but I pushed them down. This was for Zander, who held one hand and in the other, I was armed with a container of cookies. Summer had told me not to bring anything, but I couldn't very well go without something.

Zander dropped my hand and very enthusiastically knocked on the door, before hitting the doorbell way too many times.

I was about to tell him that it was rude when the door swung open and Summer and her son Dexter were standing there. It took about two seconds before Dexter and Zander were off to play. Giving a small shrug and a laugh, I held out the cookies.

"Come in," Summer said as she took them from me, opening the lid and peeking inside. "Thank you, but you didn't have to bring cookies."

A deep voice interrupted before I could reply.

"Sunshine, did you say cookies?"

Gyth came up behind his wife and peered over her shoulder. "Yes, I did. Take them in the kitchen and don't eat them all before dinner," she told him, handing him the container.

"Aww, are you worried I will spoil my meal?"

"Smartass." She smacked him on the ass as he walked away.

"Hi, Brinley. Thanks for the cookies!" he yelled over his shoulder.

Laughing, I replied with a hello and then looked at Summer. Her eyes sparkled with love and humor.

"What do you want to bet they are gone before the night is over?"

Maybe the evening wouldn't be so bad. I may have had some anxiety around going over there, but the couple was a hoot.

The laughter they brought may be just what I needed.

Chapter Ten

ROWAN

I JUST WANTED A GLIMPSE OF HER.

A week had gone by and I knew she'd been carefully avoiding me. While I didn't want to push, I had wanted to see her and make sure she and Zander were okay. It hadn't happened though and I needed to find a way to rectify that.

I knew anyone, including her, who knew the way I'd behaved wouldn't understand why now after all that time I cared.

I'd never stop caring. It was because I cared so deeply that I had to run before.

But I never forgot anything about Brinley.

The way she smelled, how beautiful she was, her sweetness, and the way she…

I groaned, shoving the last thought away. It just might be the death of me.

Chapter Eleven

BRINLEY

MY LUCK HAD RUN OUT.

It seemed childish sneaking around over the past week, but I didn't know what to do with all the emotions that Rowan had brought to the surface and I was overwhelmed. There was a tug-of-war going on inside me every second.

Should I stay or should I go?

Do I hate him or do I still–

I didn't get to finish the last thought because it was interrupted when I slammed into a hard wall of muscle. My hands came up instinctively to try and save myself, but it backfired because I wasn't safe at all when I found that they were planted on the sculpted ridges of Rowan's hard abs. A tingle started in each finger and zipped right through my palms and up my arms as I looked up and met his gaze.

Something brewed in his dark, intense eyes and I sucked in a breath. It had been so long since

I touched a man and my face flushed with embarrassment. I hadn't had my hands on anyone since—

"Mommy, is Rowan coming with us?" Zander asked from beside me.

When I heard his voice it jolted me out of the daze I had been in and I snatched my hands off Rowan's body as if I had been burned.

It was Saturday evening and we were just heading out the door to get pizza with some of the gang. Summer, Gyth, and their son were going, and Alley, Landon, and their sweet little girl. It sounded like the others were not going to make it, but that was okay. I was adjusting to everyone and smaller groups of people at a time felt less intimidating.

I was, however, feeling more nervous being around Alley again now that I knew she was an author. Talking about books was my thing, but I didn't want to babble like an idiot and make a fool out of myself.

"*Mommm*." My son drew out the word and I looked down at him.

"Honey, I don't know what Rowan is doing." I brought my eyes back to the man standing in front of me who was watching the exchange and lifted one eyebrow in question.

"Well, I was just about to knock on the door when you assaulted me," he said with a devilish smirk. "I was going to check to see if you wanted to ride over to the pizza place with me since you may not know your way around."

Damn, the man was infuriating. Always had been. He needed to wipe that smirk right off his rugged, intriguing, and seriously handsome face. But it was all those things combined that always had all the girls in school, and I am sure the women later, falling to their knees around him.

"I didn't assault you," I scoffed, making a disgusted, unla-dylike sound.

His smile just got bigger. *Ugh.*

"Mommy, I want to go. Dexter will be there waiting to play games and I won't be there." Zander tugged on my hand. "And I'm *soooo* hungry."

My son had been dramatic lately, but it was great seeing him thriving and coming out of his shell. Back home he'd played with other kids at preschool, but he seemed to be happier with his new friends. More comfortable and certainly animated.

It had a smile tugging at the corners of my mouth.

That was all I wanted. For Zander to thrive and be happy.

I grabbed my purse off the hook by the door and looked at Rowan again.

The look he gave me was almost pleading and unsure. He held his ground while he waited for my reply.

I knew I was losing my mind when the words that came tumbling out of my mouth went against everything I'd told myself I would never do again. But they did get a hooray out of Zander though of course.

"We'll ride with you."

Rowan's eyebrows hit his hairline in surprise and then a small grin spread across his face. He held his arm out to gesture for us to walk ahead of him and I found myself for the second time in a week with my back turned away from him and heat trickling up my spine knowing he was watching me.

What had I done?

THE RIDE in Rowan's truck was worrisome and uncomfortable.

It was a good thing the pizza place wasn't too far and my son was such a chatterbox. He asked Rowan endless questions about the Army and random stuff. That had allowed me just to listen, but I was worried about what might come up in their conversation and started to panic a smidge.

Somehow we'd made it to the restaurant without incident.

I saw Rowan start to round the front of the car after he got out and I scrambled to get out quickly because there was no way he was helping me from the vehicle. I'd already caused a scene when I told him a little too abruptly that I could get in his truck myself when he'd opened the door and looked as if he was going to help me inside.

He was being nice, but I couldn't handle it. Everything was such a mess. After jumping out, I went to the back passenger side myself and got Zander out. He immediately ran to Rowan's side and slipped his hand into his.

I noticed the shock on Rowan's face, but he went with the flow. As they headed toward the doors of the restaurant, my feet stood frozen in place, and my heart was in my throat. How was I supposed to keep it together when things like that happened?

Because I felt like I was about to lose my mind.

Rowan glanced back over his shoulder at me. "You coming?"

All I could do was nod. Coaxing my feet to get a move on and saying a silent prayer I would make it through the evening, I followed.

When we walked inside, everyone was already there. I couldn't help but notice Summer and Alley's eyes had gone straight to Zander and Rowan's hands. Then they glanced up at me and it was easy to see they were looking at me to see if I was okay. I didn't think these ladies missed much and that was also a bit concerning.

Saving me from the panic attack I was about to have, Alley clapped her hands and asked the boys if they wanted to play some games while we ordered? That did it. My son released Rowan's hand as he and Dexter bounced in front of her excitedly with their hands out as she distributed coins she already had ready.

"You big boys go play with them too," she said to Gyth, Landon, and Rowan.

When the guys walked up to Alley and held their hands out for money, we all started laughing.

"Get your own money, you big buffoons," Alley told them.

The grown men whined like they were five years old and then wandered off with the boys, but then Landon came back to take his daughter in the stroller with him.

"He can't stand to be away from her," Alley said. "He is such an amazing dad."

It was sweet but I also couldn't help the pang that hit my chest. I'd always wanted that for Zander. But that wouldn't be possible. I'd only loved once and it wasn't happening again, so there wouldn't be someone brought into our lives to make a family the way Alley and the other ladies had.

"I'm sorry," Alley rushed to say. "That was insensitive of me and I am so sorry about Luke."

Another direct hit.

Nausea swirled in my gut at Luke's name. Why did he have to be gone? He sacrificed so much and got so little in return and it was all my fault. But not only that, all the things I had shoved down inside, hidden away, clawed to break free because it was eating me alive.

How was I supposed to keep up the front I'd been putting on?

I was so tired.

"Anytime you want to talk, any of us ladies are here for you," Summer said. "Now, who's ready for some fun?"

"Me, I'm starving," I told her.

Pizza, games, and laughter followed. Watching the guys play games with the boys was a hoot. The ladies and I sometimes wondered if they were all not the same age the way they carried on.

Seeing Zander bond with Rowan was the only part that had me twisted up inside.

It was bitter-sweet.

All in all it was a good night, until the dreaded ride home. Once we said goodbye to everyone and got back in the truck, I let Zander do the talking again, until he'd fallen asleep. Those last few minutes were silent torture. I also didn't make it out of the truck fast enough to get my son and before I knew it, Rowan had come around and picked up Zander to carry him in.

I did my best to protest and tell him I could do it myself, but Rowan didn't budge and I had no choice but to follow him inside. When I unlocked and opened the door, he stepped right in and carried Zander toward the hall to his room.

"Just put him in my bed, please."

Without argument, he did as I asked, but I still found myself explaining. "There have been a lot of adjustments and changes. Right now he doesn't feel comfortable in the other room alone."

After laying him down and heading back to the front door, he said, "You will get no argument from me. I am sure it has been tough."

He turned to me as he opened the door and stopped, his face full of pain. I'd seen it on him many times when things were eating at him, but he never did anything about it. Rowan clammed up and closed himself off during those moments. At least most of the time. There were only a couple of times I could remember when he let his emotions show.

But then the wall was always back up.

So his next words seemed out of character. "We need to talk, Brin."

He took a few steps forward, his tall frame towering over me as his eyes pleaded with me to say yes. But I couldn't. His being so close scared me for so many reasons. I didn't know if I wanted to scream or cry. Being yanked in two directions made me feel as if I was a rubber band about to snap.

"I can't." My voice came out weak.

"Please, Buttercup."

Up until then he may have said Brin, but he hadn't dared to use the other nickname he'd had for me since we'd met. It had been so special to me and for just a second I faltered. Almost caved. But then the anger kicked in and I snapped like I'd been worried about.

"Don't you dare call me that!" My voice was raised and I took a big breath trying to calm the storm brewing inside. I didn't want to wake up Zander. "You left without a backward glance and broke my heart. Not only that but you hurt Luke too."

A few tears trickled down my cheek and I furiously swiped my cheeks to brush them away. I never thought I would be having this conversation and I honestly couldn't go on.

"Go. Just please go." I pointed to the door and with a stricken look Rowan walked away.

It was what he always did. It was what he was good at.

No fight, just flight.

Chapter Twelve

ROWAN

YOU LEFT WITHOUT A BACKWARD GLANCE.

Five words that replayed in my head for days like a broken record.

But they were not true. Yet, Brinley didn't know that and I hadn't told her. Just because she didn't see me every time I'd been home didn't mean I wasn't ever there.

I'd watched from afar and it had been excruciating.

Especially after the last time she and I had seen each other. But there wasn't a time when she was far from my mind.

When she muttered those words after our pizza outing, they burned, but the hurt that had poured off her in waves had me doing exactly what she asked. She'd wanted me to leave and once again I'd walked away. How was I ever going to repair what had happened between us?

Was fixing things even possible?

I was at work contemplating what I should do and was caught up in my head so I didn't hear Gyth walk in. While I should be focusing on my job, all I had been doing was thinking about Brinley. She didn't want to talk so how would that work with both of us in the same place? And she needed these people now more than ever.

"Maybe I need to leave," I mumbled to myself, but it was a little too loud.

"What the fuck, man?" Gyth sat down in the brown, leather chair in the corner of the room, with a frown on his face. "Why would you say that?"

He didn't understand. How could he? Gyth didn't know all the particulars, and if he did, he might ask me to leave himself. He'd been close to Luke. Thinking about what I had done made me feel physically sick. I had screwed up many times and deep down I knew I didn't deserve to be forgiven.

Even if I wanted it more than my next breath.

There was also no way to talk to Luke about it now and the way I treated my best friend had screwed with my head so bad that at a time, I wished I could take his place. He should be here right now with Brinley, not me. I was just the guy she barely could stand to look at.

"You don't understand," I find myself telling Gyth.

"Then how about you tell me?"

Maybe that is what I should do.

With Brinley and Zander showing up, the truth would almost likely either surface or one of us would truly end up leaving. I'd already known if it came to that it would be me to go. I wouldn't let those two suffer or lose out because of me.

"What is it he's supposed to tell you?" Braxton said, walking in and sitting in the other chair next to Gyth.

Great, now it was like a tag team and I was bound to lose.

Although, if anyone should know it was probably those two. Braxton was the first one of the guys I'd met. We had run into one another at a bar while on leave. We'd hit it off right away even though we were in different branches of the military and he'd told me about his plans with Gyth to head back to his hometown and start their business. By the night's end, and before parting ways he'd told me to look him up after I was out if I was interested in a job.

If I decided to leave it would suck, but I'd do what needed to be done.

"Rowan said maybe he needed to leave and we all know he's been off his game for over a week now, so I think it's time he explains some shit and gets it off his chest."

Braxton frowned. "You don't like it here? Is something not working?"

I hated that he thought that. It had been awesome working with Braxton and the other guys. It was just the job and change I needed when I decided my military days were over. I'd been thinking about it for years before I'd met Braxton, but honestly, I didn't know what I was going to do and I didn't have a place to go home to.

Not able to make something up or deny giving them an answer, I let it fly. With no finesse at all, I blurted, "I slept with Brinley."

I sucked in a breath as shock crossed both the guy's faces. But they masked their expressions quickly and both looked to be thinking. They studied me like an insect under a microscope before either of them spoke.

"I knew you guys were friends at one time, but it didn't look as though you were getting along. How did this happen in just a week? And what's the problem?" Braxton asked.

Shit, that was not what I'd meant, but the thought of being with Brin again had my brain thinking about the time we'd been together and wondering what it would be like again. That was never going to happen, though, the first time shouldn't have either.

I just hadn't been able to stop myself.

"I guess I should have explained that better."

Both stared at me, waiting for an explanation. Sighing deeply, I dug deep for the right words, but the truth was, there weren't any. Nothing I could say would make what happened okay.

"Not this week. It was years ago when she and Luke were still married." I was explaining this poorly but I wasn't one to talk about myself, my feelings, or my life. There were maybe a handful of times in my life I'd ever had a long, serious conversation. A couple of times because my mother made me, and I loved my mother. She was also not someone you told no or you might get whacked upside the head. Of course with me it would be done with pure love. The woman was full of heart, soul, and an amazing lady. The other times were with Luke and once with Brinley.

The rest of the time, I shut that shit down. So the talk I was having with Braxton and Gyth, or *attempting* to have, wasn't going so well. When Gyth spoke up, I was the one to be shocked. Instead of beating my ass or kicking me out, he gave me the benefit of the doubt and asked for more information.

"That doesn't sound like you. In the short time I've known you, I've come to believe you're a stand-up guy. Maybe you need to back up and explain more."

"I agree," Braxton added.

I should have said more from the start instead of throwing myself under the bus from the beginning. But all the technicalities of Brin and Luke being separated and finding out they truly didn't have a husband-and-wife relationship, still didn't make me feel okay about it in the end.

I did, however, need to explain better to the two guys in front of me who were not only my co-workers but also people I considered friends. Something I never allowed myself for such a long time when the best ones I had, I'd let down.

"You're right. But before I tell you the story, keep in mind that I still don't feel right about it at all."

The guys nodded in agreement but stayed quiet. With another deep breath, I let my mind wander back in time, and laid my heart bare as the past came forth.

"First, I need to tell Braxton about my sister. Gyth already knows as it came tumbling out when Brinley showed up at his house looking for him. It's not something I like talking about but pertinent to the story or maybe understanding why I am the way I am. Maybe I should have already told you."

"No sweat, man. You will get no judgment from me. It's not always easy to share personal stuff, we all know that."

So I began.

"Jelena always wanted to be with me and my friends. As much as I adored my baby sister, my friends thought it was annoying. Everyone except Luke that was. And while most of the time I allowed her to follow me around like a puppy dog and didn't mind at all, that day I was acting like a little shit. On the cusp of thirteen, I guess I'd decided I needed to play it cool at my age."

I rubbed the spot over my heart that was breaking all over again with each word.

Then, I was transported back in time as the details of the day I lost my sister came free as if they were happening to me all over again.

~

TWELVE-YEARS-OLD

"Rowan," my sister whined. "I want to come with you."

"Jelena, stop being a cry baby. You can't come with us all the time."

My sister was the queen of attitude and knew how to get her way. With her arms crossed, she stomped her foot. "Why not?" she asked in a snotty tone.

Frustration set in as the other boys waited, snickering as my sister and I bickered back and forth.

"Rowan, let your sister go," my mom said as she walked into the room. Her sharp tone held no room for debate and I watched the others scramble out of the house in fear.

"Fine, but she has to keep up." I huffed and walked out of the house, my sister hot on my heels trying to keep up.

"It's okay if she's with us," Luke said from beside me as we all headed out to the field where the treehouse was.

Jelena shoved her way in between Luke and me, then she slipped her hand into mine. When I glanced down I noticed her looking up at us with worship in her eyes. She loved Luke about as much as she did me and she had placed her other hand in his.

Luke didn't seem to mind at all and with the other boys up ahead, I let out a sigh and kept walking. When we reached the treehouse, the others were already up inside and calling out for us to hurry up.

One of them leaned out the front window. "I can't believe your mom makes you bring your little sister. What a drag, man."

"He's mean," Jelena said. "I don't like him."

Dropping my hand from hers I looked over to Luke who was scowling up at the kid shooting off his mouth. We didn't even know him well. All the kids that had come were a year older than Luke and me. They'd overheard us talking about our fort and wanted to see it. Luke had told me not to show them, but I thought it would make us seem cooler and let them come.

I should have been a better brother and also followed

Luke's lead. He was always the nicest kid around and helped out anyone who needed it. But I made one of my first biggest mistakes that day and didn't follow suit.

"You go first," I told Luke. He glanced at my sister reluctantly but then went up the ladder.

Then, instead of letting Jelena go, I scrambled up behind him. That was a big no-no. My mother said she had to always go ahead of me, but I thought if I got up there that maybe she would just go back home.

"Wait, Rowan, I need help!" she called out to me.

"Jelena, just go home with mom."

Her lip jutted out. She was stubborn and I could see in her eyes she wasn't going to listen.

"Fine if you want to come up you need to do it yourself!" I yelled out to her.

And that was exactly what she did.

She was almost to the top when her foot missed a rung on the twelve-foot ladder and it startled her. Her hand lost possession of the one it was holding at almost the same time and backward she went.

Fear sparked in her beautiful green eyes, her hand outreached as if I could save her, and she screamed out my name.

"Rowan!"

Everything felt as if it was in slow motion as terror exploded into every part of my soul.

She hit the ground with a hard thud, her body flopping like a rag doll from impact. I heard a sharp breath leave her lungs and a grunt.

Then... nothing.

My baby sister's eyes were closed, her body lifeless, and she didn't make another peep.

I jumped out onto the ladder and climbed down as fast as

I could, Luke right behind me. Kneeling at her side I gently tried to wake her, but nothing was happening. Her tiny head lay against a rock, blood pooling from the back.

"Luke, hurry, go tell Mama to call 911!"

I didn't have to tell him twice. He was already racing across the field faster than his twelve-year-old legs should have been able to go.

The other boys were still in the treehouse, but I didn't pay them any attention. How could I when the world was crashing down around me? Tears poured down my cheeks and I couldn't have cared less that they all saw me crying.

Every part of my heart and soul was breaking into a million pieces and when I heard my mother's wails as her small frame raced across the field, screaming out for her baby, I knew nothing would ever be the same.

"Please…. Please, Jelena, you have to wake up." Holding her hand in mine, I rocked back and forth. "I promise I will take you everywhere with me always. Just wake up for me."

But she didn't open her eyes or make a sound.

My baby sister never woke up again.

And it was my fault.

I LOOKED over at Braxton and Gyth as tears streamed down my face while I recalled the events of that day. The sorrow in their own eyes made it ten times harder, but I kept on.

"We'd already lost my father who'd died while serving in the Army. That was the reason I'd chosen that branch. My sister had only been one at the time so she didn't remember him, but I did. And because of me, my mother lost her daughter too."

Nausea and guilt swept through me.

"My mama was sick with grief, but she never made me feel as if any of it was my fault. She would tell me time and time again it was an accident and accidents happen. But it didn't have to. If I had told the other boys not to come at all. Or I had been behind her on the ladder. If–"

That was when I was interrupted by Braxton. "You can't predict the future and you were a kid yourself. I am so damn sorry about your sister. I can't imagine if anything would have happened to Alley when we were kids what I would have done. But your mama was right."

I was shaking my head. How could I ever agree or forgive myself for that day?

"That day shaped me into who I was from that moment on. Luke stood by me even when I changed. I didn't let anyone in. I certainly didn't talk about my feelings. And I closed myself off to everyone but him and my mother."

Even they didn't get all of me after Jelena died.

"Until *her*."

Brinley had shaken me up that's for sure.

"Brinley showed up when her mom went to work for Luke's family. She and her mom lived in a small room in their massive house, off the kitchen. Luke being Luke, took her under his wing. It became the three of us instead of just him and me."

"Brin was with us all the time, whether I liked it or not, and at first I was irritated. But just like she had with Luke, she finally nuzzled her way into my heart and carved out her own spot."

My jaw was tight as I kept going and a headache started to surface from the tension. There were good reasons I didn't talk about that kind of stuff.

"I can see how that could happen from just the times I have been around her," Gyth told me.

While I knew he meant nothing by it, a little jealousy crept in at his comment. Which was silly, he had a gorgeous wife and an amazing little boy.

"She is a sweetheart," he added. My dumbass breathed a sigh of relief when all I heard was a friendly tone in his voice.

Get a grip.

"She didn't just bury her way into mine though. Brin also stole Luke's for a time. I tried to steer her in his direction but something was always brewing between us. I just couldn't ever let it happen."

Which was another reason I had to get away as soon as I graduated.

"After a while, Luke realized that he and Brin would only be friends. He'd tried to get me to give Brin a shot, claiming there was always something simmering between us, but I couldn't. And later, when I finally told her about my sister I think she realized just how broken I was. It also didn't help that every girl in school seemed to be falling at my feet."

"Casanova," Gyth muttered.

"What?" Braxton asked, confused as hell.

We got off subject for a moment while Gyth told him about Luke calling me that. Braxton chuckled and then they looked back toward me to keep going.

"Yeah, not my finest of nicknames but even though I didn't take all those girls up on the offers they placed in front of me, I just let Brin think I did."

"Shit," I heard Gyth mutter.

"Yeah well, I didn't say I was a smart guy. All I knew was I needed her to move on. Have a life. Not hope for something that couldn't be." I ran my hands through my hair, frustrated with myself for being so dumb even for a teenage guy.

"Dude, it may not have been the best tactic but I get you were trying to do the right thing in your mind," Brax said.

A sigh escaped from deep in my throat. "I was trying to do the right thing. Then, one time when I had come back home and was on leave, I fucked up and did so many things wrong."

My chest hurt and I rubbed it again. This was so damn hard to relive while I talked to the guys.

"You see, Brin was a year younger and we left when she was going to be a senior. Her mom was already not doing well and just after she graduated her mom passed away. She had cystic fibrosis. Brinley was so young and her mother was all she had. Except for Luke and I. Me, well I was being a selfish bastard and trying to not feel anything. Luke, however, went home and married her."

Looking at Gyth, I could see the wheels turning. He knew more than anyone about Luke but still didn't know what I'd done. Yet, I could see him putting a few things in place. The guy was smart. And if he was figuring it out I knew that Braxton was probably jumping to the same conclusions.

"When Luke's mom was ready to push Brin out, Luke played the hero. He convinced Brinley to marry him so she would have his insurance and he then could help her out. His mom let Brin stay then but it wasn't long until Luke bought them a house. His mother was a nightmare and Luke knew it."

I made a disgusted sound at the thought of that woman. How she raised Luke and he turned out to be so damn honorable and such an amazing guy, I didn't know.

"Luke was the best person I'd ever known. That was obvious from the day we met, but when Jelena passed away and I thought back on that day, I knew he was always a far better human being than I was."

Sometimes the truth hurts.

My palms were sweaty from anxiety and all the emotions

running through me, and I rubbed my hands on my pants as I went on.

"They stayed together for many years and I kept my distance. I wanted them to try and have a real life. The one I told you they deserved. Because you know how the military is. I wasn't on leave much or didn't always choose to take it."

I shook my head at the thought of how I behaved when others needed me. How many times had I been disgusted with my action or non-action but still kept making the wrong choices?

"I'm sure it hurt both my mother and Brinley. I didn't come home more often, but all the memories there killed me. And knowing Brin was married was harder than you probably think."

With the way I acted, I'm sure people thought I was a cold person with not many feelings but that wasn't true. I was just good at hiding them.

"When my mama died I had to come home. And with no questions asked or attempts at trying to make me feel bad for not coming more often or keeping in touch better, Brin helped me handle my mom's passing."

When Gyth said she was sweet he wasn't kidding.

"That time, while I was home, was when I slept with Brinley for the first and only time."

I closed my eyes at the memory. I felt so many things later, but at the time it had felt so right.

"We were talking one night at my hotel after everything had been handled with my mother and Brinley told me that she and Luke were getting a divorce. I knew why they'd gotten married, I just thought maybe over time they'd fall in love but she said they hadn't."

It had felt wrong to be happy about that back then, but I couldn't help the fact that it did.

"They'd separated and would finalize everything the next time he was home, but she admitted it was what they both wanted. She needed to set him free and wanted him to find the kind of love a husband and wife should share. And he wanted her to have the same."

Don't get me wrong, if Brinley would have stayed with him, Luke would have done their song and dance forever just to take care of her. And later they did end up making that decision to salvage the marriage. It wasn't as if I led her to believe there was any future with us.

"One thing led to another and for the first time with my emotions over losing my mother so raw, as well as being in Brinley's arms as she consoled me, I gave in to what had always been between us."

It felt like heaven, but I didn't need to give the guys all the details. Those were ours and ours alone.

"After, even though they were separated, the guilt of them not being divorced still set in. She mentioned wanting a family one day and how that wasn't going to happen with them. But it scared the shit out of me because I was never having kids. Then as she fell asleep she muttered she loved me. I don't have a clue if she knew she even said it, but I panicked."

"I don't think you're the first guy to freak at those words. Hey, I even had my moments of doubt, denial, and worry when I first met Summer," Gyth said. "Then one day I pulled my head out of my ass and knew she would be mine."

I'd served in the military for years and had been in war zones but hearing the L-word had terror running through me more than anything I'd been through during my time. Gyth telling me that he had his own freak-out moments helped me to feel a little more normal. Especially after witnessing how his relationship with his wife turned out.

"So you see, I should have walked away earlier. I was good at that. But I waited until we shared what we had and then when the most amazing woman I'd ever known fell asleep, I ran like a coward in the middle of the night."

"We all make mistakes but it seems to me that what you keep forgetting is that sleeping with her wasn't one of them. She and Luke were never really a couple from what you just said. It was only on paper. And they were getting a divorce."

Gyth was animated, his hands doing half the talking as he got his point across.

"Leaving without talking to her was probably the only thing you should have done differently. But we don't always think when tested and put in a place that is uncomfortable to us. Lord knows if you ask any of us guys, we can tell you a story or two as well," he continued.

I nodded. "Somewhere down inside I know you're right and I can't imagine what Brin thought when she woke up and I wasn't there. But in the end, maybe seeing what a douche I was is the very thing that led her and Luke into giving it a real shot."

Even if I'd realized I made a mistake and wanted another chance it had been too late.

"Because that's exactly what they did. I'd gotten calls that they needed to talk to me and I tried to ignore them all. Then one day I went home to visit my family's graves sites and decided to go talk to Brin. Luke was home."

I rubbed my hands in my hair again. If I had any left by the end of this conversation, I'd be surprised.

"God what a sight they made." I sucked in a breath as I envisioned it like it was yesterday.

"Standing in their front yard, they hadn't seen me, but I saw them. They were laughing, hugging, and she was teasing him. I could tell because she swatted at him playfully and then she turned so I could see her better. That's when I saw her round belly. They'd finally made a life and a family. No way was I going to crash that party."

With the picture of them in my head again, an invisible knife felt as if it had been plunged into my chest. My breathing was a little rapid and the headache was on its way to a ten, and about to slit my head open. But I was almost done.

"Once again I left and I didn't go back. That was until Luke's funeral."

Gyth squinted his eyes and studied me for a second with a puzzled glance.

"Brin said his best friend didn't make it. At the time I didn't know it was you, but you were there?"

"I stayed in the shadows. Honestly, I didn't think she'd want me there and I wasn't doing well knowing I hadn't been there for Luke. Which sounds like an asshole thing to say when I wasn't there for Brinley either."

Rubbing my hands down my face, I couldn't help but be glad this conversation was almost over. It wasn't easy at all.

"My head was in a bad place. I would have done more harm than good. And that was the case later too."

"How so?" Braxton asked, leaning forward. "I'm sure she would have forgiven you and been happy to have you there while raising Zander."

Another direct hit. It was like a game of Battleship and all my ships were sinking as more memories slammed into me.

"I'd lost some guys I served with, fucked up with Brinley, lost my mother, and then Luke. All while never forgiving myself for causing my sister's death. When I say I was in a dark place, I mean it was pitch black, and I didn't know that I wanted to be living anymore."

"I'm sorry, man. I shouldn't have just pushed—"

I put my hand up to stop Braxton. He didn't do anything wrong and he should have known more about me before hiring me in the first place. That too was on me for not being more straight with him.

"It's okay. It took me a while to dig myself out of that. And truthfully, I don't know how I did. When I met you and you told me you had a place for me here if I wanted it, I think it gave me some new direction and I could start a new life. I hope knowing that at one point I wanted to end mine, doesn't change your mind about me being able to handle this job."

"I know you can handle it. We're good," Braxton said.

"And now that you know all the other shit, do you want me to leave?"

It was a question for them both, but it was Gyth I looked at for an answer because he was the one that had been closer to Luke than Braxton had been, and also who Brinley came seeking help from.

"You knew Luke better than I did," Gyth started. "But I knew him well enough to know that he wouldn't be mad at you and he'd want you around to help Brinley and Zander out."

When he said that, an odd look crossed his face just as it had back in his yard the day Brinley showed up and I wondered what that was all about, but he kept talking so I didn't ask.

"So, no I don't want you to leave and I think I can speak for Braxton here too. Right, man?"

"Of course I don't. We're a team. I'm sorry about all the losses and what you went through but remember we are always around to hear you out," Braxton said.

"I think I might be talked out for another decade or so, but thanks," I told him. We all laughed at my dry attempt at humor.

"That brings me back to one more thing," Gyth said. "Was that why you thought you should leave or is there more?"

"I thought that would make you want me to take a hike but when I said that I was thinking that Brinley didn't want me around. She pretty much hates my guts." Not that I could blame her. "And I think she needs all of you and your women in her life. I don't want to scare her off."

"She'll come around," Gyth said, confidently.

"You think so?" I cocked my head to the side pondering his words. "How do you know?"

"We've seen it happen multiple times around here and it started with me," Braxton said, grinning.

It was kind of odd the way he'd put it.

But a guy could hope.

Chapter Thirteen

BRINLEY

DECISION. DECISION.

Sometimes it was a toss-up on how I felt about being a grown-up.

Two more weeks slipped by and I knew I had to make a choice. I couldn't just sit around and not work even if spending quality time with my son was the best thing in life. And it kept me busy. However, I wasn't wired that way and had been taught how to be a hard-working responsible person. Something my mother instilled in me early and led by example herself. But it was time to create a new life with stability for Zander and me.

So, one evening I sat down and made a list of all the pros and cons of staying in Portland. But it didn't seem like much of a list because in the con column there was only one word.

Rowan.

My hand hesitated when I'd written his name because even though I didn't know that I could ever forgive him and I was scared to death about our past rearing its ugly head, part of me wished I could have my friend back.

But how was that even possible?

I had a lot to think about, but right then I had to get Zander over to Summer and Gyth's place to play with their son. Gyth was going to watch the kids while I went to lunch with the ladies.

It was something they liked to do from time to time and I guess they wanted to talk to me about something. What that was, I had no clue, and I was a bit nervous to find out.

I'd been around them several times and while nothing seemed amiss to give me any indication that what they wanted to say was bad, I was still worried.

One thing I noticed was that the few times everyone had been together, most recently at a barbeque at Braxton and Jurnee's place, Rowan had been very quiet. He'd also been giving me a wide berth and not pushing me to talk or interact with him.

What if the ladies wanted to tell me they didn't think me being around was such a great idea? I mean Rowan was their friend before I ever stepped foot in town and he had his job with the guys.

While I may be overreacting or conjuring up issues that were not there, the fact remained that I needed to make up my mind anyway. Maybe after hearing what they had to say it would sway me in one direction or the other.

"Mommy, are we going yet?" Zander asked, looking up at me with his head cocked back dramatically as he inhaled deeply through his nose.

Before responding, he carried on.

"I like it at Dexter's because Gyth is funny and plays with us. Can we get a daddy too?" he pleaded.

I'd never lied to my son about Luke being his father. He knew as he got older that I was married to him and he would have been a good daddy, but he wasn't his biological dad. Zander wasn't quite old enough to understand it all along the way but recently had been asking more questions and now being around other fathers, who happened to be amazing, it seemed he was wondering more.

I couldn't blame him and knew the day would come when the harder inquiries would arise. I just wasn't prepared for them to come at me like flying darts right then and hit me like a bullseye to the heart.

Taking my son's hand, I led him to the sofa in the living room and sat down, taking him with me. With him on my lap, I turned him sideways so he could see me when I spoke.

"Baby, I know it isn't easy to understand but we can't just go out and get a daddy." His lip jutted out a fraction and the sadness in his eyes killed me.

"Why not?" he said in a small voice.

"Well, Mommy would have to find someone that she liked and you liked before they could be a daddy."

Heck, I was explaining this like crap but I was struggling myself. Then, the next comment shook me to the core.

Zander seemed to think for a second and then said, "Let's ask Rowan. I like him, he's nice." A triumphant smile split his face as if he'd figured it all out. "Can we ask him today to be my daddy?"

Everything in me stilled, then my pulse picked up and emotions slammed into me like a sneak wave that had me sinking in despair.

"Mom!" Zander called out, trying to snap his little fingers in front of my face to get my attention. Not able to snap yet, his skin just brushed together, leaving a swooshing sound in their wake. "Are you listening? I want to ask him today."

Popping out of the daze I was in, I closed my eyes for a second and tried to get my bearings. A question I never thought would come and my worst nightmare all happened in the blink of an eye. And it was my fault for coming to the town to find Gyth. But how could I have ever known Rowan would be in the same place?

"Honey, we are going to be late getting to Dexter's so we will talk about this later, okay?" Nice deflection I know, but I seriously had not known what to do. It scared the crud out of me.

"Yay, let's go." Zander jumped from my lap and ran toward the front door.

And just like that, because he was a kid and wanted to play, the fire was diverted for the time being, but I knew it would come back to burn me later.

I FELT like I was in the hot seat.

After dropping off Zander, I rode to lunch with Summer and we met up with all the other ladies at a cool Mexican restaurant called Who Song & Larry's on the Columbia River. It was a beautiful summer day and we'd been seated out on the deck under a large umbrella.

While everyone ordered drinks from the waitress, I gazed out at the sun shining off the rippling river and tried to shake off my nerves. Jurnee, Summer, Alley, Teal, and Gemma were there and it was a little intimidating. When they had get-togethers and the guys, Jurnee's parents, and more people were mingling, it hadn't been so awkward.

But it felt different with just the ladies. And all of them too. Sometimes not everyone made it to stuff and it had only been a few times. I hadn't seen Gemma since the first time I had arrived. From what I heard in conversation she was not only busy, but the ladies said she had been a little quiet lately and nobody knew why, even if she insisted everything was fine.

"So," Alley started.

Here we go. Shit.

"I was really the one that wanted to talk to you, but the other ladies just used it as an excuse to have a girl's day," she added.

No denial came from anyone, they just laughed.

"You know we'll use any excuse for a day away with our friends," Summer added.

Hearing her use the word friends made me wonder if I was included in their group. I was there with them so my body fluttered with hope and some of my worries disappeared.

While the others commented on Summer's reply, Teal who was seated on one side of me leaned over and softly said, "It wasn't that long ago that I was right where you are, but trust me, we already think of you as one of us."

Her smile was so sweet and genuine, along with her words, that I found myself relaxing even more. "Thank you," I whispered back.

The waitress snuck in and took our orders before Alley could get back to business, but as soon as that was done, she launched in with her spiel. It wasn't bad at all, in fact, it was an amazing offer, and excitement raced through me.

"As you know I'm an author and you love books. I recently lost my editor due to personal reasons with her family and have also been searching for a PA to help me out. Now that I have a family I want to free up time for them." A loving smile swept across her face. "I was thinking maybe you would like to take one or both on as a job until you decide if it is for you or you are going to open up another bookstore?"

I had revealed that I had an English degree, thinking I would teach but decided that the bookstore was more my dream. While I hadn't edited before, I knew I could do it. But why did she want me?

"You look stunned. Don't be. The job, either one or both would be perfect for you. And I pay good," Alley said with a big smile and a wink.

Hadn't I been thinking just that morning I needed to be working? But I also hadn't determined where that would be and yet I wanted to say yes. Still I hesitated. Rowan's name still sat in that con column and Zander had thrown me for a loop with his questions. Even more than before, staying may not be possible.

"I don't know if I am staying," I blurted out and every-one's eyes zeroed in on me.

"You have to stay," Jurnee said sweetly. "We want you to."

"Why wouldn't you stay?" Teal asked.

"I think you'll like it here and you came to seek out Gyth for a reason," Summer added.

"You fit in," Gemma told me.

Everyone fired off questions or comments one by one and my head was spinning. But when Alley spoke again, well, I thought about running.

"If we are being honest, we all have our theories about you and Rowan. It may not be our place to butt in, but as we said before we've all had our share of hard times, reunions, and pasts to get through. Reconciliations too." She looked at me but I remained quiet, not sure what to say. "No matter what happened before or didn't, and what could in the future, we'll help you through it."

Everyone nodded in agreement.

"Why don't we eat, have a nice time, and you think about my offer? But just know we all want you to stay," Alley said.

With the emotional lump in my throat and fighting back tears, I couldn't speak. I croaked out a small, "O-Okay."

Everyone smiled, food arrived and the rest of lunch had gone on without any more intense conversation. But my mind never stopped spinning or thinking about everything that was said.

What was I going to do with it though?

.

Chapter Fourteen

BRINLEY

....

I FROZE WHEN I WALKED INTO SUMMER'S FOYER.

While I expected my son to come flying at me, excited I was back, I wasn't prepared for him to be dragging Rowan along with him. Hand in hand they came toward me, and with every step panic swept through my entire body.

Oh crap.

After my conversation with Zander earlier, I intended to grab my son and get the hell out of the house as fast as possible.

But that didn't happen.

"Mommy, you're back. Look, Rowan came over so now you can ask him."

All the air left my lungs in one big swoosh.

Rowan's brows knitted in confusion. "Ask me what?"

Finally getting my feet to move, I closed the last few inches that separated my son and me, reaching over to take his hand so we could leave. My fingers brushed Rowan's and an electric shock raced up my hand. How could he have that effect on me?

After pulling my son from his grasp, I tucked him in close

to my body and turned to leave. Summer was right behind me, a puzzled look on her face. I couldn't blame her, I was acting a bit crazy. Before we moved, Zander broke free and ran right back to Rowan.

Looking up at him, he asked, "Can you be my daddy?"

Shock stretched across Rowan's face, Summer gasped from behind me, and Gyth had just walked into the show with a strange look across his face. As for me, well I didn't have the first clue what to do, but none of that mattered because my son was on a mission.

"I want to have a daddy too. Like Dexter does."

I didn't know where Dexter was right then but I was glad he wasn't there because it would probably have confused the poor kid. The audience we had was hard enough and it spiraled even further out of control from there.

"Luke was going to be my daddy and Mommy said he would've been a really good one, but he went to Heaven. Since we don't know where my real daddy is either, I thought maybe you could do it?"

Zander didn't know the bomb he had just dropped at Rowan's feet. While he didn't come out and tell the full secret I carried, he had told enough that it wouldn't be long before either Rowan put pieces together or he'd demand the answers to the questions I could clearly see on his mind.

Rowan's gaze met mine and I didn't like what I saw. Right away so many emotions flashed through his dark eyes and a storm was brewing in their depths.

For the first time since I had gotten pregnant with Zander, I wanted to lie. I know some people would say I had already done that, but that wasn't exactly true. However, if lying by omission was what they believed, then I would be in contempt of that. But I tried and failed to do the right thing a long time ago. It wasn't all my fault it didn't work out. What

I hadn't done was blatantly ever lied to a single soul, including my son.

I wouldn't start now. So when Rowan opened his mouth and asked his first question I knew would only be the start of the ones to come, I answered with nothing less than the truth.

Honestly.

"Is he mine?"

Tears streamed down my face. My body shook uncontrollably. And I said one little word that was so complex it would change everything in the blink of an eye.

"*Yes.*"

Then Rowan did what he did best.

He walked out the door.

But this time there was only me to blame.

I SHOULD BE USED to it by now.

But it still pierced my heart all over again.

And this time when Rowan left and I saw Zander's tears, I thought nothing in the world would be right again. I wasn't the only one that was hurting as we watched him walk away. It was ten times worse this time when I knew it affected my son.

There I was with my Zander, who'd just found out the man he wished was his dad, was actually his father. But Rowan left without a word, leaving me with a broken-hearted little angel who didn't deserve that. I knew he must be confused and I had a lot of explaining to do. Not only to him, but to Summer and Gyth, who stood silently as the scene had unfolded.

"Maybe we should sit and finally talk?" Gyth said.

Straight to the point might be the best approach to take, but I needed to take care of my son first.

"Hey Zander, why don't we go check on Dexter? He probably wonders where you went," Summer asked him softly.

They both seemed to be reading my thoughts. I didn't think when Zander was upset that it was such a good idea, but the mention of Dexter perked my son up and he took Summer's hand she had outstretched to go find his new friend.

"I'll be back, Mommy." His tears dried up and a small smile lit his face. One thing about coming to Portland was that my son, and even me, had met some amazing people. For now, getting to see Dexter was like a Band-Aid. But the time would come when the wound would open and the hurt would flow again.

Summer gave me a soft smile as they left the room.

Following Gyth into the living room, I took a seat on the plush, beige couch. Scooting myself back into the arranged, dark brown and yellow pillows, I let out a sigh.

Gyth didn't push, he let me get my bearings, but once we sat down it felt wrong to explain everything, but I could address a couple of things. The person I should be talking to first may have left but it was his story to hear before anyone else. I owed him that at least.

Rowan and our son that was.

"I know I sought you out. You had been so kind when you came to see me and the truth is, besides Luke's parents, I don't have anyone. And I didn't even want to be around them, so it's just Zander and me."

I blew out a breath because I was so bad at explaining anything. All my life my mom, Luke, and Rowan were the only people I truly let my guard down around or spoke about my feelings with. Two of them were gone and Rowan had been until recently. There was also a good chance he would be again…

Or maybe it was me that would walk away this time.

"To make one thing clear, Luke's parents knew Zander wasn't Luke's baby. And they always made it well known what they thought about it." I bit my bottom lip as I worked to get control of the anger that swept through me at the mention of her. "My son also knew Luke was going to be his daddy but wasn't his biological father. It was when we got here that he started zeroing in on wanting one."

When I was doing the pros and cons list, I knew that if I stayed I would have had to come clean. I never wrote that down, but like Rowan's name, it would have also gone into both columns. Pro because I wouldn't have to hold it in anymore and con because it could upset many lives and I didn't know in what way. Good or bad? I was still wondering which way that would go after the scene that just played out by the front door.

"Anyway, when our home and my business burned down, it was time for a new life, and I don't know why but this was the only place I could think of going after you said you would always help. I had no idea what I needed and I wasn't really thinking, but all of a sudden we were here."

My hands clenched together where they sat on my lap and then I continued with the last part I would say for the moment.

"I don't know what is going to happen from here, but I need to get my son home to talk to him, and then the next person I need to have a conversation with is Rowan. It is only right that I tell him more first."

Gyth nodded his head. "I understand and agree. Just know that my offer of help still stands. I don't care what the situation is or was, I promised Luke I would be there for you two and that doesn't change."

I thought about that for a minute. And it was sweet, but there was a factor that I thought might switch that up.

"Even though you are friends with Rowan and work together?"

"Of course, that doesn't change a thing," Summer said, walking over to her husband where he sat and placing a hand on his shoulder. "We can support both of you any way you need. Right, Big Guy?" she said lovingly looking at her man.

A little jealousy at what they had swept through me.

"My wife is right."

A small laugh escaped me even in that trying moment at the look on Summer's face that said, 'Of course I'm right, duh.'

Then Gyth continued.

"I think you both will need us and as my wife said, we can be there for everyone. But if I am being honest, even not knowing what happened with you and Rowan in the past, I have a strong feeling you will find that he has changed some and won't let Zander and you down."

I bit the inside of my cheek and my face crinkled up as I thought about the fact he'd just walked out of the house at the confirmation he had a son. As usual, Gyth hijacked my thoughts.

"Rowan leaving a minute ago could be expected from anyone after finding out what he just did. Don't let that sway your thinking that he will keep running. Give him a few to let it sink in. I think you'll be surprised."

My cheek was going to hurt, I bit it so hard.

"I will try. And thank you both," I said softly. "I think it is time to get my son home and I will talk with you guys more later."

"Let me go get Zander," Summer said, and then she was gone.

Silence sat between Gyth and me for a moment. It wasn't uncomfortable I realized. He had such a huge presence but was also like a teddy bear at the same time. Not that he'd probably like knowing I thought that.

Then, he broke the silence with a friendly reminder.

"Don't forget what I said, okay?"

"I won't. Luke was lucky to have such a great friend and I guess that trickled down to me now."

I tried for a small smile, but at the mention of my best friend's name and one of Gyth's too, tears pooled in my eyes. When I looked at Gyth, I saw a glimmer shining in his eyes too.

That was the kind of guy Luke was. He touched everyone's hearts that he met.

Chapter Fifteen

ROWAN

I HAVE A SON.

The ability to breathe left me when I heard Zander's small voice ask if I would be his daddy. But when Brinley said yes, he was mine, I didn't think I'd ever pull oxygen into my lungs again.

I have a son.

Over and over I said those words in my head, but they still didn't take hold or feel real.

We were together once.

I used a condom.

She stayed with Luke.

My head was spinning in never-ending circles.

And like I told Braxton and Gyth, I'd seen them together when I finally caved to their request and came home. But what had I truly seen?

I rubbed the sides of my temples as a headache started to take hold.

Realization hit and my stomach bottomed out. I felt sick. How stupid could I have been? Brinley was honest about her and Luke never having sex before we'd been together that night. She'd been a virgin. And even though I may have broken her heart and hurt her, she wouldn't have ever jumped into bed with someone else. Not even Luke.

She'd saved herself for someone she loved, she'd said.

Then she gave herself to me.

And because I couldn't hold myself back any longer from all the feelings she provoked in me and the way I felt when I was around her, I let her.

Now I knew what I saw that day was Luke being Luke. He was just being the best guy he always was and once again stepped up to take care of Brinley because I hadn't. Not only her but my son. He would sacrifice anything to be there for any of us.

But even knowing that I couldn't help the anger that rushed through me. Anger toward them both for not pushing harder to tell me. Could I forgive them both? Luke wasn't even around to speak his peace and Brinley didn't seem to want to talk to me at all.

Maybe the question I should be asking was, should I be forgiven?

I may not have known, but that was my fault for not staying and hearing them out. I'd taken one look at them and made assumptions that caused so many problems. And then my best friend was gone.

After rubbing my hands over my face, I pushed them through my hair and pulled in frustration. How was I supposed to sort out all these feelings?

I'd just stood there and was given the truth about my son, and what did I do? I still walked away and didn't listen.

Did Zander understand what had just happened? Was he sad or confused?

I had never wanted marriage or kids. I was too fucked up. I let my baby sister die. Putting other people's lives in my hands that I cared about and loved was not something I thought I could ever do again.

I didn't deserve it.

But Zander was my son. There was no changing that and I already adored him. Brinley was his mother and I...I what? Loved her?

Hadn't I always?

Could I be a good father?

My mind swirled with the questions. I don't know how many hours I'd sat on my couch wishing the answers would come before several light knocks at my door pulled my attention.

Did I dare answer it with the state I was in?

I STOOD STARING at the figure in the hall.

When the knocks had continued, I'd decided I better check it out.

Expecting it to be one of the guys, I was shocked when I pulled open the door and looked down to see who was there.

My son.

Alone.

"Daddy-y, c-can I come in?" His little voice wobbled and a tear trickled down his cheek.

The sight almost killed me on the spot.

Leaving the door open in case Brinley came out of her condo and raced down the hall, I dropped to my knees in front of my *son*.

"Come here, buddy," I said, opening my arms to him.

When he rushed me, his body slamming into my chest with a small oof and his tiny limbs wrapping around me, every cell in my body tingled with a feeling I couldn't yet describe.

My throat closed up as a lump formed, leaving me unable to get a word out. I held him in my arms and breathed in his scent. His hair smelled fresh like he had just gotten out of the bath. The sound of his soft cries reached my ears and I knew what I felt.

Love.

It hit me like a freight train. Fast and hard.

The impact was life changing.

He was really *mine*.

"I'm not going anywhere ever again," I whispered.

"D-Do you p-promise?"

The last promise I'd ever made was to my sister when she was still alive. She'd been scared one night and I promised her I would always take care of her.

I didn't.

Could I make another promise?

I had to. This was my son. Everything inside of me said no matter how terrified I was or even if Brinley never forgave me, we had to both make this right for Zander.

He was the only thing that mattered.

"I pinky promise," I said, pushing him back from me so I could put out my little finger.

Zander stared down at my hand and then looked up at me shaking his head.

"You have been hanging around Embry too much. Only girls do that, silly," he said theatrically.

Laughter escaped me. But it died quickly when I heard feet pounding on the floor in the hall and Zander's name cried out in sheer panic.

Then Brinley was standing at my open door.

Wearing only a short pair of sleep shorts, a tank top, and

sans bra, I couldn't help my body's reaction, even if it was not the time to be taking notice of how sexy Brinley was. I scanned her from head to toe and back up again.

When my eyes landed on hers, so many emotions were playing across her face at the sight before her that it was all I could think about. Which was crazy because Brinley was breathtaking. But those emotions flitting across her face held no secrets like the one she'd kept from me.

Relief that her son was safe, worry, how scared she was, and sorrow too.

I could feel every one of them down to my bones.

Zander turned her way, releasing me.

"Mommy. Daddy promised he would never leave again."

Brinley's sharp intake of breath echoed through the room and her eyes widened.

I nodded my head in confirmation. I'd told her once that I would never promise her or anyone anything after losing my sister and not keeping mine to her, so I knew she was shocked. She probably was also worried that I was going to break another.

And it would be to our son.

"I did make that promise," I said, staring into her blue eyes that shimmered with tears.

Seeing her cry always pulled at every one of my heart-strings.

"I think maybe you should come in," I said standing. I placed my hand on Zander's shoulder farthest from me and pulled him into my side as I held out my other hand for Brinley.

It was my turn to be shocked.

When she took it.

Chapter Sixteen

BRINLEY

Zander had finally fallen asleep.

Lying next to him, I stared at my world. I didn't know what was going to happen next or how things would play out. What I did know was that I was going to do the right thing for my son.

He was so tired when we'd gotten home, but as soon as we got onto our floor a look of longing crossed his angelic face as he glanced down at Rowan's door.

"Does my Daddy want to see me?" his tender voice asked.

His words ripped my heart to shreds and the answer was, I didn't know. But how could I tell my son that?

"Baby, why don't we go inside and I'll tell you about him and then you can get some sleep?"

"O-okay." My little guy's voice shook again with remorse. I knew he wanted to go down there right now and talk to Rowan.

I was struggling with him calling him daddy but Zander had wanted it before he knew it to be true and he was grasping on to the title like a lifeline.

How could I take that away?

As we snuggled in bed, I rubbed his back and told him about his father. There was so much he wouldn't understand, but for the time being I did the best I could at explaining about Rowan. He'd always known his real dad couldn't be around, he had just been too young to grasp or ask why. It wasn't too long before I realized I was talking to myself and Zander had crashed.

After some time, sleep finally came over me but a short while later I woke abruptly, an uneasy feeling consuming me. Then I looked over.

Zander was gone.

My pulse raced and panic shot through every cell in my body. Bolting out of bed, I shouted my son's name as I ran from room to room. When I reached the living room I noticed the front door unlocked and fear took over. I couldn't move for a second, but then I remembered Zander's words when we'd come home earlier.

He'd asked if his daddy wanted to see him. That was when I knew exactly where he had gone. Not taking a second to think about anything but getting to Zander, I hastily threw open the door and raced down the hall to find Rowan's door wide open.

I came to a halt at the threshold as I took in Rowan on his knees and Zander standing in front of him, a smile on their faces. My pulse, which had been out of control, slowed a little. That was until Rowan's gaze swept the length of my body.

His heated, inky eyes enhanced my pulse to a whole new level that left me breathless. But then something in them changed and Zander severed the connection when he told me that Rowan had made a promise.

Rowan didn't make promises.

But he stood from where he knelt, his tall, muscled frame commanding attention, and he confirmed he had in fact made my—no *our*—son a promise. That bombshell of information had an impact so strong, my knees wobbled where I stood. Then he reached out his hand and asked me to come in, and I had no choice but to take it because I wasn't sure I could walk.

Dropping his palm from Zander's shoulder where it had laid, he shut the door, and took his son's hand in his before leading us both inside to the couch. I sat down on one end and then Zander scrambled up on the cushion beside me. Rowan took a spot on the opposite end and turned slightly to look at me. Our son looked from me to his dad with droopy, sleepy eyes and then lay down with his head on Rowan's large, strong thigh, and his feet on me.

We sat in silence for a few minutes, which is all it took before Zander was fast asleep.

Apprehension took hold as Rowan and I stared at one another. The conversation we were about to have was not one I thought I would be having. Sure at one time, but then when Rowan never came home I gave up on the idea, the hope, and admitting the truth about Zander. What if the information was not received well?

"I'm scared," I whispered, dropping my head to my lap, not able to look at him as I admitted my feelings aloud.

He exhaled slowly. "Me too, Brin."

My head snapped up quickly, my eyes bugging out of my skull. He was telling the truth, I could see the trepidation in his gaze.

"You?"

"Yeah, babe, me."

I sucked in air at the term of endearment that flew swiftly from his mouth. Maybe he didn't hate me after all? Was there a way we could make this work smoothly for our son's sake?

"Why don't you start at the beginning," he said.

The beginning. My mind rewound to the moment I had met Rowan and I wondered how I would be able to lay all my feelings on the table, along with how we had gotten to the point we were at.

But I had to try.

It was time.

I BLEW OUT A FRUSTRATED BREATH.

Nothing was escaping me and I felt paralyzed. Fear did that to people. It wasn't that I didn't remember the exact moment I saw Rowan for the first time or how he made me feel. That would be the beginning where he asked me to start, but I'd never put it into words the way he was asking me to.

When we'd spent that phenomenal one night together, we talked about Luke and I getting a divorce, but he didn't want to talk about his mother. I accepted that. Rowan wasn't someone who talked about his personal life or how he felt about anything. If he did, it was a rare occurrence.

But that night, all those feelings seemed to pour out in our lovemaking. No words were necessary. However, I made a mistake thinking that the connection we had as our bodies had come together would change the future. I'd been waiting forever to feel Rowan wrapped around me the way he'd been that night and I wasn't thinking straight.

"Buttercup?" Rowan whispered, pulling me back to reality.

"I remember the day you gave me that nickname." I loved

when he called me that because it always made me feel like I was special to him.

Rowan had caught me sitting in the corner at a Halloween party I hadn't even wanted to attend, that he and Luke made me go to. The only saving grace was that they had my favorite candy in masses and I drowned myself in Reese's Peanut Butter Cups as the guys mingled. It had always been hard watching the girls fawn all over Rowan, a.k.a. Casanova, but the candy helped a tad.

"It was when I realized what a sweet tooth you have and how addicted you are to the candy. But I dropped off the front for the nickname because it sounded ridiculous and decided I was just going to call you Buttercup. But we know the truth on how you acquired the name."

We shared a little laugh at the memory, which also helped me open up a little and I tossed out the first thing that came to my mind.

"You were the first boy that ever made my heart tingle."

Rowan's eyes went wide in wonder as I shifted on the couch nervously.

Somehow I needed to barrel through the conversation and tiptoe at the same time since it was all very important, but was that even possible? Breathing deep through my nose and then exhaling through my mouth, I tried to explain the best I could.

"Luke and you were my best friends. The way you two took me under your wings when I arrived in a new place was more than I could have hoped for. But my feelings for you were different right from the start."

The look on his face told me he'd already known that. Maybe I didn't need to start at the beginning and make a fool out of myself, but I carried on anyway.

"I was aware of how Luke felt about me in the beginning

too. We talked about it multiple times, and later as well. Luke didn't shut me out the way you did. He never hid any part of himself."

Rowan winced. I wasn't meaning to sound harsh, it was just the way it always had been.

"He also knew who held my attention and our friendship grew with clear boundaries. Later our relationship was stronger than ever and Luke would do anything for me. And he did."

Rowan nodded his head. It would be no surprise to him how amazing Luke was. He was the kind of guy who would give you the shirt off his back. Only for me, Luke went above and beyond.

A sharp pang of sorrow pierced my heart as I spoke of him. Knowing I would never get to see him again hurt so much. I knew that though it may keep getting easier, nothing would ever be the same without him here. Tears gathered in my eyes. But I couldn't let them fall yet, we had just gotten started.

"You know Luke married me to take care of me after my mother died, and you know that we were going to get divorced. That night everything with you was amazing and I tried so damn hard to leave my emotions out of it, but with you it was impossible. My heart had been invested for far too long."

Rowan had been quiet for so long I hadn't expected him to respond, but when he did, I realized for someone like him why he took a run for it.

"You said you loved me before you drifted off to sleep," he said.

My body tensed and my eyes widened at the declaration. I had no clue I'd said that, but it wasn't time to start lying. So I didn't.

"I don't remember that, but I'm not going to tell you it wasn't true. I loved you for a long time." Technically it was love at first sight, but I didn't want to scare him more than he already was so I didn't include that part. "I wish I hadn't said it because maybe you wouldn't have left. But I can't take it back now. We can't change the past as much as I wish I could so Luke would still be here."

Rowan's face held so much pain when I said Luke's name.

"I wouldn't change anything between us though. You're leaving crushed me. And when you didn't answer my calls or come back, that was a really bad time for me. But you gave me the best part of my life and he is lying right here."

As I pointed at Zander, my gaze caught on Rowan's hand which was softly brushing our son's soft blonde hair. I don't think he even realized he was doing it, but the sight warmed me.

"I wouldn't want that to change either."

I wasn't expecting him to say that and be so accepting about finding out about our son after all these years. But we still had more to say.

"I'm glad we agree on that," I whispered in reply.

"Brin, I want you to know that I am sorry for not calling you and Luke back." He hung his head and sighed before bringing his eyes back to mine. "And I did come. It took me longer than it should have. I also screwed up so bad when I saw you pregnant and still with Luke."

What was he talking about?

Before I could ask for clarification, he continued.

"When I finally came back I was walking up to your house when I saw you and Luke in the front yard. You were laughing playfully at something he said and then he hugged you close. And when I saw that you were pregnant I thought it was Luke's, that maybe after I left, you guys changed your mind."

I gasped. I wasn't expecting him to say that and wasn't sure how to feel. On one hand, I could see how it might've looked since I told him we were divorcing. But on the other, Rowan was the only one I had ever had sex with and he knew how I felt about that.

"Why would you think I would sleep with Luke right after I had made love to you?"

It hurt that he thought that, but we'd both made a lot of mistakes. I was so tired and emotionally exhausted. I rubbed my eyes.

"I'm so sorry. I realized how stupid I was after I left Gyth's house tonight and I lost so much time with my son I can't get back. I also lost time with you and Luke because I was always running and trying to shut off all my feelings." His hands ran down his face in frustration.

"Then after Luke died, I should have been the one to be there for you and Zander no matter what I thought, but I was in a dark place and thought you guys were better off without me."

I was shaking my head from side to side while tears slipped down my cheeks, scalding my skin.

Rowan scooted to the side and lightly lifted Zander's head to lay it on the couch as he moved out from below him. He came in front of me and was once again on his knees. Reaching up he wiped my tears with the pad of his thumb and my breath hitched at both the contact and the sweetness of his touch.

It brought more tears until I was full-on sobbing. I gulped and tried taking a couple deep breaths to get myself under control. Waking Zander was not something I needed to do when he'd already had such a heavy, soul-stirring day.

"Luke was just trying to help," I told him, my throat tightening. "And his parents always knew it wasn't Luke's baby but that didn't s-stop his overbearing mother from trying to run everything since we were still married. Between her and the f-fire, we had to leave... We just *had* too. But I never thought we'd f-find you here." I was struggling to get it all out and hold my shit together.

A soft smile lifted. "I'm glad you did."

More sobs shook my body. "Do you mean that?"

"Yes, Buttercup," he replied without hesitation. "I want to know our son."

That was exactly what needed to happen, I just didn't know how I was going to handle being around Rowan all the time. I thought I'd hated him, but as he sat in front of me, hate was the last thing from my mind.

"Will you stay and let that happen?" he pleaded.

I quickly thought about Zander and how happy he was here. About how he would have his father and new friends. How *I* had friends and a once-in-a-life time job offer. I also wouldn't be close to Luke's neurotic mother.

The pros were winning this time.

By a landslide.

"First, I want you to know I should have tried harder to find you and tell you," I continued, further explaining Rowan deserved to know all my truths. "But when you didn't call back and I didn't see you, I thought I would just be ruining your life. I knew you didn't want kids and I understood why you always felt that way."

I reached over and softly brushed my finger over the tattoo that honored Jelena's memory. Rowan shuddered at my touch and his eyes filled with even more sadness, tugging at my already aching heart. Having lost Luke I could understand, but for Rowan, it was not only about losing his sister, but about wrongfully blaming himself too.

"We'll stay," I told him. "So we'll have more time to talk, but for now maybe I should get *our* son back to bed?" A huge yawn escaped me. I was officially drained.

"For the record," Rowan replied, "I didn't want kids. But that's changed."

My breath hitched. I could only hope he meant what he said and that he would still feel that way as he got to know his son. If he walked away again it would devastate both Zander and me.

Please stay this time…

"I'll carry him," Rowan said, interrupting my thoughts as he stood and picked Zander up, cradling him in his strong arms.

My knees weakened at the sight.

Heart in my throat, I followed suit and we walked toward the door.

It felt odd to be leaving now when there was probably more we could talk about and say, but I could see Rowan was as emotionally spent as I was and there would be more time.

We walked back to my place in silence and he placed Zander on my bed. My heart wasn't prepared when he leaned down and kissed our son's forehead before whispering, "I'll keep my promise."

I had to get Rowan out of here before I completely broke down.

At the door, he turned to me before leaving. "Thank you."

I asked him for what.

"For calling him *our* son and giving me a chance to be his father." Then, like he'd done many times before, he walked away.

Only this time I knew he'd be back.

Chapter Seventeen

ROWAN

I HAD A LOT TO PROCESS.

More than I knew what to do with.

And though I needed some time alone to do just that, the second I closed my door after returning to my place, everything in me wanted Brinley and our son back by my side.

Never in my life did I think I deserved to be completely happy.

I also didn't know I truly wanted a family.

Until now.

Chapter Eighteen

BRINLEY

So much had changed over the past month.

Even though Rowan had been working a lot, he'd still managed to spend quality time with his son. Watching them get to know each other and witnessing their similarities was a revelation. They liked so many of the same foods, some of their mannerisms were identical, and they had loads of fun together.

It might be because Rowan was a big kid?

However, even during the playful moments I caught glimpses of the sorrow shining in his eyes and could tell he was thinking about his sister while playing with Zander. He might have masked it for our son's sake, but I knew Rowan well enough and had seen that look so many times in the past. So, I wasn't oblivious to the fact there were still many hurdles to get over.

And it wasn't just what we needed to work on together so we could be good parents to our son, but also our personal hang ups that shaped how we proceeded through life. There were a lot of feelings to sift through from our past that we still hadn't fully dealt with.

I'd held a secret tucked away for many years. A big one. I'd been doing it for so many reasons, but it was never to intentionally hurt anyone. I'd thought in the long run I was allowing Rowan to live the life he wanted without taking the chance of Zander ever feeling rejected.

Like I had when Rowan walked away from me.

Some people might not understand that. And there was a chance Rowan may just be going through the motions then one day he'd wake up and decide he couldn't forgive me.

It was a constant worry.

The loss of two very special people in Rowan's life was another item to add to the list of things he had to deal with. One being his little sister. He blamed himself for her death and the agony had sat dormant in his heart since she died, rushing to the surface from time to time, only to be pushed back down so he didn't have to feel the devastation it left him with. The other loss was Luke, which I wasn't sure he'd processed completely either.

And we can't forget the elephant in the room. We'd had sex and created an absolutely precious child together, but since Rowan had found out about Zander, we hadn't talked about the intimacy we shared to bring our son into the world.

Yet something undeniable simmered between us when we were together.

But I'd wrapped my heart in a protective cocoon when it came to anything Rowan. I couldn't allow it to unravel and be set free to break again.

Keeping the focus on my son was the best-laid plan.

"Let's go," Zander said while tugging on my hand. He seemed to be doing that a lot, eager to go see Rowan, Dexter, and all the other new people in his life. "I want to see where daddy works and he said he is going to show me everything."

Zander had been waiting to see *No Surrender* for weeks

after they talked a little about what Rowan did and where he worked. Of course, Rowan was careful about how much he told him about certain aspects of the job. Hopefully, he would be leaving the guns out of the show and tell.

While I heard they started with security systems and multiple classes at the center, such as martial arts, self-defense, and also gun classes, they had recently started branching out. They'd been asked to do security for venues and also some personal security when public figures, singers, and others were attending functions.

The assignment Rowan had been on lately, seemed to bother him, but he didn't divulge many details. It was, however, easy to see the distress and concern in his eyes sometimes. It wasn't my place to ask and I assumed that he had to keep the privacy of some people.

He also seemed tired. He and Lyric seemed to be taking on more jobs so the others could spend time with their families. Rowan was fairly new to the company and Lyric, while a cop, was moonlighting for *No Surrender* on the side. But I heard they are still looking for more guys, so hopefully, that would free everyone up some.

"Mom, we have to go. Daddy said that after we see his work, he has a surprise for me. If we miss it I will be mad." He folded his arms across his chest, squinted his eyes, and gave me his best 'I'm angry impression.'

Fighting back laughter, I hid my smile with a cough and turned around to grab my purse and light jacket, which I most likely wouldn't need. It was a beautiful September day, not too hot, and not cold at all. It was perfect for Zander's surprise. I knew where we were going, but Rowan wanted me to keep quiet. It was cute he was so exhilarated to plan something special for his son.

Zander's birthday was in the middle of the week coming

up so Rowan had planned a party on the Friday before so everyone could attend. They had even scheduled all their work meetings, gigs and classes around it. It was amazing.

Each year it had been just the two of us. Except for when Luke's mom would pop in, give him a gift, and remind me how much our home was not up to her standards. I tried to understand that losing her son hurt her deeply, but she didn't like me, yet she tried using my son and me as replacements in a sense.

It was all very twisted and the whole situation had been absurd over the years.

Taking a deep breath because thinking about her could drive me to drink—like a few too many—I turned and took Zander's hand. My son and I had a whole group of wonderful people that wanted to be a part of our lives. And they appreciated us for who we were.

"Ready, Freddy."

"My name is Zander," my son said with an eye roll.

"Really?" I questioned as if I didn't know. We'd done this banter back and forth many times.

"You know that, goofy."

Ducking down, I grabbed my son, snuggling into his face and raining a million mommy kisses all over his cheeks. He giggled with laughter. I freed him from my hold but couldn't stop thinking that one day he would get older and wouldn't let me do these things.

I would get as much as I could while he still let me.

Hand in hand, another thing I wouldn't take for granted that he still allowed without question, we walked out the door to spend the evening with Rowan.

I hoped that I could keep my heart locked up tight, but it was getting harder by the day.

～

"CAN I come to work with you every day, Daddy?" He placed both hands together like he was praying I would say yes and looked at me with big puppy dog eyes. "It's so cool."

I had to agree with our son. *No Surrender* was a great set up and it was easy to see all the guys had taken great pride in building the best business they could. Also in hiring the people that worked there. They weren't just partners, co-workers, etc. .They were a family.

Teal had greeted us as we walked in the door and from that moment I knew that anyone who walked in would get the best treatment and attention during their time there. If that was the case inside, then I knew the second they were working outside their domain they would be just as dedicated.

But I had to admit I was a teensy bit jealous and maybe a little thrown off guard when Zander asked if he could spend every day with Rowan. It had been the '*Zander and Mommy*' show since he was born, and I wasn't used to sharing.

"Who's gonna take care of your beautiful Mama then if we are both here," Rowan asked as we headed back toward the front doors to leave.

My head snapped sideways in Rowan's direction. A funny feeling swept through me and my belly fluttered with butter-flies at the soft, heated look in his eyes. He'd thought of me and I truly believe he understood how hard all the changes were for me. But it was the word *beautiful* and the expression on his face that had my pulse ramping up.

He hadn't said things like that out loud before and I wasn't quite sure what to make of it but having Zander as a buffer when I felt out of sorts helped. And he did well as he chimed in, saving me to find something to say.

"I'll do it. I can take care of her." His little brows crinkled in thought. "But can I come on Monday and Friday? That would be fair, right?" Zander was a sweetheart, but he also knew how to negotiate like a seasoned lawyer.

We'd stopped in the middle of the reception area and Rowan threw his head back as he roared with carefree laughter that echoed off the walls. I stared at the tight cords in his neck and the enormous smile on his face, then shivered as a tingle raced through my body.

Rowan was a seriously attractive, well-made man and I needed another damn distraction before I embarrassed myself and started drooling. Besides, I was still protecting my heart. Pulling my eyes from him—which wasn't easy—I looked toward Teal to see what she was doing. That was a big mistake. She had a knowing look on her face and gave me a wink.

"We'll see what we can work out, but we better get going. We have plans, remember?" Rowan told Zander.

I rolled my eyes at Teal and looked down at my son who had curiosity written all over his face. Appeased with the work subject, for the time being, he bounced on his feet, and asked, "What are we doing?"

Rowan ruffled his blonde hair and took his hand again. "It's a surprise so I can't tell you, but we have to run by the condos first so I can change and we can drop off a car. That way we can ride together."

That would give our friends time to get where they needed to be, so it worked out perfectly.

"Okay, sounds like a decent plan."

Sometimes my little guy seemed a lot older than five and I still couldn't believe he was that old already. I sighed and looked up to catch Rowan's gaze. My stomach sank when I thought about how Rowan missed the first five years altogether and once again I found myself hoping we'd get through the messes that had been made.

"Are you good with that too?" Rowan asked me.

I nodded once. "Yeah."

Zander took my hand and started pulling us toward the door. I glanced down at his little hands cupped in each of ours and my heart fluttered. I may at one time have pictured the three of us holding hands like this, together, but I never in a million years thought I'd see the day.

"Bye, family," Teal said, once again bringing my attention to her as she waved.

Rowan and Zander shouted goodbye. I was still stuck on her saying *family,* so I muttered a lazy, "See ya," as we kept walking. Even if we were not together, we'd still be family, right?

I finished the walk in a trance and realized we made it out the door when the bright sun beamed in my eyes.

"Daddy?"

"Yeah, bud?"

"You were right about mommy. She is the most beautiful girl in the world."

That wasn't quite what Rowan had said, but I smiled at my adorable child. He sure knew how to make my heart pump with love.

"In all the world," Rowan echoed, causing my wide eyes to snap to him once again.

The sun had nothing on Rowan right then. My face flamed and my body temperature skyrocketed as the intense stare between us simmered and flared to life.

How was I going to guard my heart when he said stuff like that?

Chapter Nineteen

ROWAN

I'D MISSED FIVE YEARS.

But I would be damned if I'd miss anymore.

I had been wrestling with all the things I hadn't got to see him do and be a part of, but I was happy I got to throw him his first big birthday party. Brinley had told me it had been the two of them alone every year and that was another punch to the gut.

I should have been there.

There were so many feelings to work through and I had been doing my best not to shove them down the way I'd always done. Not only my son, but Brinley, deserved more than that. But it wasn't that easy and completely out of my comfort zone to face things head-on when it came to my emotions. And while I was working to do that with the ones surrounding Brinley, Zander, and me, I had others that I just couldn't manage to let myself truly address.

"Daddy, where are we?"

My heart stumbled a beat, then warmed at Zander calling me Daddy. I was still getting used to the title in some way, but I'd be lying if I said it didn't feel fucking amazing.

I pulled into a parking spot and turned off the truck, then swiveled around to look in the backseat at my little man. "Ready for your surprise?"

Zander's gaze roamed to the doors where people had been streaming in and out. I was glad we had reserved a party room because Bullwinkles was seriously busy. As a family amusement center with mini-golf, laser tag, go-karting, bumper boats, zip-lining, an arcade full of games, food, treats, and more, it was the place to go.

"We are going to this place with all those people?" His forehead wrinkled in confusion.

I chuckled. "Well, we're not going with them exactly, but it's a place lots of people can go at once." Our friends should have all been in there by now so we would have a large group there to celebrate with Zander. "Want to go check out your surprise now or should we head home?"

"No, no, I want to go see," he said, bouncing on his butt on the truck seat.

Brinley had been quietly watching the exchange from the passenger seat and I looked over at her to find her watching me intently. "You're good with him," she said.

My eyes widened at the compliment. She hadn't said anything bad over the last month, but she also hadn't said a whole lot of anything about how she thought I was doing as a dad. I could read emotions cross her face so I knew it was going okay but hearing her acknowledge what she just had felt great. It was different hearing it out loud, especially coming from her sweet lips.

Lips I shouldn't be thinking about, let alone how sweet they were, but I couldn't help it. I should've been thankful she couldn't read my mind and went on without knowing where my head was.

"Why do you look so shocked?" she asked me.

I shrugged a lone shoulder. "I guess because it's the first time you've said anything and I'm glad you think so."

"Honestly, I am a little surprised." She threw both hands over her mouth, but the words were already out. When she pulled them from her face, she hurriedly said, "I don't mean that mean, but—"

"I know what you're saying, don't worry about it," I broke in, interrupting her. "We both knew I was a screwed-up mess after—" I stopped abruptly, not able to say it. I wasn't kidding when I'd told Gyth and Braxton I thought I was all talked out. At least where my sister was concerned. That was hard enough getting it out then and I had been raw ever since.

"I know what you're saying," she said, echoing the words I just used.

"Can we go now, *pleassse*!" Zander shouted.

Brinley and I both laughed.

"Yeah, buddy, let's go check this place out." I hadn't been here, but some of the others had and recommended it when I mentioned doing the party. I was hoping Zander would have fun.

We all got out of the truck and started toward the door hand in hand.

Again.

"Swing me," Zander begged.

Brinley and I lifted Zander's arms a little, swung him forward off his feet into the air a bit, and then brought him back down to the ground.

"Do it again!"

One day when we all had been walking into the condo I had told him about my mom and dad swinging me like that and we did it. He obviously remembered. Brinley and I obliged and swung him again. Then we made it to the building and I used my free hand to pull the door open.

When we all walked through, the noise level was crazy. Kids were screaming with glee, people talking, games dinging and bells going off everywhere. Zander stopped in his tracks and his eyes bugged out of his head. I chuckled at his expression.

"This is so cool," he finally said. "Do we get to play?"

"You bet we do," I told him. "And there is *a lot* more."

"There is?" he asked in wonder, staring up at me, mouth slightly agape.

"Yup, but we need to go find our spot to sit before we go check everything out, okay?"

"Okay."

My son was a good kid. Sure there were moments, but I was so damn proud of how well he behaved. "You did good, Brin." Because it was all her and she needed to hear it.

She looked at me and a sparkle shone in her baby blue eyes. I didn't want her to cry, but I did want her to know. "You're an amazing mother and did a great job."

"My mommy is the best, but can we go now?" Zander pleaded, tugging on our hands.

He never seemed to miss a beat, our kid. And while he was very well behaved, he was still just that. A kid. One who happened to be in a child's dream place right then, so I couldn't blame him for wanting to start playing.

"You bet. Let's get this show on the road," I told him.

"But I don't want to see a show, I want to play games."

Brinley and I burst out laughing at him.

"No, buddy, it's just an expression that means to get going," I told him.

Zander puffed out a small breath and started pulling on our hands dragging us along. I veered him toward the party room I had reserved and maneuvered him in front of us so he walked in first.

"Surprise!" a chorus of people screamed as he walked through the open door. "Happy Birthday!"

Our friends had gotten there earlier to decorate and it was fantastic. Even if Summer, who was in charge, may have gone a little overboard. It looked as if she bought out the entire store of decorations. But it was for Zander so there were no complaints from me. I was so thankful for the people that had come into my life, as well as Brinley and Zander's.

They were damn good people.

"This is for me?" he asked, looking up at me and then his mother.

"Daddy planned it for you," Brinley said.

And once again my heart took another little stumble at the word Daddy. Only this time it was because it had come from Brinley's mouth.

"Thank you, Daddy."

Then he was rushed by all the kids and I knew it was time to get the party started.

"It's time to make a wish," Brinley told our son after everyone finished singing happy birthday.

We had pizza and had been playing for a couple hours, but the kids were ready for cake. Which happened to be perfect and had Zander clapping his hands in excitement because it was designed like a forest with army men hiding throughout the trees as if on a mission.

I was impressed and I knew it would be good since it came from my favorite little bakery. I'd brought Brinley and Zander cinnamon rolls from there the first morning after they moved in and she was addicted to them. Although she said she hated me because she is going to gain too much weight.

Personally I thought she looked amazing and over the last month had filled out generously. She had needed it and it rattled me to think the stress in her life had caused her to lose any weight before coming to Portland.

Brinley's body was—shit, not something I should've been thinking about at our son's birthday party with a room full of kids around.

"If you don't hurry and make a wish it will be our bedtime pretty soon," Embry told Zander, bringing my mind back to where it should be.

"But I already got mine. I got my daddy," Zander said, looking right at me.

I heard several intakes of breaths and had a feeling Brinley was reeling from the statement like I was, but I couldn't look at anyone but my son right then.

The first night I'd looked into his gaze and sensed that I was missing something important... something familiar. I'd realized later it was his eyes. They looked like *mine*. How I missed that the second I saw him when he and Brinley arrived at Gyth's, I don't know. I think it was because in my head he looked so much like his mother and I also thought he was Luke's.

But looking at him as we played on the bumper boats and he shouted with glee, the excitement as he dropped the ball into a hole at mini-golf, and now staring at me with a happy but puzzled expression on his face, I saw something else.

My baby sister.

In my son, I saw Jelena.

Zander's expressions were so much like hers in joy, sadness, and confusion. And they were both very dramatic. I shook my head slightly to clear my mind because it pained me to think he would never get to meet his aunt who I know he would have adored.

And who would've adored him in return.

"I know, I know," Embry chanted as she ran up to Zander and cupped her hand around his ear and whispered.

A huge smile lit up his face and he nodded his head in confirmation. When Embry moved back, Zander closed his eyes and his little lips mumbled something so quietly nobody could hear, but Embry giggled, clearly knowing what the wish was and her own smile beamed bright.

Then my son's eyes popped open and he leaned over and blew out his five candles. Everyone clapped and cheered, but Zander looked at his mom and then to me curiously.

"Uh, oh," Brinley whispered from beside me.

"What? Is something wrong?" I asked, turning toward her.

Her gaze left Zanders and caught mine. "I think I know what he just wished for with a little nudge from Embry."

Brinley's face was a light shade of pink as though she was embarrassed, but her eyes held a hint of worry. I wasn't sure what I had missed. I turned back to our son and Embry was whispering something else in his ear and it got another nod out of him.

Embry's mom Jurnee walked over and told her daughter it wasn't nice to tell secrets and maybe she should share with everyone in the room.

Zander's face turned to worry, but Embry had it handled. "I can't, then his wish won't come true, Mom. Let's cut the cake."

When the other kids cheered and crowded around them, Embry smiled in triumph. Smarty-pants knew exactly what she was doing when she suggested eating cake. Jurnee rolled her eyes at her daughter and gave her a knowing look, but let it go and started serving the kids.

Soon everyone had a piece and was enjoying the sugary

treat with a scoop of ice cream to top it off. The kids would likely be bouncing off the walls for a while and then crash hard later. But when I heard the soft moan that vibrated in my ear, I knew sleep wouldn't come for me for a very long time. When I turned to see Brinley licking her spoon, her eyes half closed, delight written across her face, my pulse picked up speed.

Averting my gaze, I tried to think of something that would throw cold water on the fire burning inside me before I had to leave the room.

I'd managed to get myself under control just as Dexter walked up to Zander and asked him to open his present first. There was a whole table of gifts but I was astonished to realize that Zander hadn't even paid them any attention.

"Why don't we move closer to the gift table and everyone can gather around it while Zander opens his birthday presents?" Summer said.

All the kids moved that way and the adults too, but Zander stayed in his seat, staring at the table.

"Hey, Buddy, don't you want to open those?" I placed my hand on his shoulder and gave it a squeeze, nodding toward the table of gifts.

A tear slid down his cheek and Brinley rushed to his other side, squatting down next to him. "Baby, why are you upset?"

He was worrying me when he didn't speak at first. Then in a small voice he whispered, "I never had a party and so many people get me gifts before." A couple more tears trickled down his face.

I wanted to kick myself repeatedly for what Zander had missed out on. I had been upset about the five years I had missed, but what about my son?

Fuck.

Brinley looked up at me and then back at Zander. "You

have that now and everyone wants you to open what they brought you. Do you want to do that?"

He nodded as Dexter rushed back over. "Yes, I want to open them."

"Come on, you're going to love what I got you," Dexter told him.

Zander swiped at the salty liquid on his face and jumped out of his seat to follow his friend. I believed the tears were a mix between knowing what he never had and happiness all rolled into one. He was working through stuff like the rest of us, so there were going to be times ahead when he got upset.

I knew I sure the hell had my own struggles I was trying to get through and needed to face. I looked over at Zander already tearing into his first gift and then my gaze locked with Brinley's and she gave me a tentative, soft smile.

They were worth it.

Chapter Twenty
BRINLEY

WHO KNEW A KID'S PARTY COULD KNOCK YOU ON YOUR ASS.

I was exhausted, but it was a spectacular party and I had Rowan to thank for setting it up, as well as the ladies for helping out. Looking around the room at our new friends, the decorations, and the presents, I understood how my son had felt a short time ago.

Neither of us was used to the help, affection, or having others in our corner who would be there at the drop of a hat when needed. It was overwhelming at times, but it was such a blessing too. Now that Zander and I knew what it felt like I was scared.

I didn't want to lose it all.

Was that how Zander felt too?

And then it hit me like a ton of bricks. It wasn't just the friends he and I had found in our new home. It was Rowan too. I didn't want either of us to lose him now that we finally found him. The thought scared the crap out of me and I started to breathe rapidly, as panic started to seep in. We were getting in so deep and if Rowan was yanked from our lives we would never recover.

"Hey, girl. You okay?" Teal asked, placing her hand softly on my back, rubbing in a soothing, circular motion.

"Crud, I'm sorry. I'm supposed to be cleaning up."

"Forget about that and take a couple of deep breaths to clear the panic," she said.

Doing as she said, I turned to look at her and her hand dropped from my back. "How did you know?"

"Honey, I'm the queen of panic attacks."

I hated to hear that but knew she'd had a hard past. A hell of a lot worse than mine. What Teal had been through made my heart ache for her.

"I suffered from them all my life, but they increased in intensity and frequently after my mom died. When I first started working at *No Surrender,* everyone had witnessed a few doozies and it wasn't pretty. But my life has changed in exceptional ways and they have gotten so much better."

She smiled at me and gave me another of her signature winks. "And a hot guy who worships me is icing on the cake. He has many ways to get my mind off the panic when it sets in."

Not able to control the laughter that burst free, I almost choked.

"I'm telling you, this woman here has seriously come out of her shell," Alley said, joining the two of us.

"Eavesdrop much?" Teal asked Alley.

"You know it. It's one of my superpowers," Alley sassed in return.

Teal stuck out her tongue at her friend.

Correction, at *our* friend.

"See what I mean," Alley said, looking at me and rolling her eyes.

"Hey, what is everyone doing over here? It's not nice to leave us out of the private party," Summer said.

Before I knew it, everyone was gathered around, Jurnee and Gemma too, and they were throwing a load of sass each other's way.

It was hilarious and my panic had disappeared.

While I knew it wouldn't stay dormant forever at that point, with the help of my friends I could get through it.

And maybe Teal had a point about a hot guy?

Shit, no I couldn't go there.

Then all the kids and guys walked back in, and my eyes immediately landed on Rowan. He had always been an extremely good-looking boy, but all grown up, he was a sexy, lethal man.

God, it was getting harder not to cave and throw myself at him.

Rowan's eyes met mine and he gave me a knowing smile. I felt my face flush with heat.

"See what I mean," Teal said, nudging my shoulder.

"You are trouble," I told her.

"Well, that title, *Queen of Trouble*, is reserved for Alley, but I am happy to be of assistance," she said.

"Heard that!" Alley yelled.

"We maybe should call her *Bionic Ears,*" I said, laughing.

"I told you, superpowers!" Alley shouted.

I was about to add loudmouth to the mix but was interrupted as a tingle raced up my spine and goosebumps broke out along my arms from the deep voice that sounded from behind me.

"Need some help?" Rowan asked, placing his warm palm in the center of my back.

I shivered at his touch and this time it was Teal who gave me a knowing smile.

"You bet she does," Teal said and walked off.

I turned around and lost Rowan's touch immediately as

his hand dropped away. My eyes went to his lips and all I could think about was what Teal had said about a hot guy being able to take one's mind off things. I licked my lower lip wondering what his mouth would feel like against mine.

Glancing further up to find his gaze, I found him staring at the path my tongue had just taken and a low growl rumbled from deep inside him. I let out a little squeak of surprise at his reaction, and I squeezed my thighs together to curb the tingling sensation the sound ignited in my lady parts.

It was not the time or place. If there was ever one, it certainly wasn't our son's party. And I couldn't believe I even contemplated it.

I was pretty damn sure there could be more than one *Queen of Trouble* in our group because Teal was for sure a runner-up in my book and pushing for the head spot.

"We better clean up," I announced and ran off.

Rowan chuckled as I walked away and the sound sent another shockwave of desire straight to my core.

I had to occupy my mind before I threw caution to the wind and kissed him right there in the middle of the room with everyone watching.

That would be bad.

Wouldn't it?

~

"WAKE UP, SLEEPYHEAD."

I felt someone touch my arm gently and give me a slight shake.

My lids came open and I was staring into a pair of eyes the color of dark obsidian, the outer edges lighter and more transparent, holding a ray of emotion. Some may have thought Rowan's eyes were scary, but I thought they were beautiful. His eyes were like a mood ring, darkening and lightening with his moods.

They were mesmerizing and hypnotic. And I was so lost in them I hadn't heard a word he'd said.

"What?" I asked.

He smiled., "I asked if you could walk while I carry Zander or do you want me to come back and get you?"

Oh Lord, I was not letting him carry me.

"I can get in by myself."

"Maybe next time then." He winked before getting out and rounding the truck to grab our son.

Was Rowan flirting with me?

Abort. Abort.

I needed to stop thinking about how cute that was and wishing for more. What we needed to concentrate on was just parenting Zander and letting Rowan get to know him more. And while we were doing that together, we weren't a couple.

We never had been.

And we never would be.

I best remember that so I didn't find myself disappointed at some point, because I had been there enough times in my life where he and I were concerned. In truth, I was struggling. One second I wanted to take a flying leap and see what happened if I flirted back, and the next I wanted to take a play out of Rowan's book and run away.

Instead, I pretended nothing was going on and followed them inside. When we entered I watched Rowan carry Zander to the spare bedroom where he'd started sleeping, instead of with me, and my heart did a flip flop at the sight of the two of them. We had another surprise for him, hidden behind door number three that had been shut up, but it looked like that would have to wait until he woke up.

Coming into the room behind them, I told Rowan I would

get Zander changed for bed and pulled Pajamas out of his drawer.

"I'm just going to go start bringing his gifts up while you do that."

"Crap, I forgot about those. I could have grabbed a few and brought them with me."

"You were still half asleep. I got them." He walked out of the room.

After getting Zander settled and back to sleep, snug as a bug in a rug, in the Army blanket that Rowan had bought him a week ago, I went to my room to change too. That blanket went almost everywhere with him and he loved it. Throwing on a pair of sleep pants and a tank top, I padded out to the kitchen to get a glass of water.

Looking around the room, I frowned. Where could Rowan be? He would have to make a couple of trips and should be back by now with the first. I grabbed my cell phone out of my purse that I had hung on the hook by the door when we walked in and checked it to see if there was a text. Maybe he had to go to his place or something happened?

There was nothing.

I paced around the room waiting for him to return and finally he entered, a load of gifts in his hands and a storm brewing in his eyes.

When I said you could see his mood in his inky globes, I was right. And right then Rowan looked beyond pissed off, but also a dose of worry shined in them too.

Walking over to him to take some of the presents from his hand, I asked, "What happened?"

Setting the items on the table for now so we didn't wake Zander, I noticed his free hands clenched into fists at his side. I was thoroughly confused and wondered if I had done or said something wrong. I racked my brain to think about what we may have said to one another in front of the truck to the house twenty minutes or so before. Truth was, I wasn't sure how much time had passed but it had to have been at least that.

"Did I do something wrong?"

And his eyes changed again. Remorse glistened in them.

"Brin, it's not you, I'm sorry to have made you think that." He took a deep breath and rubbed his face. "Some stuff happened that I believe has to do with work and I need to go talk to Braxton," he said. "I'm gonna grab the other stuff first really quickly before I go."

Disappointment struck me hard. I shouldn't have thought he would be sticking around but hearing him say he was leaving I knew that deep down it was what I'd been hoping for. And again, I realized how messed up I was with my push and pull of emotions when it came to him.

"If you have to, I understand," I said quietly, my eyes cast toward the floor.

Rowan sighed and walked closer to me so he was mere inches away. His warm hand went under my chin, tilted my head back so I could meet his gaze, and then he slid his palm around the back of my neck.

I sucked in a breath at his touch. He hadn't touched me so sweetly, and intimately since the night we created our son. It was the one time, for a short moment, that Rowan let his guard down and let himself go. He'd allowed himself to just feel.

Why now? What was going on?

Those magical eyes of his told me something big was brewing and I was a little scared. Not of Rowan, but for what was coming.

"Rowan," I whispered.

His shoulders tensed. "I have to go, even if I don't want

to." He took a deep breath trying to control some sort of war going on inside him. But seconds later the battle was lost.

Rowan's mouth crashed down on mine and claimed my lips in a frantic, desperate, mind-blowing kiss. My eyes closed and I moaned into his mouth. Bringing my hands up, I gripped his shirt in my fists, pulling him closer to me so there was no space at all.

Our tongues tangled, and I nipped his lower lip. For the second time that evening, a deep growl rumbled from the depths of his soul and he pulled back, breaking the kiss. Close to crying in outrage, my eyes popped open.

Rowan was staring at me, both of us panting, and our breaths mixing as one. His woodsy scent surrounded me and I felt intoxicated by the smell and the taste of him still on my lips as my tongue darted out to swipe across them.

"If I didn't have to leave I wouldn't," he said in a gruff voice.

"Okay." My mind and body were in overdrive still and I couldn't say much more. I wasn't sure what the hell had just happened.

All I knew was that it felt incredible and whether it was smart or not I wanted a repeat.

"I really have to go. I told Braxton I was on my way." He looked as disappointed about leaving as I felt. "I will be right back with the other gifts. Lock up until I get back and I'll knock three times so you know it's me. But make sure you also check the peephole before opening."

Rowan was acting strange. I mean he'd told me many times to do the same thing, but something in his gaze and tone came off differently that time.

"What's wrong?" I rushed to ask.

"Maybe nothing. We'll talk later. I'll text you when I get home, okay?"

I could tell something was going on, but also that he needed to leave so I didn't push.

"Promise?" I didn't mean to ask him that, it just slipped out. He'd made Zander a promise, but that was different. I'd told myself I would never ask him to promise me anything because my heart couldn't take him breaking his word. But before I could take it back he replied.

"I promise, Buttercup. I will text you when I get back. If you need anything, call my phone."

He dropped his hand from my face and then said he'd be right back as he moved toward the door. Then, he was gone.

This time he was only absent for a few minutes, but after the kiss we'd shared, it felt like an eternity and even longer than the first time.

Once he knocked three times and I checked the peephole, he walked in and laid the rest of the presents on the table with the others. Still in a fog, I followed him toward the door as he went to leave for the third time.

He put his hand on the knob, but then dropped it and turned toward me. With not much space between us, he reached over and cupped my cheeks with both of his hands.

"Lock up. I'll talk to you later. Promise." He kissed my forehead softly and once again turned to leave.

As he walked out the door, he said, "What just happened with us… It's not over, Buttercup." With a flirtatious smirk, he waited for me to shut the door.

My face turned pink as I closed it and threw the locks into place.

I heard him mumble, "Good Girl," from the other side of the door and sighed.

Did the man have to be sexy even when he was being bossy?

Chapter Twenty-One

ROWAN

I SCREECHED TO A HALT IN FRONT OF BRAXTON'S HOUSE.

Driving probably hadn't been a good idea. Between being filled with rage over what I'd found on my truck when I went to get Zander's gifts and the lust racing through me after the explosive kiss Brinley and I shared, I wasn't in the right state of mind. But I'd made it and now I needed my friend to weigh in on the note clenched in my hand before I lost my shit completely.

The door flew open and Braxton stood there urging me to come in. I hadn't even remembered getting out of my truck and approaching his house. Once I stepped into the entryway, I waved the paper in the air and then lost it.

"If anyone thinks they can threaten my *family* then they better think again. Nobody better get within inches of Brin and Zander or they will see what I can do with my bare hands!"

Braxton's face lifted with a small smile.

He'd always been level-headed and easy-going since I'd met him. Although, I'd heard the story about when Jurnee, his now-wife, was in a bad situation, and Braxton himself had come unglued. I didn't blame him one bit. But right then I was counting on him to talk me down and stop me from tearing up the town to find the fucker who dared cross me.

What I didn't need or understand was the smirk on his face.

My body was shaking with fury.

"Why the hell would you be smiling right now?"

"Let me see," Braxton said, motioning to the paper in my hand.

"You didn't answer my question."

"I was smiling because I'm finally able to welcome you to the club."

He was making no damn sense.

"What fucking club are you talking about?" I squinted my eyes at him in frustration.

"The family club, you idiot." He shook his head at me telling me with his actions to get with the program while I remained confused. "You don't even realize it because it came out naturally, but you said, 'If anyone thinks they can threaten *my family*.' That is who Brinley and Zander are for you and I smiled because I was happy to see you finally admit it out loud."

I thought about it for a minute and it was the truth. I wasn't sure I deserved them, but they were mine and I'd make sure nothing happened to them. I'd failed my sister and I couldn't do the same with them.

"I see it's sinking in. Now hand me the note," Braxton said. But he didn't wait for me to give it to him, he swiped it out of my hand, ninja fast.

As he read it, his face contorted into worry, and then anger vibrated off him as he pulled his phone from his jean pocket.

"What are you doing?" I asked him.

"Calling an emergency meeting at work with everyone including Lyric. He works for us, but is also a cop, so he's a good guy to have in our corner."

Braxton fired off a text and then shoved his cell back in his pants. "I need to tell Jurnee I'm leaving, I'll meet you outside. We're all in this together and will figure this out. Nobody in this group stands alone." He gave me a pointed look. "Ever."

He turned to find his wife and I wandered outside. The fresh air hit my face, but it did nothing to calm me down.

I had a family again.

And I would go to the ends of the earth to protect them.

EVERYONE HAD LOST THEIR MINDS.

I sat at the large conference table as five sets of eyes stared at me inquisitively with the same stupid smirks on all their faces that Braxton had on his earlier at his house.

"You guys are a bunch of jackasses. We have shit to talk about and you are all wrapped up in Braxton's announcement that I used *one* word, so you're acting like some lovesick girls."

The truth was when we got here I was so riled up that their stupid bullshit was actually causing me to calm down just a little bit. Bantering with these men had become something I was getting used to and we could all do it in an easy, playful way. We'd bonded, which surprised the hell out of me.

"Well, it's so damn awesome to watch someone else fall when I was recently sitting right where you are now not so long ago. And Lord knows you will still fuck it up at some point, but I for one like my front-row seat," Kace said, laughing like a mad man.

"Hey, I'm not gonna be the last one you get to mess with," I told them, but my gaze landed on one person in particular.

Braxton, Gyth, Landon, and Kace's eyes followed mine as I zeroed in on the only single person in the room.

Lyric.

"Dude, don't try and get these guys off your back by throwing me under the damn bus. Besides I don't have anyone in my life so you won't be seeing me joining your little club anytime soon," Lyric mocked.

I raised my eyebrows. "Really? I may not have been right there but don't think I haven't heard the ladies talking about your exchange with the red-headed nurse at the hospital. Tell me. Have you pulled your head out of your ass and went back to talk to her?"

The room erupted in a round of laughter from everyone except for Lyric, who shook his head. "Deflection isn't going to work with me and that was nothing. Now let's move on."

"I call bullshit," Kace chimed back in. "I was right there and the sparks that were flying off the two of you almost burned us all. And my wife is not gonna let what she saw that day slide."

Lyric groaned and I laughed. "How does it feel, man?" I asked him.

"Everyone will forget about me by the time they are done watching your love life unfold, so it's all good," Lyric replied.

Love?

I'd said family and they were, but where did love come from?

I was shocked when Landon opened his mouth. He was the quietest one out of all of us.

"Don't fight it. Admitting to being in love may be scary as hell, but trust me and just embrace it," he said looking at me before turning his gaze to Lyric. "And you," he said, pointing at him. "You've met my wife. Alley doesn't forget shit. Trust me when I tell you that she and the other ladies have probably been plotting how they will get you with the nurse again."

"It's only a matter of time Summer has said," Gyth added. "She said they are just busy with Rowan right now but it won't be long."

"Geez, your guys' ladies are crazy meddlers," I said to the room, laughing.

Nobody took offense, they knew I liked every one of their wives. It was said in complete fun. But then my gaze landed on the paper laying on the table and my mood soured straight away.

Everyone else must have noticed and they sombered all at once. Braxton grabbed the paper, walked over, and handed it to Gyth first.

"Pass it around so each of you can take a look, then I am open to hearing what anyone has to say," he told the group.

It didn't take long for everyone to read it, the note was short, threatening, and to the point. And as each man looked it over, their demeanor changed and each of their faces looked as pissed off as I felt.

This was family.

It wasn't just blood relatives, the mother of your child, or your kids alone. It was everyone who had your back. The people who looked out for you and you looked out for them. Those you could count on to take something like that note as personal as it was and be ready to kick someone's ass for you and those you love.

And I had just said love without a second thought.

The whole day and night were turning into a revelation.

I tilted my head back and blew out a breath, sending a silent thought out to not only my mother but my baby sister. I was battling so many feelings right now. The usual one that tore me to shreds inside of how I let my sister down and what that loss did to me. How I should have been a better son to my mom who had lost her husband, my father, and then lost her daughter because while we were close, the grief that consumed me always had me holding back.

Then Luke and Brinley deserved more of me growing up as well as after I joined the Army when they had stood by me no matter how I acted. And of course, when I finally let myself cave to the intimate feelings I had for Brin, I shouldn't have walked away scared later.

Why didn't I stay? Or fight for what had always been there?

I'm sorry so damn sorry to everyone I let down.

But I was going to be different. I had the chance to be there for Brin, Zander, and all my friends. And that was what I was going to do.

"Rowan." I heard my name being said but didn't know who said it. My thoughts had been spiraling like a winding, never-ending staircase.

"Sorry, what was that?" I said to the room.

It was Gyth that spoke. "We've filled you in on everything that our ladies have gone through and some have had similar situations, so I can without question feel this is not random, but very personal."

Everyone nodded in agreement and then Lyric picked up the conversation. "Do we know if there are cameras in the parking lot where you were parked?"

I had been so wound up I hadn't been thinking clearly and that hadn't even crossed my damn mind yet. I was slipping for sure when it came to using my head and I couldn't afford to do that when people could get hurt *again* because of me.

"There is," Gyth said. "They had the entry gate and the cameras in place, but Braxton and I double-checked it and also lent a hand on some updates to them as well. While we don't monitor those as you know, we work closely with the company that does."

"When can we take a look at those?" Lyric asked. "If I need to jump in I need to do that."

The cop in him was shining through. For a moment, I feared he'd try to warn us all not to get mixed up in this and tell us to let the police handle everything. But that wasn't what he did.

"I will help any way I can with my connections, but I know you will all do what you need to do and I respect that. Just don't get in trouble," he said with a glint in his eyes.

It was obvious he knew us well and we would do whatever was needed to protect any of our families but were all highly trained. We could handle this properly unless pushed into a corner and then it was all bets off because nobody would hurt the two most precious people in my life. Even if it meant I got myself in trouble making sure they were okay in the process.

Braxton jumped in. "I will get a hold of one of the owners over there in the morning and get the footage. There will be no issues retrieving the images. Anyone who's available tomorrow afternoon can meet me back here around two and we can go over it."

The gym was open so I knew Braxton would be here and I believe Kace had some classes going on, but I still hated for everyone to take time out of their weekend away from family.

"Wipe that look off your face." Kace's eyes were zeroed in on mine when I turned to look at him. "I can see you worrying about us taking time out of our schedules, but nobody is going to blink a damn eye helping with this, you hear me? You are family. So are Brinley and Zander."

I nodded because a lump of emotion in my throat kept me from speaking.

"I'm not sure how I can help, but I'll be here," Landon blurted out.

"You're our lawyer so if we murder anyone you get to get us off," Braxton said, letting out a deep, crazy chuckle.

Landon laughed as well as the room, while Lyric groaned, putting fingers in his ears and humming like a child who was pretending not to hear what was being said. That caused more laughter and I couldn't help but join in. It was funny as hell honestly.

"The other thing we need to do is think about the jobs you have done or are doing now that could've pissed anyone off," Braxton said to me. "Also if you had anyone that could have followed you to town when you came that you made mad in your past or since you got here. Anything from military time, ex-girlfriends, lovers, and so on."

I winced. I didn't like thinking anything that had to do with me was bringing this to my family's doorstep. And besides work, I couldn't think of a single thing. There had been a few jobs I helped on that I had been worried about because the security we were putting in was for issues much like this where women and children didn't feel safe from their exes.

A shiver went up my spine at the thought. One in particular that I had just been dealing with bothered me the most. Was it possible it was related?

Other than those I had no struggles with people in the military so it wasn't that and some may not believe me but there were no ex-girlfriends or lovers.

Whether I could admit it in the past or not, Brin was it for me and there had not been anyone since her. Not a single person that may have tried after she and I were together compared to her and was not given the chance. If I didn't give her one, I certainly wasn't going to give that to someone else. Even if it was just sex.

"It has to be work, there is nothing else," I said.

All the guy's eyebrows raised in unison and the sight was pretty comical. I wasn't going to explain my personal reasons on the matter. And right then I was itching to get back to my place. Braxton seemed to pick up on my unease and jumped in to wrap stuff up.

"Okay, well we'll go over all the jobs tomorrow while we check out the camera footage. Let's conclude for now so we can all get home, it's late and I know Rowan is worried, which is understandable."

"If anything else happens you call me no matter what time. I don't give a shit whether I am off duty or not, this is about having your back as your friend," Lyric told me.

"That goes for any of us, day or night," Braxton added, and again everyone nodded.

I let out a big breath I felt like I had been holding in the whole meeting. "Thank you. All of you," I told everyone. "I appreciate this more than you know."

Braxton picked up the note. "You want to take this or leave it here?"

"I'll take it. As much as I hate to show Brinley and scare her, I am not going to keep her in the dark so she doesn't pay attention to her surroundings."

"Understandable and smart, even if it is hard," Braxton said, handing the paper over to me. Then he rapped a couple of times on the wooden table with his knuckles and everyone stood. "See you all tomorrow."

As we walked out of the conference room, Lyric slapped me on the back. "Anytime something feels off you give me a call."

"Thanks, man," I responded with a lump in my throat. It felt odd having people care so much but damn good too.

We all walked out of the building and Braxton locked everything up, setting the security system with his phone.

"Thanks again, man," I told him as we reached our vehicles. Everyone else had gotten in their own cars and were pulling out of the lot.

"No thanks needed. It's what we do." Giving me a chin lift, I gave him one back and then jumped into my truck.

Before pulling off, I glanced at the paper in my hand and another wave of anger raced through every cell of my body, along with fear as I read the words again.

You made a mistake sticking your nose where it doesn't belong. What is mine is mine. You had no business messing with my personal life, but since you decided to do just that, you better watch the people in yours. Real close. Especially that pretty lady and cute little boy.

I pounded my hand on the steering wheel.

"You're not fucking touching them!" I shouted to the empty car.

It may have been late but I needed to get home and see both Brin and Zander with my own eyes.

I needed to touch her. Not in an intimate way, although that had been amazing.

But just to know she was safe.

Chapter Twenty-Two

BRINLEY

I COULDN'T SLEEP.

As I lay there staring at the ceiling, my phone chimed from the bedside table, and I rushed to grab it. The screen lit up with a text from Rowan letting me know he was home and at my door. My heart started pounding for two reasons. First, because I knew something had happened before he left and it wasn't good. Second, because I could still feel his mouth pressed to mine and couldn't help but want a repeat.

In his text he said he needed to see if Zander and I were okay for himself, which scared me a bit. But after the way he worded it, I couldn't say no.

And I didn't want to because I wanted to see him too.

I climbed out of bed, padded down the hall on bare feet and peeked out the peephole when I reached the door. Standing up on my tippy toes so I could see, I said, "Who's there?"

A huge smile broke across Rowan's face. He was strikingly handsome. The man could have any woman swooning and if he ever graced the cover of one of the romance books I read, he'd have every lady one-clicking in the blink of an eye. Maybe even the men.

"You know who it is, Buttercup, you're looking right at me."

I giggled. "Do you know the password?" My toes were starting to hurt but the flirting was too much fun to care. At least at the time that is what I thought we were doing. Then with Rowan's next words, I was sure of it.

"Spanking." I saw him wink. "Because if you don't open this door right now, that is exactly what you are going to get."

My breath caught and the damn tingles were back in my lower region. Rowan could charm the panties off of anyone. Including me I realized as his sexy voice washed over me.

"Since the door is still closed, maybe that is exactly what you want," Rowan growled.

I dropped to the flats of my feet and stared at the wooden door. A strange feeling rushed through me. Was it a yearning? Anticipation? I wasn't sure. It then hit me that the idea of him actually spanking me was appealing. What was wrong with me? I had told myself to stay away and not get hurt. I also had no clue how to act when I opened the door.

"You're thinking way too much, sweetheart. Let me in, Brin."

If I didn't he was going to wake up all the damn neighbors. That would be even more embarrassing than facing him after the banter we'd shared. Not to mention him seeing me red-faced from the desire that rushed through my body at his comment.

I pulled open the door and my face flamed even more when I saw him without the barrier between us. Rowan smirked and walked inside, planting a quick peck on my lips when he got beside me.

"Hi," he whispered.

"Hi," I said back breathlessly. Even just his lips on mine and a simple hello got to me when it came to Rowan.

Then he leaned back, glanced up and down the hall before shutting and locking the door. Another niggle of worry seeped in. Rowan was nervous about something and that was not like him. It immediately put me on edge. One second I was flirting and the next ready to jump out of my skin.

"What's going on?" I sighed. "You have to tell me. You're worrying me."

He grabbed my hand and guided me down the hall.

"Where are we going?" I asked.

"I'll tell you, even if I wish I didn't have to, but I just need to peek at Zander first," he told me.

I didn't press him right then for why because it was easy to see his nerves were frazzled and he needed to set his mind at ease.

Once he got a look at his son, he let out a big breath of air and then he led me back down the hall to the couch.

He pulled me down next to him leaving no space between us. I felt heat radiate from his thigh and yet even with the warmth I shivered at the lust-filled sensation his closeness brought on. He turned his torso a little so he could look at me and I did the same. When he dropped my hand, that's when I realized he held a piece of paper in the one that had been free.

The lust was gone and dread took its place. It sat like a greasy hamburger in the pit of my stomach and I felt sick. We'd had such a good day and it had changed after he'd gone to get Zander's gifts out of his truck.

I nodded to the paper in his hand. "What do you have there? Is it the reason you left earlier?" Everything inside me said it was and that I wasn't going to like what was on it.

Rowan tilted his head back and took a deep breath, then brought his gaze to mine. "Yes. It was on my truck window when I first went out there to bring stuff in. I want you to know before you read it, that I'm so damn sorry that anything that has to do with me would bring problems to you and Zander." A small tick of his jaw told me he was fighting to keep his emotions in check. "But I promise I will not let anything happen to either of you."

With reluctance shining in his eyes, he handed me the paper.

It didn't have much on it, but the small amount that was there had my blood running cold. It was clear it was meant for Rowan, but whoever put it on his truck must have been watching us to know that we were in his life and they could get to him by taking aim at my son and me.

"Why?" I dropped the paper and it fluttered to the floor. "Who would do this?"

"I don't know, but me and the guys are sure as hell going to find out. After talking tonight, the only thing we can think of is that it is tied to one of the projects I've worked on recently." He rubbed his hands over his face and I could see the stress of the situation was getting to him. "Everyone is meeting tomorrow to see if Braxton got the footage from the cameras in the parking lot."

"Someone had followed us, Rowan!" My blood pressure was rising and I felt a little frantic. "Whoever it is knows where we live. So what else do they know?"

"That's what the guys and I will figure out. Take a deep breath. I am right here."

Another thought crossed my mind and I shook my head, confused. "How did he get through the gate?"

"That I don't know either, but I have to think he walked in when someone opened it, or something. We'll figure this out, Brin. I didn't want to show you and scare you, but I need you to be aware so you watch your surroundings and never get caught off guard."

I took the much-needed breath that Rowan had just asked me to take and my body relaxed a little. "Thank you."

He looked at me perplexed. "Why are you thanking me? This is all my fault."

I took his hand in mine. "Rowan, you're just doing your job, if that is what this is. You can't control what other people do. I was thanking you for not shutting me out and letting me know."

He glanced down at our joined hands and sighed.

"You were always so understanding when we were growing up, but after the way I fucked up, I have to say I am surprised you're being that way with me now." His head came back up and his eyes seemed to search mine to see if I was telling the truth.

When his body sagged a touch and the storm in his irises vanished a fraction, I knew he could see I was being honest.

He brought the hand I was holding to his chest and my skin burned with the urge to run my palm up and down his solid muscles. His heart was thumping rapidly and he said something so unexpected. "Go out with me?"

"What?" I squeaked, caught completely off guard.

"Brin, I want to take you on a date. One that is long overdue and I should have done back in high school."

God, how many times had I wanted him to ask me that very thing? But how could I risk getting my heart trampled on like a stampeding herd of bulls?

"What if—"

He cut me off. "I know you must have a bunch of what ifs. But what if it wasn't our time back then and now it is." His other hand ran up and down the top of his jeans that covered his powerful thigh. Rowan looked uneasy and he was usually so sure of himself. "What if you were made for me and this is our second chance? Say yes? At least this once, then we can see where this goes."

At my hesitation he said more.

"No matter what, I swear we'll always take care of Zander together. You'll never have to do it alone again. Seeing you again and finding out about my son has made me look at things differently, Brin. I was an idiot before. All our lives actually, but I'm here now."

Hearing him say no matter what he was still going to be there for Zander was amazing. And I would get to go on my first true date.

With Rowan.

"Okay, yes."

The smile that stretched across his face blew me away. But then something crossed my mind.

"What about Zander? How can we go out when someone is sending you notes? I can't let anything happen to our son."

His thumb circled on the top of my hand, soothing away the worry that was racing through every cell in my body.

"Honey, I work with some badass men. He will be well protected at Gyth and Summer's place. I will ask them myself. And I will be with you." Keeping hold of the hand on his chest, he let go of my other and cupped my cheek in his palm. "I get this may not be the best time when we just found this note, but I don't want to miss out on making any more memories with you, Buttercup."

I turned my cheek further into his palm and soaked up the moment. It felt insane. I should have been scared about the letter, which I was, but this chance was a once in a lifetime for me.

Because Rowan was always it for me. Always had been.

There had never been anyone else and I never thought there ever would be.

I just never imagined I'd have him.

As long as Zander was safe, I was taking my shot.

Rowan leaned over and kissed my temple. "I know I already said this, but I'm going to protect you and Zander. I promise." He gave me a little tug and tucked me under his arm so I was plastered to his side. Resting his chin on the top of my head, he sighed.

I mimicked the sound with a sigh of my own, feeling safe and warm in his embrace.

And that's how our son found us the next morning.

Chapter Twenty-Three

ROWAN

"Daddy!"

My eyes popped open when Zander yelled. I was able to move the warm, sexy woman from my arms a second before my son landed on my stomach like it was a pool and he was doing his best version of a cannonball.

"You and Mommy had a sleepover," he said, giggling.

His face inches from mine and blond hair in disarray, he grabbed my cheeks and smashed them in his palms.

"That's not fair. I want to have a sleepover with you too," he whined.

A cute, sleepy groan from beside us had Zander and me looking over at Brin. Her arms went up in the air as she stretched and a monstrous yawn escaped her. My son and I both laughed. Then my eyes seemed to catch and be transfixed on her pink-tinted, bow-shaped lips that I craved to kiss.

"Mommy always sounds like a bear in the morning." Zander's humorous voice stopped my thoughts from tumbling to a place they shouldn't be going with him in the room.

"I heard that," Brin mumbled and Zander giggled again.

Well aware that it was an accident that she and I had

fallen asleep together, and unsure if I would ever have this moment again, I soaked it all in. I pulled Zander closer to my chest with one arm and Brin into my side with the other, giving them both a squeeze.

Then I launched a tickle war and all hell broke loose.

Zander kicked and screamed with glee, while Brin fought hard to set herself free from my embrace. She was ticklish everywhere. A memory from our past came back to me.

We'd been picking out a movie to watch one evening as we waited for Luke to get to my house with food and Brin had said something sarcastic. Knowing she was extremely ticklish, I set forth to get her good and tickled her every-where. We ended up off the couch and onto the floor where I hovered over her as she cried out mercy.

When I finally stopped I became aware I was straddling her middle, our cores touching, and looked down into her mesmerizing blue eyes that shimmered with desire.

Brin lifted her hips, pressing up into me even more, and the bulge in my pants grew like a weed on speed. A groan erupted from deep in my soul just as Luke walked in waving the bags of cheeseburgers he had picked up from our favorite diner in the air. I'd jumped off Brin making some comment about her smart mouth and how she deserved her tickle torture before heading to the bathroom to get myself under control.

That was when I was sure there was something between her and me that went beyond friendship. But I never acted on those feelings until that fateful day I came home to bury my mother.

Had that been a mistake?

Even though I felt like I screwed up and I missed out on time with Brinley, I also couldn't help but feel like if we'd gotten together earlier on, then we wouldn't have what we had now.

Zander.

And while I'd only had a very short time with him, I couldn't imagine life without him.

"Earth to, Daddy? Can I have my other present now?"

We'd told Zander we had another gift for him when we got home the night before, but he'd fallen asleep. Apparently, he hadn't forgotten about the present.

"Brin?" I raised my eyebrows in question.

It was her house. Plus she and Zander may have had plans, or a routine, so it was only right I asked.

"Sounds good to me as long as we can get some breakfast right after because I woke up hungry." She smiled at the same time as her stomach growled and we all broke into laughter again.

I could get used to this.

As in *forever.*

"Yay, where is the present?" Zander dug his knee into my stomach as he used it as leverage to push himself backward off me.

My son bounced around like a superball that was out of control. "Does he have Red Bulls stashed under his bed he drinks before he comes out of his room in the morning?" I asked Brinley, pointing to Zander.

Her soft chuckle was adorable and the sound swept through every cell in my body, lighting a flame of desire that needed to be extinguished before I had to explain the growing hard-on pressing against the zipper of my jeans.

Damn, everything about the woman that was next to me turned me on. Had it always been that way and I was just better at ignoring it?

I realized the answer was yes. Brin had knocked me for a

loop from the moment I'd met her and I'd always been hers even if I never could admit it. That didn't seem to be a problem now though.

I was happy to shout it from the rooftops and make a fool of myself letting anyone know she belonged to me.

"Daddy, come on," Zander pleaded. He grabbed my hand and pulled, grunting in the process of trying to pull me to my feet.

Playing along, I acted as if he was managing to drag me up. "You are so strong," I told him and a huge grin spread across his face.

I turned and snatched Brin's hand on my way, making her stand at the same time. When she smiled, I couldn't help myself. I leaned over and whispered, "You make it hard to concentrate on anything else." I placed a quick kiss on those perfect lips. Our son didn't miss it.

A dramatic gasp slipped from his mouth and I looked over to see his eyes bugging out of his head. "You kissed her," he whispered as if it was a secret. It was hilarious and adorable all rolled into one.

"Is that okay?" I asked him.

He was nodding his head vigorously and when I looked back at Brin, she looked skeptical and nervous.

"He's okay, Buttercup. Look at him for yourself."

She glanced at our son who was smiling like a loon and the hesitant look left her face.

"Why is she a Buttercup, Daddy? That's a candy," he stated matter-of-factly.

Brin's face flamed red and I knew I was in deep shit if we didn't get on with the present part of the morning. Because I had a feeling she would be sweeter than the candy and I was dying to get a taste.

"Let's go check out your gift." Hands still all clasped

together I veered the three of us down the hall until we got to the bedroom that used to be a nursery.

"I thought we couldn't go in here?" Zander said.

We'd told him that the room was off limits as we had worked on it at different times when Zander wasn't there. I was seriously proud of my son because he listened and hadn't even attempted to breach the door.

"Well, we can now." I turned the knob and pushed open the door and watched my son's eyes bug out for the second time that morning.

"Happy Birthday, Bud," I said.

Then Brin leaned down and hugged our son. "I hope you like it."

Zander gave her a tiny squeeze and unleashed himself from her grasp, running to the middle of the room where he spun in circles. "This is awesome!" he shouted, happily.

"So I assume that you like your new room then?" I asked.

He climbed the ladder to the top bed of his new bunk bed and a small shudder ran through me. Watching him go up each step brought on a wave of fear. What if something ever happened to my son? I couldn't lose him like I lost my sister. My stomach twisted. It was a very small ladder, but that didn't seem to matter when the past came floating back. Then, Zander flopped himself down onto his back and yelled, bringing my focus back to him. "I love it! Now Dexter can come over and we can each have a bed."

Zander and Dexter had become fast friends. I loved that for my son. As I watched him take in the room and thought about the sleepovers he would be having, a wave of sorrow washed over me.

I felt Brin lean in and rest her head against my arm. When I looked down at her, she was watching our son with a smile on her face, but then she glanced up at me.

"I miss him too," she said. Somehow she knew I'd been thinking about Luke. While we had talked about him, we were still both struggling on that front.

Luke and I had many sleepovers through the years growing up. I swallowed the lump that formed in my throat thinking back to those days and hearing Brinley's sad tone at the loss of a truly spectacular friend.

"He was the best," I whispered. "I let him down. But now isn't the time to talk about that."

The moment was about our son and when I looked back at him, his laughter and glee were contagious. "Let's go join him," I said.

Brin pulled her head from my arm and I missed the contact immediately. She was starting to warm up to me and maybe the idea of us too. At least I'd hoped so. When she touched me on her own accord, it felt amazing.

Like I'd won the lottery.

We both walked further into the room together and I asked Zander, "What do you like best about the room?"

"Everything, duh," he said. His little tongue came out and he cocked his head as he rolled his eyes. Clearly he thought I was dumb for asking.

I had to admit Brin and I had done a damn good job with the room with some serious help from Landon. "Maybe I need a room like this," I mumbled.

"You're a goof," Brin said in response.

The mural Landon had painted that resembled the scene on Zander's cake was remarkable. He was seriously talented. A forest scene with many trees, Army men lurking behind their large trunks, a river running through the middle of the scene, darkened sky above, and some animals in the mix made it all look so real. I couldn't thank him enough for what he had done for Zander.

Then Brin and I found the bunk beds, camo bedding, a couple of bean bags, a toy chest loaded with new toys, a dresser, lamps, and a small desk with a chair. Everything matched and blended so well.

"Daddy, will you be the first to have a sleepover in my new room?" He slid down the slide on the opposite side of the small ladder that took him to the ground and ran up wrapping his arms around my legs.

My heart swelled at the request.

"I sure will. As long as your mother is okay with it?" I looked at Brin. "You mentioned the girls wanted to do a sleepover soon, so what if I stayed here with Zander so you could go to that?"

"That's perfect, Mommy. We have a sleepover and you go to one too. Okay?"

Brin hesitated. I knew she wanted to go, but had said she didn't know about leaving Zander, and having never gone to a sleepover with girlfriends before, she wasn't sure she would know how to act even though she'd become closer to all the ladies. But I knew she would say yes not wanting to have her son miss out on something he wanted.

"I think we can work that out," she told him.

"When?" Zander immediately asked her.

"Soon, I promise. Now how about that breakfast?" she asked, smiling.

I hated to put a damper on the morning we had so far but I had to meet with the guys today. "I have to go into the office soon." Brin's smile fell and a worried look entered her eyes. Exactly what I wished I could have avoided.

"How about this? We go to get some breakfast, then I'll drop you two back here to get ready while I go meet with the guys, and as soon as I'm done, I will come back to pick you up so we can go to the zoo?"

Besides the party the evening before, it would be the first big family outing with just the three of us. I knew how Zander felt about it since he was jumping up and down, as usual, begging his mother to say yes.

"We could do that," she said.

"Yay! I'll go get dressed." Zander was off with lightning speed to the other room.

"I almost forgot for a minute," Brin said quietly.

It killed me that she had to think about it at all. Turning to her, I lifted her chin with my fingers and looked into her crystal blue eyes. "I'm sorry, sweetheart. I told you last night, but I'm going to figure this out."

When I dropped my hand from her face, she nodded and then changed the subject, making it clear she didn't want to think about it anymore right then.

"Do you seriously want to have a sleepover here?" she asked.

"Of course I do. Are you worried about staying over with the girls still?"

Brin bit her bottom lip as she paused for a minute before saying, "A little I suppose. I've never done sleepovers."

"I beg to differ. Me, Luke, and you had sleepovers all the time." All innocent, except for the one time I'd thought about earlier. However, there was nothing innocent about the things I'd like to do with Brin if she agreed to what was brewing in my head.

"That was different." Brin glanced down at the floor.

"How about after our date we practice having a sleepover?"

Brin's head popped up so fast I would be shocked if she didn't have whiplash. Her eyes mimicked her son's from earlier and were bugging out. With a red face and shocked look, she said, "That wouldn't be even close to the same thing."

Smirking, I leaned in and gave her another quick kiss. Leaning back, I gazed into her eyes. "Exactly. If you can get through our sleepover, you can make it through any others."

She gasped, but interest shined in her gaze.

I wiggled my eyebrow suggestively and she laughed, playfully swatting my arm.

"Mmph. Men," she murmured.

Grabbing her hand, I pulled her toward the doorway so I could feed her and Zander.

"I think you'll like what I have in store for you during our sleepover, Buttercup."

I was going to arrange that pronto.

Chapter Twenty-Four

BRIN

WHY HAD I DECLINED TO GO SHOPPING?

The girls tried coaxing me into going out during the following week to pick up something new to wear for my date with Rowan, who'd wasted no time getting it planned after asking me out.

We'd been busy with our trip to the zoo which went fabulously well and had been a lot of fun. I was apprehensive at first about us all going together as a family, but I'd worried for nothing. At least not as far as the outing went. Rowan was fun, carefree, and attentive to Zander, along with me the whole time. I suppose it was as if I was always waiting for something to go wrong or for things to change, even though they seem to be progressing instead.

Then during the week, we had Zander's actual birthday to celebrate, which we'd done with just the three of us also, and besides Rowan's work, I was also busy doing some work for Alley. So in the end I said that I was good with what I had. But I was second-guessing that decision as I threw what minimal clothes I had all over my room.

A frustrated sigh escaped me as I threw myself backward

on my bed. Flat on my back, my legs dangling over the side, I willed something magnificent to magically appear that would be suitable for a first date.

It was the beginning of October so not too cold yet, but the summer heat had tapered off. I also wasn't sure where we were going and was told to dress in whatever made me happy. Rowan's words were, 'Anything you wear will look spectacular on and off you, Buttercup.' Thinking about it as I lay there, my body temperature rose, just as it had when he said it.

I had a feeling that Rowan was going to succeed in charming my panties right off me as the evening progressed.

Nervousness bombarded me and I contemplated texting him to say I couldn't make it. Suddenly feeling queasy, I was sure I was getting sick and could use that as my excuse. As I was about to reach for my phone the doorbell rang.

"Oh no, no, no," I whispered to the empty room.

Rowan couldn't be early, I wasn't ready at all. I sprang to my feet as Zander hooted and hollered that we had company while running down the hall.

"Don't you dare open that door when you don't know who it is!" I told him, following hot on his heels.

My legs were longer than his and we reached the door at the same time. I glanced down at my fuzzy bathrobe I'd tossed on while looking for something to wear and groaned. It was not how I wanted to start the date.

"Mommy, pick me up and let me check the peephole," Zander asked.

Doing as he requested, I grabbed my son and hiked him up high enough for him to put his eye to the hole.

"Let me down!" he said excitedly as he wiggled to get out of my grasp. Setting him on the ground he turned to me. "It's Summer and Dexter so it's okay, right, Mommy?"

Well someone was early but I sighed in relief that it wasn't Rowan. After opening the door the boys cheered enthusiastically and ran off toward Zander's new room.

"Sorry we're early, I thought maybe you might like some company while you got ready and I brought some clothes just in case." Summer held up a cute yellow bag that looked stuffed to the brim. "If you're anything like the rest of us when we had our first dates with the man of our dreams, your room probably looks like a war zone." She gave me her usual, sweet smile, but this time there was a know-it-all smirk lurking behind it.

I giggled. "Like World War III."

She nodded. "I got to get a look at it, but I can't promise you won't be teased about it later, and not just by me."

"Oh geez." I groaned as I shut the door and then we headed toward my room. When we entered, Summer busted out laughing. "I knew it!"

"Oh, hush," I sassed. "Show me what you got in the bag. I need serious help here."

As she laid out all the clothes she had in the bag, I thought not for the first time that Summer had some serious style. I rummaged through the selections and held up the outfit that called to me.

"You sure you don't mind if I borrow it?"

Summer rolled her eyes. "Are you kidding? I would mind if you didn't. That's what friends are for."

"Well, since you want to be such a good friend, how about helping with my hair and makeup?" I asked her with a pleading, but unsure look.

"I thought you'd never ask." She squealed and clapped her hands. "And wait until you see the gift from the girls and me," she added with a smirk.

I was almost scared to find out what the present was, but

we set out to get me ready for my date and I hoped Rowan would like what he saw.

~

"Are you going to come in?" I asked Rowan, who stood outside the door in the hall, not moving.

"Just give me a minute, Buttercup." His gaze roamed up and down the length of me. "Let me appreciate the view for a moment."

The thorough assessment that was coming from his dark, potent eyes had a quiver racing through my body and dampness settling in the sexy, pink-laced undies the girls had bought for me, along with a bra to match.

I bit my lip in anticipation as Rowan finally walked toward me like a cat on the prowl. With a gleam in his eyes, I had a fraction of a second to register what was coming my way. One strong arm circled my waist as he pulled me in close to him, his other hand going to the side of my neck, and his mouth landed on mine.

Without thought, I opened automatically and he deepened the kiss. Our tongues dueled, teeth nipped, and the taste of Rowan's minty fresh breath, mixed with his earthy scent was an aphrodisiac that had me going wild in his arms. I moaned into his mouth and I felt his desire pressing into me. Then he softly broke the kiss and a whine of protest left my lips.

I wanted more.

Leaning his forehead against mine, we both fought to get our breath under control. "If we don't get the date started I won't be letting you out of here."

An unladylike snort escaped me and I buried my face against his hard chest in embarrassment. *Way to go, Brin, I'm sure he can't wait to get into those sexy panties now.*

"You're adorable," he said, causing another snort.

What the hell was wrong with me?

"You're funny," I told him, my words muffled with my face still pressed against his massive chest.

Rowan moved his hands to my shoulders and gently pushed back, looking me straight in the eyes. "I'm serious, Buttercup. Everything about you appeals to me and if we don't get the show on the road I'm going to show you just how much."

Goosebumps broke across every inch of my body.

"Would that be such a bad thing?"

My mouth blurted out my thoughts before my brain got the memo to keep my trap shut. As I had said, obviously I was not in control.

"Trust me, sweetheart, I would like nothing more than to strip you bare and have my way with you while I explore every inch of your amazing body, but you got all dressed up and it's way past time I take you out on a date."

I guess the outfit I borrowed from Summer was working and Rowan hadn't even seen the gift the girls bought me that was underneath the flowy, flowered dress, jean jacket, and brown cowgirl boots.

"You might change your mind if you saw what was under my clothes."

With a sexy grin and his signature wink, he replied, "We will get there." He grabbed my hand and pulled me toward the door that had been open the whole time.

I grabbed my purse on the hook by the threshold as we walked out and then my heart fluttered with warmth when he spoke again.

"How was Zander when he left? Do Summer and Gyth know to call us if he needs us to come to get him?"

Summer had left with the boys just before it was time for

Rowan to show up. Zander was a little disappointed he wasn't going to see his dad before heading out but was also stoked about spending the night with his friend. And while he was excited to go, he'd never stayed at other people's homes overnight so I wasn't sure how it would go.

It was sweet and an eyeopener into how much Rowan had grown to love our son when he'd offered to end the date if we needed to get him.

Even if it meant he wouldn't be getting any.

I tried to tell myself before we left that I wasn't sure what would happen when it came to the end of the night, but after the start we'd had, I knew exactly how I wanted the date to end. And there was no question in my mind about what Rowan wanted.

"They do know. Thank you for caring." It was probably an odd thing to say when he'd been showing me how much Zander meant to him since he'd found out he had a son. Well, shortly after. He had to get over the initial shock first, but that only lasted a matter of hours. Then he'd been amazing.

"I care a lot," he said, turning his head in my direction as we walked hand and hand toward his truck.

I gave him a megawatt smile.

"About *both* of you," he added.

My stomach fluttered and my heart beat faster as his words sunk deep inside.

WERE DATES ALWAYS THAT MEMORABLE?

It was perfect.

I didn't have anything to go off of since I'd never been on a date before. I mean Luke had taken me out all the time, but that was two best friends hanging out. Him trying to do nice things for me.

Going out with Rowan, sparks flying between us the whole time, was a completely different feeling. And I was sure it wouldn't feel the same with anyone else. Rowan had told me that he should have taken me on a date when we were teenagers and so we were going on one that normal teenagers would. First, we had dinner at a Mexican restaurant that sat on the edge of the Columbia River. We ate delicious food on the heated patio, talking and laughing the whole time.

Then, he took me to the movies where he bought me popcorn, proceeded to play coy, and wrapped his arm around the back of my chair as he inched closer to me in our seats. Before long the movie was forgotten and he had me making out with him in the dark theater. I'd been glad we were in the far back seats at the end so there wasn't anyone paying attention to us.

Something I figured he'd planned all along.

After, he took me for ice cream where I decided it was time to turn the tables. I tortured him with every lick, swirl, and moan as I devoured the two scoop, waffle cone as slowly as possible.

When he told me I was going to pay for what I'd done, I giggled and he swatted my ass right there on the sidewalk for the whole world to see.

'Foreplay, baby,' he'd said as my face flamed red and my body caught fire.

How we made it to my place and into the house before I spontaneously combusted, I wasn't sure. And the trip to my bedroom was a blur. But once there I agreed that there had been foreplay all night and I was ready to get to the main event.

"Let the charming begin," I mumbled.

"What's that, Buttercup?"

My eyes widened realizing he'd heard me but then I also realized I was way past caring.

"Oh, to hell with it," I said out loud plain as day.

The jean jacket came off and I threw it toward the corner of the room. Next went the boots. And then I ripped my dress over my head and tossed it in the same vicinity as the jacket. Standing in nothing but the pretty pink, laced panty and bra set, gifted by some truly amazing friends who somehow knew I'd be needing them that evening, I looked into Rowan's eyes feeling a little vulnerable.

I hadn't thought that striptease through and had let lust drive me. But once I got to that point I couldn't help but wonder if Rowan would like what he saw? While we were together one night, that was a long time ago. I was older and I'd had a child since then. Even had a few stretch marks to prove it.

But the look I was getting from Rowan was telling me that he indeed liked what he saw and I relaxed. He put his hand in the air and with his pointer finger at a downward angle, he did a little twirling motion urging me to spin around. Doing as he asked, I heard a deep groan, and that was when all the nervousness was gone.

"That is fucking sexy," he said.

"I'll let the ladies know," I told him as I was in motion. "It was a gift from the girls."

"Remind me to thank them later."

Once facing him again, he was on me in no time and fused his lips to mine while his strong, warm hands wrapped around my back, flicking the clasp of my bra and adding it to the pile of clothes on the floor in two seconds flat. This time I broke the kiss and backed away a couple of inches. Grabbing the tops of my panties, I slowly slid them down my thighs and kicked them to the side.

"I knew you could charm the panties off of anyone," I said breathlessly. "I'm just glad it was mine."

"Your panties are the only ones I want to see hitting the floor."

I could hear the sincerity in his voice, but I asked the question rumbling around in my head anyway. "You mean that don't you?"

"I don't say things that I don't mean, baby. You know that."

Rowan had always been very careful about what he said, making no promises, and keeping so much to himself, so I did know that.

"I do," I agreed.

He smiled and it lit up his gorgeous face. "Then believe this too. I'm not walking away from you again, Brin."

My breath caught and my heart was doing crazy things in my chest. I wasn't sure what to do with all the emotions, but I knew what to do with the desire so I said, "You can have your way with me now."

His eyes heated, the smile he was sporting turned into a devilish grin that said I was going to like what was coming. In a flash he was in my personal space again plucking me up into his arms and tossing me onto the soft, pillow top mattress behind us.

I bounced a couple of times and he came down over the top of me.

"I can't promise this first time I won't explode like a rocket. You're fucking sexy as hell and so damn beautiful. I've spent years wanting to be inside you again. But I promise the second time we will slow it down. And you will love it both ways, sweetheart."

I was nodding my head yes, needing him to get on with it.

He scooted back off the bed, got to his feet, and started to remove his shoes and clothes. It was the sexiest thing I'd ever seen in my life. Rowan was a magnificent piece of art. I wanted to feel and explore every inch of him. Especially the nine inches jetting out from his swoon-worthy, masculine body that was ready and willing to rock my world.

Leaning over he plucked something from his pants and straightened with a single condom in his hand. "I may need to run home because one time won't be enough."

I motioned to the drawer in my nightstand and watched as he opened it. Grabbing the box of condoms that lay inside, he held them up with raised eyebrows.

"Another gift from the ladies," I told him, giggling.

"They are my new favorite people. I'll have to let the guys down easy," he said. "Gyth may be the most pissed he isn't my fave anymore."

We both laughed and then Rowan was over the top of me again.

"Now we're getting to the good stuff," I said, staring into his eyes.

"It's just the beginning, baby. Hold on for the ride."

Chapter Twenty-Five

ROWAN

I WANTED TO NOT ONLY OWN HER SEXY BODY BUT HER beautiful heart too.

By the end of the night, Brinley would realize I was meant to have both.

From that day forward it would be clear.

And it would be forever.

Chapter Twenty-Six

BRINLEY

Rowan had told the truth.

The first time had been quick, but I was sure it was going to be just as memorable as the times to come in the future. And I was hoping there was in fact a future, because I couldn't imagine him not being in my life. Losing him twice would be unbearable.

Besides, I wouldn't have been able to handle going slow either. Rowan and I had chemistry and it had been smothered for far too long. We'd been doing a song and dance around one another for so many years. But the embers of the fire inside us when we came together ignited and were burning out of control.

We'd both gone up in flames.

When we finally came down to earth, I lay spent, the weight of Rowan's body covering me like a warm blanket. He, however, recovered instantly. I watched his glorious naked body move off the bed to discard the condom in the bathroom. His backside was mouth-watering as he walked away, but upon his return, the full-frontal view staring me in the face was newsworthy. Only I wasn't about to share it with anyone else.

Ever.

He slid back in bed and showed me he'd meant it when he said the slower version would be just as earth-shattering as the first.

My body sizzled, then sparked to life again as he pressed down on the mattress with both hands beside my head, hovering just above me, and gave me a smoldering look. His shaft grew to its full length and once again sat heavily between my thighs, with the potential to tear another mind-blowing orgasm from my body.

When I felt the sensation he'd created slip away, I almost cried from the loss. But then Rowan's powerful body slid down the length of me and his face replaced his cock between my legs, an all-new sensation had taken hold. His facial hair rubbed against my clit and my pulse sped up at the friction he was generating.

He'd been worried about going fast the first time we'd had sex, but it was nothing compared to what had happened next. He parted my folds and with the initial swipe of his tongue from top to bottom of my lady bits, I saw stars. My breath came out in quick pants and I grabbed hold of his hair, pressing his head closer as my hips launched upward at the same time. When his tongue speared inside and his thumb pressed against my ass simultaneously, my second orgasm of the evening sparked to life. My hands dropped from his head and my palms hit the mattress, clenching the sheet tight in my grasp. A rumbling sounded as my body shook uncontrollably before I erupted as explosively as a volcano that had been dormant for centuries and had been waiting to be set free.

There was only a small recollection of him sliding on another condom before he was above me once again. Grabbing his manhood, he slid it through the wetness he'd created. Still coming down from my last orgasm, I felt another surge forth. Rowan pushed the head of his cock into me a few inches and then pulled free, teasing, playing, and all the while he watched with stormy black eyes that commanded every inch of my body, mind, and heart. I begged, and pleaded, asking him to finish what he started.

Doing as I wanted, he played me like a fiddle so perfectly and effortlessly. One hand came up to pinch one of my nipples, his warm mouth wrapped around the other, and he drove forward. In one fluent motion he slammed home, burying himself so deep inside me I wasn't sure I'd ever be the same.

The third orgasm was building rapidly and I scraped my nails down his back. I was sure it would leave the aftermath of our lovemaking on his beautiful, tanned skin. But he paid it no mind and it seemed to fuel the fire inside him. He pistoned his hips in and out of me, setting a grueling pace that I tried matching thrust for thrust until he slammed home one last time. With a powerful roar from the pits of his stomach, and while I screamed out his name, we fell over the edge together.

I was sure we were never coming back.

"BABE, ARE YOU OKAY?" Rowan asked, his voice muffled in the crook of my neck as he lay beside me, one strong arm wrapped around me.

Umm, that was a big fat no. He'd wrecked me from there on out. I already wanted repeat performances whenever I could get them. How would that even be possible?

But a tinge of fear took hold and that little voice in the

back of my head whispered, *What if he walks away again?* A shiver ran through me.

Misinterpreting the shake of my body, he asked, "Are you cold?"

"No, I'm fine."

Pulling back and raising up on his elbow, I found myself face to face with the man of my dreams. Now that he was looking at me I could see in his eyes that he was reading me like a book. Never missing much and capable of always knowing what I was thinking, he ran his hand softly through my hair. "I'm not going anywhere, Buttercup."

My breath hitched and my body trembled.

"And I don't mean just for right now. I mean I'm never leaving you again." His hand came to my cheek and his thumb caressed the side of my face. "I'm going to prove that to you and one day you won't question it. But I know I have some work to do and believe me, baby, when I tell you I will do it."

I grabbed onto his words and tucked them deep inside my heart while I sent a prayer to the heavens above asking my mama and Luke to watch over me. Both of them had loved Rowan and I could picture them smiling down on us now, telling us it was about time. Maybe even his mother too.

When I realized where my thoughts had gone, I made a sour face and shuddered. Hopefully, I was wrong and they were not watching right then or both may be vigorously washing their eyes out.

"Are you going to let me in on what put that look on your face when all you should be feeling is pure sexual bliss?"

I rolled my eyes. "You're pretty proud of yourself, aren't you?" I didn't need words, his sexy smirk confirmed the answer was yes. So I decided to knock the hottie down a peg. "I made the face because I was thinking my mom, Luke, and your mom may be happy and watching over us. Then I realized they may not have wanted to witness what just happened between us."

Laughter consumed me and broke free loudly when Rowan's whole body looked as if it convulsed at the thought. And then for the third time that evening, I snorted. Only I didn't feel embarrassed as I had before and it felt amazing to be me without worry.

Besides, Rowan seemed to like me the way I was.

"That was not funny, woman." Without warning, he jumped out of bed and scooped me up as if I weighed nothing, throwing me over his shoulder like a ragdoll, and walked toward the bathroom.

Pounding on his back and yelling for him to put me down, I received a swat on my bare ass. "Stop squirming," he said.

"What are you doing?" I screeched. "You probably left a handprint!"

A deep chuckle vibrated against my belly as his shoulders shook with laughter. "There's more where that came from."

I sent up another prayer that our families weren't watching right then because if they were they would see how much the idea of another spanking sparked more desire within me.

When he dropped me on my feet on the cool white tiled floor next to the shower and turned the water on, I said, "Are you trying to tell me something? Do I smell?"

"Sweetheart, you smell like sex and I'd gladly leave the scent on you all night since we're not even close to done, but I have to wash away the image of others watching the show." He pointed upward with his version of a sour face and it was funny as heck.

I would have teased him about it, but I received another

healthy swat on my fanny. "Get in the shower, babe. I'm ready for dessert number two."

Not willing to say no to that, I did as I was told.

Rowan conjured up another orgasm as the wet spray rained down over us and I knew I would probably be sore in the morning, but it would be worth it.

FIVE.

How was it even possible to have five orgasms in one night? I had a feeling that if Rowan set out for more he could get them.

After the shower, he knocked my world off its axis once again and then we lay in the circle of each other's arms and did something else that we hadn't done before.

At least not like we had then and to the depth which we did.

We talked about his dad dying in the Army, and the loss of his sister, mother, and Luke. My mom's death and also about how our son would never forget what an amazing man Luke was.

Something shifted, everything felt different and I burrowed in and fell asleep with the man that I had always loved. Even when I wanted to hate him in my times of sorrow, I couldn't do it.

I had my best friend back.

And something a lot more.

Chapter Twenty-Seven

ROWAN

WHEN MY PHONE RANG AND I SAW BRIN'S NUMBER, I answered.

It didn't matter if I was in the middle of a meeting with the guys, I was worried. It had been a couple of weeks since our first date and we'd fallen into our own routine with just the three of us. And Brin didn't often call when she knew I was working.

Zander was with her each day because he wouldn't start Kindergarten until the next fall. Embry and Dexter were already in school so playdates happened once they were home. But with Brin working for Alley they happened to see each other more regularly in the daylight hours. She was getting more and more comfortable with all the ladies and true friendships were in place.

It was great to see.

We had dinner together every night if I hadn't needed to stay late at work and we spent weekends together too. The three of us were becoming a tight family unit. And while there had not been any more threats toward me, Brin, or Zander, I wasn't going to let my guard down and assume the issue had gone away. We still didn't know who it was so it was an active case as far as anyone was concerned.

"Hey, sweetheart, what's going on?"

Only it wasn't Brin.

"Daddy!" Zander cried. "Someone hit our car! You have to help us." His breathing was coming in fast pants across the line. "Please, Daddy."

My world spun and a million scenarios raced through my head.

"Son, it's going to be okay. Where is your mother?" My pulse raced as I waited for him to reply. I stormed out of the conference room, the sound of booted feet pounding behind me, but I was paying my friends no mind. All I could think of was getting to my family.

I put my phone on speaker as I fumbled to pull up the find my phone app so I could see where they were at.

"She is driving and trying to get away from the bad person!" Zander's voice was full of fear and I was right there with him.

I was scared to fucking death.

"Mommy t-told me to c-call you," he said, bawling hysterically. It made it harder for me to understand him, but I was getting the message.

One that had me going berserk.

I heard Brinley in the background murmuring to our son as she tried to soothe him, but I could still hear the panic in her voice. She was trying to get away from God knows who and probably terrified as hell, but her first priority was Zander.

My vision blurred for a second and I had to concentrate to keep myself upright as I raced to my truck.

"Bub, can you put the phone on speaker so I can talk to your mother?" I felt like I was coming unhinged.

"Y-Yess."

There was a pause and then his next words had my knees hitting the asphalt a few feet from my vehicle.

"Daddy, please don't let us die!"

Oh God, not again. I can't lose anyone else.

The phone crackled and then Brin was on the line

"Rowan!" she called out over the loud revving of an engine. "Someone is—"

Brin and Zander let out a piercing scream at the same time as the crunch of metal rang in my ears.

"Talk to me, baby!" I shouted, frantically, jumping to my feet.

I heard sobbing, glass shattering, and tires screeching.

Brin yelled out for our son.

And then there was nothing but silence.

.

Chapter Twenty-Eight

BRINLEY

SOMEONE WAS FOLLOWING US.

Over the last few weeks, Rowan had been clear to watch my surroundings and I'd been trying to do that.

It was a Friday night and Rowan was working late. He'd been working so hard and also worrying about the threatening note even though things had been quiet.

Quiet didn't matter though. I'd learned once before that it could mean the complete opposite. Sometimes the silence meant something bad was going to happen and your world was going to be turned upside down.

I found that out the hard way when my heart was ripped to shreds after Luke had been killed.

So until whoever put the note on Rowan's truck was found, we needed to stay alert. I'd thought I'd been doing a pretty good job of that, but that didn't always mean things couldn't go sideways.

Zander and I decided we'd pick up some food for Rowan and the guys so they could eat during their meeting. We stopped at one of their favorite pizza places and then headed in the direction of *No Surrender*.

Besides him working hard, I wanted to see and be near him, even if just for a second. Especially after the tense call I'd got from Luke's mother earlier that had me upset. I was going to wait until he got home from work to talk to him, but when our son whined that he wasn't seeing his dad for dinner, the idea to surprise him and fill his stomach sounded like a nice plan.

That was until my Spidey senses went off and a tingle at the back of my neck started. Something else that Rowan had taught me not to ignore. I was looking in my mirror for a short time and noticed a truck staying right behind us. There was always the chance they were going the same way, but something was telling me that wasn't the case.

If anything happened to my son because I hadn't been paying close enough attention, I would never forgive myself.

There we were traveling down the dark, isolated road next to a hillside and I knew that I needed to get us somewhere with more cars. Or better yet, to Rowan. As soon as I sped up a little, so did the vehicle, and then before I knew what was happening, it bumped our back bumper. A small intimidating tap as if to let me know they were right on top of us.

And there was nothing I could do about it.

Thump, thump, thump.

My heart raced and I fought to calm it the best I could so I didn't scare my son any more than he already was.

"Mommy, what is going on?" His breathing was rapid and the fear in his voice not only made me sad but pissed that someone would do something so reckless and possibly hurt a child.

My child.

"Baby, take my phone and call your dad," I said.

Carefully picking my phone up out of the console, I handed him my cell. Keeping my eyes on the road in front of me, I gave quick, small glances in my rear-view mirror to watch the truck behind us.

When I heard Zander talking to his father, frightened, and begging for him to help us, my heart crumbled to pieces. Then my son told me Rowan wanted to talk to me and placed the phone on speaker.

I took a deep breath and hearing his voice calmed me for a second because I knew he would help us.

"Rowan, someone is—"

We were rounding a curve when I started to tell him what was going on and the next thing I knew the truck didn't just tap us, it slammed into the back of us at a startling high speed. Zander and I both screamed, the phone went flying, and my car spun out of control.

I tried. I really did.

Working to keep the car on the road was my goal, but it wasn't in the cards. The impact was too hard and the truck was so much bigger.

"Mommy!" Zander's tearful voice called out.

"Baby, hang on!" I cried out in response, hands gripping the steering wheel so tightly I was surprised it didn't bend in half. "I promise I'm gonna take care of you!" I prayed that was the truth and it wasn't the last time I ever got to hear my baby's sweet voice or look into his beautiful face.

As the words left my mouth, our car left the road completely and flew off the deep embankment.

It was impossible to do anything as it was happening so fast. Bumps, bangs, metal crunching, glass breaking. Each horrific sound registered in my head as the world around us imploded and we went over rocks and tree limbs slammed against the car. And then the car came to a sudden stop as we smashed into a huge tree trunk with substantial force.

And it was lights out.

~

"Mommy, wake up."

The sweetest sound drifted to my ears. I moaned and lifted my head from the steering wheel where it lay, a warm liquid trickling down my forehead.

Raising a hand to my head I placed it on the spot that hurt and it came away crimson red. Sucking in a breath and squeezing my eyes closed as pain sliced through my head, I fought to get my bearings.

"Mommy…"

Zander's small voice snapped me to attention and I unclipped my seatbelt—something I was thankful for—and slowly turned around to find my son.

Witnessing the tears that cascaded down his angelic face had me seeing a different kind of red and I never in my life wanted to harm another person as much as I did to the person who'd put that fear into my precious little boy. The fact that he was still in his booster seat and looked unharmed had the murderous feeling simmering a fraction. But I wouldn't know for sure until I got to him. Or even later for that matter.

"Does anything hurt, sweet boy?"

"No, but I'm scared, Mommy."

I assessed him again with my eyes once more, hoping that he wouldn't feel an ounce of pain even later on.

"Baby, Mommy is coming. Sit still and I will come and get you."

"O-okay."

Turning back around, I tried to open the driver's door and failed. It only opened a fraction before hitting against something that was stopping it from opening more than a couple of inches. I had to get to my son. The soft weeping from the backseat was killing me.

Body sore, blood dripping in my eyes, I turned back around and sluggishly crawled between the front seats to get in the back with Zander. As I was going over, something flashed and caught my attention.

A flashlight.

Up on the road, a light was shining down, scanning the area and through the trees. Alarm seized the air in my lungs. Was that the same person who hit us? I hadn't seen anyone else on the road so it had to be. Panic gripped me as I wondered why he would still be there. Were they not finished with us?

My promise to my son that I would take care of him flitted to my mind and fueled my momentum. Scrambling faster the rest of the way into the backset than my body had liked, I unbuckled Zander and tried to talk to him in calm, soothing words.

"It's okay, baby. Shh." Working overtime to keep myself calm as well, I kept talking as I brought him into my embrace. "Mommy's got you."

I didn't know if the person would try coming down to us, but I wasn't taking the chance of us being sitting ducks. We needed to move.

Hugging my little man close for a second, I reached to the back door handle and prayed it wasn't stuck as mine had been. A relieved breath exited my lungs when it popped open. With my son wrapped around my front like a monkey, I slowly inched on my butt across the seat and out the door. On wobbling legs, I stood with him in my arms and froze.

At the sound of cracking tree branches and the swivel of the beam of light over my head, I felt paralyzed with terror. Once again, the small voice in my ear got me moving.

Seeming to grasp the situation, he whispered in my ear, "Someone is over there, Mommy."

On unsteady legs, I held tight to my son and moved forward one step at a time deeper into the trees that surrounded us. I shivered as the cold night air seeped into my body. My coat was in the car long forgotten since my only thought had been getting to my son. I was thankful that he had on a sweatshirt at least but knew it wouldn't keep him warm for too long.

I couldn't hear anything any longer and hoped that whoever was out there gave up, but I couldn't take any chances.

With nothing but the moon to illuminate our way, I searched for a place to hide. Before I got too far, a loud rumbling from farther away broke through the eerie silence. Then the crunching of footsteps started again and I turned to see the light from the flashlight swinging swiftly back and forth. I breathed a sigh of relief when I noticed it was going back up the hill. Then another engine started and I could hear a vehicle speed off.

Was it safe for us to try and get back up the embankment?

The sound of not one vehicle came closer, but multiple and I hoped with everything I had that it was someone to help us.

Please find us, Rowan.

My son and I must have been thinking the same thing as he softly asked, "Will Daddy find us?"

Tires screeched as they came to an abrupt stop and doors slammed.

And as if we both had conjured him up, a deep, masculine, and frantic voice boomed through the night.

"Brinley! Zander! Where are you?"

I opened my mouth to yell, but nothing came out.

He came for us.

A big spotlight shined bright and my hand flew up to shield my eyes as Rowan's voice rang out again.

"Come on, baby! Talk to me, please!"

Hearing the panic in his tone, I started walking back toward where the car was. We hadn't made it very far away in our attempt to get away from whoever was out there, but we had descended a good distance off the road when the person hit us.

"We're here!" I yelled.

"Keep talking, sweetheart, I'm coming to get you guys."

I did as he asked and we reached my car at the same time. How the hell he made it down that fast was crazy, but I was freaking glad he was there.

Zander immediately cried out for his dad and turned in my embrace practically launching himself at him and I winced at the discomfort. Rowan caught his son and also the look that crossed my face. It was dark, but the big light shined down on us, and seeing the man in front of me, I knew everything was going to be okay.

So, when he pulled me gently into his arms, trying to be careful of any injuries I had, and asked if we were okay, I lost it. The trembling started and the tears broke free.

In the distance, I heard the sirens, more footsteps coming down the hill, and people talking, but all I wanted to do was hold the two most important people in my life.

And just feel.

I WASN'T sure how we ended up in the back of an ambulance.

Everything was a blur after Rowan found us. Somehow when we got back up to the road, all the guys from *No*

Surrender were there and the cops had things blocked off, searching the area for clues.

Rowan insisted we be seen at the hospital and I shuddered at the thought. I hated hospitals after spending so much time with my mom there during her illness before she passed away. But it was important to get Zander checked over so I didn't argue.

"Stella," I whispered.

The name popped into my head and left my lips. I shut my eyes trying to think. My head pounded and I rubbed my temple trying to grasp why the name crossed my mind.

"Baby, what did you say?"

Why would a woman's name jump into my head? I wondered if I hit it so hard that something was seriously wrong. But the name wouldn't leave my mind.

Eyes still closed, a vision was coming forth. The headlights in my mirror as the truck had come closer. I'd glanced in the mirror just before it had hit us the first time and saw the license plate. I remember it seemed odd that it had a woman's name and wondered if they named their car, but when he bumped into us I'd forgotten until I lay in the ambulance.

My lids opened and Rowan was staring at me as I rested on the gurney, Zander seated in his lap, his head against his dad's chest. Our son didn't want to leave either of us and was doing okay physically so Rowan insisted we all ride in the back together to the hospital.

"The front license plate said Stella," I told him. "I forgot until now."

Rowan's eyes widened and he looked toward the door of the ambulance where Gyth and Braxton stood.

Something passed between them, but I didn't know what was going on.

The pain in my head was getting worse and I winced.

Rowan's gaze swung back to mine and he told everyone we needed to get going.

"We'll meet you at the hospital," Braxton said just before the door shut.

I reached up and laid my hand on my son's back, needing to touch him. Things could have gone even worse tonight.

"Don't go there, Brin. You protected our son and you're amazing," Rowan said, placing his hand over mine where it lay on Zander.

Even with my head feeling as if someone was banging a cast iron pan against it repeatedly, I could tell that Rowan was working to keep his cool so he could soothe both Zander and me. I appreciated it more than I could say, but not going off the road at all or knowing someone was watching us before we left that night would have made me feel better.

It would be hard not to beat myself up about it for a while.

I started to close my eyes once more and I heard the EMT tell Rowan he needed to try and keep me awake until we got to the hospital and got checked out because he thought I had a concussion.

"Baby, open your eyes. You need to stay awake."

I attempted to do as he asked, but it wasn't working. My body was so tired and I just wanted to sleep for a few minutes.

"I love you, Brin."

My eyes snapped open and I sucked in a gulp of air.

That woke me up.

Chapter Twenty-Nine

ROWAN

I NEEDED TO GET HER ATTENTION AND IT SEEMED TO DO THE trick.

But I meant each word as if they were my last.

I loved her.

So damn much.

And I loved my son too.

Brinley lay in stunned silence as we finished our trip to the hospital, words not leaving her beautiful mouth until we'd gotten inside and they wanted to take our son to another room to check him over.

That's when Mama Bear showed her claws.

Her son was not leaving her sight; she'd roared, making sure everyone there knew it. I couldn't help but chuckle, she was absolutely marvelous to watch when she was on a rampage.

Truth was, she was something special to see all the time.

When she glared at me, I had to hide my smirk with a cough or I knew there'd be hell to pay.

I leaned in and kissed the two people that owned my heart before they took them away to look at them. With her son lying next to her, Brin watched me until they were out of my sight.

"Sir, can I ask you a few questions?" a lady at the desk said, drawing my attention.

Before I could move in her direction, a commotion sounded behind me and I swiveled around to see a mass of people coming through the doors as others around them parted like the red sea to let them through.

They were an intimidating group and they demanded attention. Sometimes they could be a little scary too, but they were amazing, caring people, and I knew that was why they'd come.

Family.

Every last one of them was also part of my family. I wasn't sure how it happened. When my family died and I walked away from Luke and Brinley, I thought for sure I was meant to spend the rest of my days alone.

But the group that came toward me and the two that were waiting for me to come to find them said otherwise.

"Excuse me, Sir."

I'd almost forgotten about the lady at the desk until she called out to me again. Holding up a finger to my friends, I walked over to the desk and answered what I could.

"Can I go back to the room now?" I asked her as we finished.

"I'm sorry, only family can go back," she said sympathetically

"They are my family. That's my son and…" Girlfriend? Was that what I was supposed to call Brin? It didn't seem like enough, she was so much more, but I settled on, "and the mother of my child. I will be going back."

The woman looked at me, paying no attention to my unyielding tone, and said, "So you're not married then?"

"Not yet, but we will be soon." I let that settle for a minute and knew it to be true. "She's my fiancée."

I heard a throat clear from behind me and turned to come face to face with Alley. A sheepish look crossed my face as she raised her brows at me.

"Does Brinley know about this or were you just going to demand it, lock her in your room, and then chain her to your bed while someone marries her off to you?" Then she snapped her fingers and her eyes lit up. "Hey, Kace and Gyth, both are ordained. One of them may do it for you."

Leave it to Alley and her sassy mouth to cause a stir. I heard the woman behind me laugh and I couldn't help but laugh along with her. Alley was a force of nature.

Then I winked.

"She will know soon."

~

"THEY'RE ALL HERE?"

Brinley looked flabbergasted when she found out everyone was in the waiting room. And when I'd said I meant everyone, I wasn't exaggerating.

"Even Dexter?" Zander asked.

"Yup, even Dexter. Every man, woman, and child we know is in that waiting room. I don't think there is room for anyone else."

Brin laughed and then closed her eyes in pain. What hurt her, hurt me, and I reached for her hand. Rubbing slow circles on it, I tried to soothe her.

Zander still lay beside her on the bed. He may be sore over the next week or so, but he checked out without having any major injuries. But he didn't want to leave his mother's side and the emotional damage that was caused would take longer to heal.

He was still scared but was also worried about his mom. Same as I was.

Brin didn't walk away from the accident as easily as Zander had, but it could have been a hell of a lot worse.

I shuddered at the thought. I'd been working on not playing the *what-if game* and focusing on just being there for them. Then I'd find the motherfucker who dared to cause my family any trauma and he'd better hope Lyric was with me to put him behind bars, because if he wasn't, they may never find his body.

Shit, I could never do that, or I'd have to leave my family and that wasn't something I was willing to do. But I was so fucking angry it sounded good for a minute.

When my son told me to not let them die, images of my sister falling to her death flashed in my mind and the guilt, the sorrow, and the pain consumed me. Then, the faces changed and I saw Brinley and Zander. I couldn't let them down and yet at the time, I didn't know if I could save them.

I'm not sure what would have happened if the guys and I hadn't pulled up when we did. I'd seen the flash of taillights in the distance and Brinley had told police at the scene that whoever hit them had been headed down the hill, possibly in search of them, until our vehicles could be heard in the distance. Then the person took off.

It didn't matter, we knew who he was. And I knew it was a man because when Brinley mentioned the license plate I realized the dirtbag who owned it was the husband of one of our clients.

The wife had us install security systems, she was taking self-defense classes, had a restraining order out on her husband who refused to divorce her, and had been both physically and verbally abusive.

She was his property, he'd told his wife.

The name of the license plate was her name and it was not sweet, but creepy after finding out all about him. He was, however, not as bright as he thought he was since that stood out like a sore thumb and he used it in a hit and run.

As Brin told me all the details she could remember, it was clear she was the true hero that evening. She was going to protect her son no matter what and she had. With a concussion, a sprained wrist, stitches in her head, and a lot of bumps and bruises, she still managed to be everything Zander needed at that moment.

She was a badass and she was *mine*.

Once she healed I'd convince her to make it official. Or I could just go with Alley's plan? At least then I'd know she would be safe.

"Can we go home now?" Brin asked. "I hate hospitals." I saw her quiver and could tell another bout of pain swept through her.

"You're not going to leave us, right, Daddy? Will you stay at our house?"

The worry in my boy's voice sent my rage skyrocketing again.

My hands clenched wanting to punch something. No, I wanted to punch the someone who put fear in my son. "I promise I will be right there with you both." My words seemed to ease his mind and he rested his small head on his mother's shoulder as she rubbed his back.

They let us go after she was all stitched up and with a brace on her wrist. We were given clear instructions that someone needed to stay with her. We were just waiting for a nurse to come back with her discharge paperwork and prescriptions for her pain meds.

"We should be out of here really soon," I told her, having not answered her question about going home yet.

When I looked into her crystal blue eyes and saw her biting her lip, I wondered what was going on. Usually, I knew what she was thinking, but right then I didn't.

I didn't get to find out either. The nurse walked in a second later to give Brinley and Zander their walking papers and wheel them out front.

With Zander perched on Brinley's lap and me walking along beside them, the friendly nurse escorted us down the hall.

We reached the waiting room and everyone but the little ones that had fallen asleep stood up, happy to finally see Brin and Zander for themselves.

Looking around at the group I was thankful to have them all in our lives. But when my eyes landed on Lyric, it looked like he'd swallowed his tongue. Then I saw Teal nudge Alley and a 'Told you so' was murmured, but I didn't know who said it.

What in the world was going on?

I looked back to see what everyone was staring at and that's when I noticed the blush on the redheaded nurse's face. I'd totally missed it with everything going on. I wasn't there the first time Lyric and the nurse met, but I'd heard all about it. Enough sparks were flying to keep the fourth of July going for a whole damn year.

And Lyric thought he was immune from biting the bullet and joining the club? He was full of shit.

"You're next buddy," Landon said, clapping Lyric on the back. "I told you that my wife wouldn't let it go."

"What did I miss?" Brinley asked.

She couldn't see the nurse's face go from blush pink to bright red, but everyone else had. Lyric fidgeted, and because I needed to get my lady home, I saved him.

"I'll tell you later, baby. It's time to get you two home." The nurse nodded and began pushing them to the doors.

As I passed Lyric, I whispered, "That lifeline I just passed you won't last long. Should just give up now."

I didn't wait for his response but heard the guys chuckle and the ladies giggle.

Then Gyth added, "Don't fight it, brother, it's no use."

I smiled to myself thinking he was definitely in for a ride.

We got out to the front and I was glad someone had driven my truck from the scene to the hospital. One of them had also already pulled it up to the loading area. The guys and I were all on alert and checking our surroundings as we got situated in the vehicle, Brinley riding in the backseat with Zander.

Right before we took off I looked back to check on them. It was hard to keep my eyes off of them for fear something else would happen.

Brinley was looking at me in the mirror as if something was still on her mind. I gave her a questioning look and she solved the mystery.

All the air left my lungs and happiness swelled inside me. And my heart, well, it mended as her words sunk in.

"I love you too. Always have."

"Me too!" Zander exclaimed as he bounced a little in his seat. "I love you both this much," he added, throwing his arms out to the side, wide. I was glad to see him happy but hoped he didn't hurt himself or Brin.

Flashing them both with a bright smile, I started the engine.

And we headed *home* together.

Chapter Thirty

BRINLEY

Rowan hadn't left our side but a few times over the last week.

And if he couldn't be right there then one of the other guys was.

Since the accident, they hadn't caught the man responsible. I'd found out they knew who it was by the name on the license plate that had burned its way into my brain. He was some pompous, abusive asshole named Michael that seemed to have it out for Rowan because he installed Stella, the wife's, security system. The jerk didn't like someone else interfering with what he deemed was his.

Michael seemed like the name of a nice, ordinary person, but these days you just never knew. I cringed and my body shook just thinking of him. I'd forever shudder when I heard that name in the future knowing it would always bring back bad memories.

Although I was still scared and hurting, my priority was making sure my son was safe. God, I didn't want him to be fearful of everything, and yet since the incident he hadn't wanted to sleep in his room alone at all. If I was being honest,

I hadn't either. Having him by my side made me feel marginally better. And even better than that was the fact every night Rowan had been in bed with us.

I felt a smile lift my cheeks.

It had been hard to be happy and smile over the last week, but the image of the three of us cozying up together in my bed did the trick. I was hoping that the get-together and trick-or-treating that evening would be another.

Zander had been looking forward to the day for months, ever since he and Dexter started talking about their costumes. My son had always been with me for Halloween and this was the first time he got to celebrate with other kids. But he was hesitant and worried that someone would come for us.

This wasn't fair.

He was a little boy. My son shouldn't have been looking over his shoulder all the time. And although we could never predict when our time on earth would come to an end, the last thing I wanted was my precious baby worrying that his mommy was going to die. Something I knew he was doing because of the way he was acting, along with the nightmares he'd been having.

At least he had his father. He thought Rowan hung the moon and was some kind of superhero. So if his dad was with us, then he said we'd be safe.

I never thought Rowan and Zander would be together, but now that they were I couldn't imagine them ever being apart. Luke's mom, however, made it clear by her phone call earlier in the day before we left to take Rowan food and got run off the road, how she'd felt about it. A conversation I had to relive when I told Rowan about it.

Not pleasant at all.

In a nutshell, she'd called to bitch about the type of mother I was, going on about how Luke would have wanted more for his family than what I was providing for my son. Anger boiled inside me. She may be his mother but she didn't have a clue what Luke had truly wanted because she only cared about being the best and having the best. Her son would have wanted Zander and me to be happy.

And Rowan was doing that.

Luke had always encouraged me to keep trying to get in touch and talk to Rowan, never once had he tried to pretend Zander and I belonged to only him. He was my best friend and, God, he would have loved Zander, but he'd always hoped one day Rowan and I would find our way together. Luke was an exceptional man.

Anyway, when I'd taken a deep breath and worked up the courage to finally tell Luke's mom who Zander's father was and that we were with him, she'd exploded. And then I matched her fire for fire. Always looking down on Rowan, who was not good enough for her son to be best friends with her choice of words and things to say about him was the last straw.

Needless to say, I don't think we'd be hearing from her again and we were better off that way. But it still hurt for some reason as I replayed the things she said in my head.

"Mommy, lookie, I'm all ready." Zander came running into my bathroom where I'd been thinking and getting ready to head to Braxton and Jurnee's place.

Another smile lit up my face in just a few short minutes. Because the cutest little Army guy was standing in front of me, actually excited and fuller of life than I'd seen him in days. He looked great in his combat uniform and camouflage face paint.

"Do you like it?" he asked.

"I love it. Your dad did a good job."

"Wait until you see him!" Zander shouted just as Rowan walked in behind his son.

When my gaze took in the man dressed to match his son, I was at a loss for words. I'd never seen Rowan in person in his uniform and it sent a jolt of desire racing through me. He looked like a sexy badass.

Suddenly I was feeling a whole lot better.

Between Zander in my bed, which neither of us would have changed, and my injuries, Rowan had made it clear there would be no whoopee. I cracked up laughing so hard at his choice of words, I'd let out another of my unladylike snorts, and I figured I'd set my healing back a day.

But it was worth it since it was one of the few times I'd laughed over the last week.

I wasn't laughing now though as my eyes scanned Rowan from head to toe and wondered how to get him alone just for a few minutes.

"Like what you see, Buttercup?" He waggled his eyebrows at me.

"You look okay," I said nonchalantly with a shrug of my shoulder. "We better get going."

Zander turned and raced out of the room. "I got to get my candy bag!"

It was so good to see him excited about going.

Rowan was staring at me as I moved through the bathroom doorway, passing him.

"Just okay?" Rowan's deep voice asked. I paused, my back to him, and giggled.

He moved closer and leaned in next to my ear. "Well, you look hot, Wonder Woman. I can't wait to get my hands on you again." His husky voice in my ear sent goosebumps pebbling all over my body.

Everyone was dressing up and Zander and Rowan had

come up with the costume I wore. I was feeling a little exposed, but the man behind me was enjoying it.

"We better go before I lock you in the bathroom and have my way with you, baby."

I shivered right before he swatted my ass to get me moving.

"DAMN, GIRL, YOU LOOK—"

Alley stopped abruptly, not finishing her sentence, and looked around at the children present. She, however, slipped on the cussing and a certain someone picked up on it as usual.

"Pay up, Auntie Alley," Embry told her, the palm of her hand out in waiting.

I knew where to go if I ever needed to borrow any money. That girl made a bank for her swear jar with all the potty mouths around her.

"Haven't I given you enough to buy a damn car already?" Alley threw her head back and sighed realizing her mistake.

"Probably since your favorite word is the one you just said twice in a row and now you owe me double," Embry sassed.

Between the look that Embry threw Alley's way and her comment, I couldn't hold back the laughter. Besides, she was as sassy as her Auntie Alley and it was fun to watch the two of them banter.

"I don't have any money hiding in this outfit, we'll have to get it later, girlfriend," she told Embry.

All the ladies decided we would dress up as some badass woman for Halloween. Alley was rocking a sexy Catwoman costume.

"Fine, but don't think I will forget," Embry told her.

More laughter bubbled up and I held my arm across my stomach, cupping one hand under my wrist that was in the splint. Working to not jiggle my arm too much was a chore and my head was still hurting, but I would be okay.

My son and I were alive.

The little girl was intuitive and also as sweet as she was sassy. Coming over to me she wrapped her arms around me softly and looked up with a soft expression.

"I'm sorry you're hurting. My daddy, Uncle Rowan, and the rest of the guys will make sure you and Zander will be okay, Auntie Brin."

My breath hitched hearing her call me that. I kept saying they were family, but when she said that it truly sunk in. I loved that girl as if she were mine and I knew all the other women felt the same way about each other's kids.

"Thanks, sweetheart."

She smiled at me and then with no filter at all—true Embry style—she said, "When are you and Uncle Rowan getting married?"

I didn't get a chance to answer before the woodsy scent of Rowan filled my nostrils and goosebumps broke out across my neck. The heat of his body wrapped around me as he moved up next to my back. Leaning in, his mouth close to my ear, he peered over my shoulder at the little girl. "Hopefully really damn soon if I have my way."

Looking at Alley, she gave me a knowing look and I wondered if she knew something I didn't. We hadn't talked about anything like that. Was he being serious? Maybe it was the accident talking and he was just scared, but once things settled down and they found the man responsible he would forget all about that.

"You guys are hopeless," Embry said.

I thought she was talking about the marriage bit until she carried on.

"Maybe I should make the D word exempt from the money jar fund. You all like it way too much and are bound to be broke real soon."

"She's right about that," Alley said.

"Or maybe I should double the fine for that word," she said, giggling.

The girl was smart.

There was no time to keep pondering the marriage thing between Embry's antics and Zander running up with Dexter to ask if it was time to go trick-or-treating yet.

Everyone else descended on us. Jurnee in her Black Widow costume, Summer dressed as Elektra, Gemma looking amazing as Batgirl, and there was no way to forget Teal as Scarlet Witch.

I shook my head as I took us all in, truly impressed. "Us ladies, look da—darn good," I said, correcting myself in the middle of my sentence.

Embry giggled. "Almost had you," she said. "I know there will be more to be made tonight."

"Trick-or-treat," Hudson's sweet little voice rang out. He held out his candy bag letting us know he was ready.

The kids looked so adorable too. I was so glad we got a ton of pictures. Everyone laughed and worked their way toward the door.

"Did I already tell you how hot you look, Buttercup?"

"You did, but no funny business. We need to get to trick-or-treating. We need to find some Buttercups."

I gave him a cheeky smile and he laughed.

Rowan leaned in and gave me a quick peck on the lips.

"I already have mine so I'm good."

Butterflies fluttered in my belly. Rowan was still himself,

but also so different in the way he expressed his feelings. It didn't feel like he was holding back at all. I didn't want to either, but part of me was still worried it would all vanish one day. Not wanting to think about that right then, I tried lightening the mood. It was a party after all.

"If you want to keep it that way you need to find me some candy, Army man."

I sensed that he knew what I had done but he went with it. Putting out his hand toward the open door, gesturing for me to proceed ahead of him he said, "Your wish is my command, sweetheart."

WE WALKED MILES.

Or at least it felt that way. My feet were killing me.

I moaned as Rowan rubbed my feet propped in his lap. He'd just put Zander to sleep in my bed, which shocked me. My little man was so tired that he didn't care that nobody was in there. He'd still wanted to sleep in there and not his room, but it was the first time he went in alone.

"Those noises are killing me."

I lifted my head from the pillow on the other end of the couch and smirked at the gorgeous man with the masterful hands. He and Zander had both showered, having to work hard to get all that face paint off. Smelling fresh, looking sexy in a pair of sweats that hung low on his hips, and shirtless, I was struggling just as much as him.

"Then do something about it," I challenged.

"Baby," he took a deep breath. "You're still hurt and need to be careful. It kills me to know I wasn't right there to make sure you two were safe. And now you have to heal."

The strain on his face and the guilt in his tone broke my

heart. It wasn't his fault and I'd told him that a million times. I wanted to forget it all right then.

Pulling my feet free from his hold, he watched as I tucked them under me and moved to my knees, crawling slowly across the couch. Swinging one leg over his legs, I sat on his lap and wrapped my arms around his neck. I leaned over, pressed a kiss to his chest right over his heart, and felt the rapid thumping against my lips.

It was good to know I had that effect on him.

Straightening, I looked into his stormy, black eyes, that swirled with emotion after emotion.

"I need you, Rowan. I want to feel alive. You can do that." I pleaded with him with my stare. "Make love to me, please."

He was breathing rapidly, fighting with himself about what to do.

"You can be gentle this time. I'll be okay." I ran my hands up and down his smooth, muscular chest and pressed my core down on him, swirling my hips.

He sucked in air. "You don't fight fair, Buttercup."

"Is that a yes?" I asked in a hopeful tone.

He put his hands under my arms and turned me to lay me down on the couch, where he followed me over.

"How can I say no to the woman I love?"

The truth was he couldn't.

And thank gosh for that.

Chapter Thirty-One

ROWAN

"WHAT'S THE OCCASION?" BRIN ASKED.

We were in the truck headed to the bakery where I bought all the goodies from and had gotten Zander's cake. Since I always picked them up and brought the goodies to the house, she'd never been in the shop herself.

Glancing over at her briefly, I smiled. "No occasion, baby. I just thought we could do something altogether today before you leave me for your sleepover."

It was clear I was dreading her being gone and maybe it seemed silly, but I had my reasons. Not only was it because we still didn't know where Michael the crazy husband was, but also because I hadn't spent a night away from Brin since he'd run her off the road.

My jaw tightened thinking about it every time and I was surprised I hadn't broken a tooth with how hard I clenched. I wouldn't rest until we found him. And even after that, I wasn't sure if I would ever relax completely. I knew what losing someone you loved felt like and after the scare with Zander and Brin, I constantly worried it would happen again.

I felt a soft hand rub across my arm where the tattoo for

my sister was placed and looked over to see a soft, sympathetic look on Brin's pretty face. She always knew somehow.

"Jelena knows how much you love and miss her."

My heart squeezed.

Brinley and I had talked about her and Luke many times over the last few weeks. We'd even told Zander more about them too. He loved to ask questions and I liked to answer, but I wish it didn't still feel so raw.

"Daddy," Zander called from the back seat. "Do you think Auntie Jelena would have liked me?"

And that was one of his favorite questions. For some reason, it was important to him. Brin had done an amazing time making sure he knew about Luke and how much he would have adored him but finding out about Jelena was new.

Brin moved her hand and grabbed mine where it rested on my thigh in silent support.

"You bet she would, bud. She would have loved you and you two would have had so much fun."

I could picture it in my head. She would have been the fun aunt, but also the one that caused chaos, and let him get away with everything.

"I'm going to talk to her and Luke in heaven," he said.

Getting choked up, I couldn't respond so Brin did it for me.

"They would *love* that, baby."

Then she did what she did when things got hard and changed the subject. Sometimes I wished she wouldn't do that, but I understood why she did and respected her when it was what she needed to do. Right then I was thankful for it.

"What are you going to get at the bakery?" she asked our son.

I looked in the rearview mirror and saw Zander put one

finger to his lip and tap it in thought. "Hmm. Can I get two things?"

I was about to say yes because looking at him in the mirror with his adorable smile and hopeful look was hard to deny, but Brin wasn't looking at him and she told him he could have just one.

"You have your sleepover tonight and will probably have way too much junk then."

He was a good sport and didn't argue. Zander was looking forward to Dexter coming over and I was on kid duty. It had been three weeks since the accident and tonight would be the first night he was going to sleep in his room. With Dexter there, he'd feel safer and maybe it would help going forward.

I wanted to be with Zander but also by Brin's side. All the girls were sleeping at Alley's but Gyth would be right outside the whole time since Summer would be with the girls and his son would be with me. Lyric was planning on being there too so It made me feel better. And because Alley and Landon's little girl was so small, Landon was banished to the bedroom for the night to care for his daughter. What could happen with all three guys there? Logically I knew not much, yet I still felt uneasy.

We pulled up in front of the bakery and Brin glanced over at the storefront. "Capri's," she murmured. "That's her name right?"

"Yup. Let's go in. I think you'll like her."

After getting out of the vehicle, Zander's hand in each of ours, we started toward the door and Brin stopped suddenly, glancing at the place next to the bakery.

"What is it?" I asked.

"It's for lease," she told me.

I'd seen the sign the last time I was in and I'd guessed

it was still available, but I wasn't sure why Brin cared. Then it hit me. She hadn't talked about it a lot since arriving, but one time she'd said maybe someday she would open another bookstore. When she started working for Alley and with everything happening, she'd never mentioned it again.

But I could see the wheels turning as she stared at the empty space.

"If you're interested we could call and check it out?"

Her gaze snapped to mine. "I—"

Cutting her off, I placed my free hand on the side of her face. "You can do anything you want to, Brin." I dropped my hand and pulled out my phone, then snapped a picture of the number on the sign. "We'll call later. Let's get some sweets."

"*Finally*," Zander said dramatically.

I held the door open and ushered them in.

"Oh my goodness it smells heavenly in here." Brin's breath caught when she looked at the woman behind the counter who had a big, bright smile on her face.

Turning to me, she whispered, "You didn't tell me how stunning she is."

"That's because I only have eyes for you and you're the most beautiful woman in the world to me."

"Flatterer." She playfully swatted me.

"It's true, baby."

"I love you," she said.

I sighed. "God, I will never get tired of hearing that."

"Then I will never get tired of telling you." She stood on the tips of her toes and kissed me.

When she pulled back, I smirked. "Are you marking your territory?"

"You bet I am." This time she gave me a wink and my pulse ramped up a few notches.

I chuckled and when I looked over Zander was already at the counter chatting with Capri. "Guess he's hungry."

I took Brin's hand and guided her to the woman waiting. I had a feeling they would get along great and if my girl was serious about the spot next door it just might be perfect.

"I'm hungry too," she whispered seductively.

"You can have extra dessert later," I told her and winked.

"ONE MORE," Brin said, fusing her mouth to mine.

Gyth had brought Dexter over to the condo and he was currently in Zander's room talking to the boys. Since he was staying outside Alley's place he was taking Brin over with him. I trusted the man immensely and knew she was in good hands but was having a damn hard time letting her go.

And she was struggling too.

We'd been standing at the door for ten minutes and every time she was about to tell Gyth she was ready, she'd asked for another kiss instead. Hell, I couldn't complain about that, her lips were like soft, puffy clouds that felt like heaven against mine. And the taste of her mixed with the cherry ChapStick she'd put on had me going back for more.

Brin was an addiction that I was happy to have.

Between the two of us, she may never get out of here.

"Are you two done yet?" Gyth said, coming toward us. "We gotta get going. You two will have to pick this up tomorrow."

I heard the little ones giggle in the background and we broke apart.

"They are always kissy-kissy now," Zander said.

"Tell me about it, my mom and dad do it all the time too," Dexter said.

And then they giggled again and ran back down the hall.

I raised my eyebrows at Gyth. "You're giving me shit and yet your son just outed you about lip-locking habits?" I pointed to the hall. "Give us a minute."

Gyth's deep chuckle shook his huge frame. "Hey, what can I say? When we fall, we fall hard." He walked past us and opened the front door. "I'll be right outside waiting. Don't take too long, it's been forever since my wife has kissed me." He winked and shut the door.

Brin's sweet laughter settled my soul.

"That guy is something," she said. "I'm glad I came to find him."

"Yeah, why is that, baby?"

"Because it led me back to you."

Her words jump-started my heart and had it beating furiously.

"I guess we kind of owe him. Remind me to thank him later. But I draw the line at naming *our* next kid after him," I teased.

Brin froze and her ocean blue eyes rippled with emotion and then everything she was feeling crested like an enormous wave.

I realized what I'd said and while it had just popped out, I knew after a few seconds that I meant it. Our true feelings came from our hearts and sometimes our minds had to play catch up. I'd spoken without thinking and it came from the right place.

She studied me with her gaze and seemed to find what she was looking for. "You mean that, don't you? That you would have another child?"

I brushed away a strand of hair that had fallen into her face and rested my hand on the side of her neck. "With you, yes."

"Rowan," she whispered. "You never wanted children. Not after—" Stopping abruptly, she bent her head. "I'm sorry, I didn't mean to bring it up."

Moving my hand under her chin, I raised her head so she was looking at me again.

"It's still hard, but I know now I can't hide from it. Doing that before cost me a lot." I slipped my hand around the back of her neck and rested my forehead against hers. "Anything is possible with you, Buttercup. I see things differently now."

She placed her lips against mine again and I slid my other hand around her back. I guided it down to her sweet ass and pulled her as close as I could get her. When she removed her warm lips from mine, the loss was immediate.

"I better get going," she said softly. "Gyth is being very patient out there, but I don't want the big bear to start growling."

"One more for the road," I begged.

It took a couple more minutes to extract ourselves from one another, but we finally managed. And then after calling out to Zander and saying one last goodbye she pulled the door open.

"About time," Gyth said, tapping his watch.

"Brother, don't make me shut the door and have you waiting again," I joked. "Now take good care of my girl."

Brin walked, then she and Gyth started down the hall. He yelled back over his shoulder.

"Like she was my own."

"You sound like Kace," I told him. That guy was always stirring the pot. "Don't make me come kick your ass."

"Many have tried and failed," he said.

"You two are something else," Brin told us, shaking her head.

Both Gyth and I said, "I know," at the same time, and Brin rolled her eyes.

When she looked back, I mouthed, *I love you* and she mouthed it back, then blew me a kiss.

I'd hold on to that forever.

Chapter Thirty-Two

BRINLEY

"GIVE US THE DEETS GIRL," ALLEY SAID.

I felt my cheeks heat as everyone let out a loud 'whoop' in agreement.

"This is the portion of the evening when we all spill our secrets and talk dirty. By the time we are done, we are either laughing, crying, or missing our men. Well, all three actually, but not necessarily in that order," Alley added with a wink.

When Gyth and I first arrived, he indeed got his kiss from Summer. I was a little jealous as I was already craving another from Rowan. But as the evening went on I'd been having a blast.

We'd stuffed ourselves with some amazing Thai food, dessert from Capri's, which seemed to be the place everyone loved, and superb wine. There had already been an abundance of laughter but I missed my guy something fierce, so I was worried the crying portion would sneak up on us. I decided to shoot for more laughter. They did say they wanted the deets.

Taking a deep breath I went for it. I wasn't used to talking this way with anyone, except with Rowan. It was getting easier with all these women though. And it was a good thing Embry had retired to the bedroom and was fast asleep.

"The one-eyed monster is not a myth ladies. I found him and he is alive and well. And boy howdy, he sure does know how to rock my world."

You could hear a pin drop, it was so quiet. Jurnee, Summer, Alley, Teal, and Gemma all stared at me and I thought I had botched the whole sharing at the sleepover part of the evening. But then all five of them roared with laughter at the same time and I joined them.

"Lady, I knew you had it in you!" Alley clapped, rubbing her hands together and giving me a cheeky smile before continuing. "Now tell us all about how your fine specimen of a man got you in the sack. And don't take that wrong, all our men are hot. We're not blind." She gave a little shutter and corrected herself. "Well, I'm talking about everyone but my brother. That's just gross."

"Hey now," Jurnee started. "Your brother is smoking hot and he—"

Alley threw up her hands and covered her ears. "Watch what you say and *don't* even go there."

Jurnee giggled as Alley pulled her hands from the side of her head.

"That goes for you with Landon," Summer said, pointing at Alley.

Alley stuck out her tongue. "Well shit, this brother thing can be a real buzz kill."

"There's always Kace," Summer announced.

"Oh no." Teal wagged her finger back and forth. "If I go talking about that right now I'll have to go home earlier than planned and jump the man."

Everyone let out another round of laughter.

Teal was sad she wasn't staying, but tonight she decided

she would hang out and then go home to the baby. It may have something to do with Kace too and I couldn't blame her.

I was having a great time, but there was just something about being wrapped in Rowan's arms when I fell asleep that made the whole night better.

"What about you, Gemma? Any prospects on the horizon for you?" This came from Teal who was surely trying to get the attention off herself.

Gemma was fun, sassy, smart, and beautiful. She should have the guys lined up around the block, but she said that she was too busy with school all the time. So when she told everyone that she had been casually seeing someone from her college, but didn't think it was going to work out, everyone looked stunned.

"Honey, you never said anything about meeting some-one." Jurnee tilted her head looking closely at Gemma as if trying to get a read on what was going on. "And you certainly haven't brought him around."

I had heard that Jurnee was the closest to Gemma after being together in foster care for a time with each other.

"That's because it wasn't a big thing." Gemma looked uneasy and I think it was safe to say everyone there was concerned by the look on their faces. "He just turned out to be too much, you know. Clingy and..." She left the sentence hanging there.

I saw Teal studying her closely. "Did he hurt you?"

"No. No. Nothing like that." Gemma waved Teal's question off and didn't elaborate any further.

It wouldn't be the last time one of the ladies spoke to Gemma about what was going on. I could see everyone, including myself, was picking up on the fact something wasn't quite right.

Gemma grabbed a pastry out of the box from the bakery

and took a huge bite. "These are so good," she announced over a mouth full of food.

I recognized the subject change, being that I was a master at it. Feeling bad, I jumped in to help save her. "Rowan took me there for the first time today."

"So you met, Capri, then?" Jurnee asked.

"Yup. She is not only beautiful but as sweet as all the treats she makes." I paused for a minute trying to decide if I should say what I was thinking and then decided Alley had said we share, so I did. "To be honest when I first saw her I was a little jealous knowing Rowan had been going in there all the time."

I rolled my eyes at how silly I sounded.

"I know, it's stupid, right?" Looking around the room, the ladies didn't seem to think I was dumb at all by the looks on their faces.

"Brin, you're in love with the man. We all have our moments when we get jealous. Don't worry though. Since Rowan got here I have never heard him talk about a woman, Capri included, in a manner of interest or look at a lady in that way."

My body settled and I smiled.

"Well, you know how to make me feel better, that's for sure." I bit my lip and wondered if I should bring up the other thing on my mind.

"What is it?" Teal's scrutinizing gaze assessed mine. "I can see there is something else going on in your head."

I sighed. "Maybe I'm reaching, but have any of you been by Capri's lately and seen the building next to her for lease?"

"Oh, yeah, I noticed that the other day when Landon and I went there." Alley nodded. "Are you thinking about opening a new bookstore?"

My brows scrunched up, confused. I didn't know how she'd thought of that so fast and was shocked.

"I don't know how you read my mind, but when I saw it, I did think about that right away. But I am helping you now and I just don't know if it is possible." My heart sank a little bit each time I thought I couldn't do it again and start over, but when I got a glimmer of hope I could, it soured.

Alley waved me off as Gemma had done with Teal earlier. This time it wasn't her trying not to answer, but more a gesture telling me I was ridiculous. "If you want a new store, don't let anyone hold you back. Certainly not me or I will kick your butt."

"If I do this, I am still going to help you." My pulse picked up. '*If I do this.*' Was I seriously thinking about it? "I will make sure I have time and if you argue I will kick your butt," I told her, throwing her words back at her.

Alley laughed.

"We'll all help you," Summer added. "It will be fun."

When everyone agreed, I realized we had gotten to the crying part of the night. Their kindness touched me. It wasn't the only time the tears had flowed either. Sometime later we had gotten on the subject of my mom and Luke, as well as the past, and a river had run down my face. All the ladies had comforted me, tears in their eyes too.

Teal had even talked more about her mom since she'd also suffered that loss, along with everything else in her life. When she went on about no good men, I saw her watching Gemma closely. Hopefully, if Gemma put an end to what she thought wasn't a good thing, it just went away.

As we went through all the emotions, the wine kept getting poured, and with everyone watching me, I picked up my cell and dialed Rowan. I guessed the missing my man thing was getting to be too much to handle. And to make the moment even funnier than it turned out to be, as well as a little embarrassing, I'd put my phone on speaker.

Only Rowan didn't know that at first. *Oops.*

"Hey, baby, is everything okay?' he asked when he answered.

Crap, I didn't mean to scare him.

"Yes, I'm good, but I miss you," I slurred.

A deep chuckle vibrated through the line. "Buttercup, are you drunk calling me?"

I looked at the ladies and put one finger up to my lips, telling them silently to be quiet. Out of the corner of my eye, I noticed another figure by the hall and realized Landon had walked out. I gave him the silence signal too and he looked like he was about to crack up as he shook his head.

Alley got up and walked over to him, giving him a quick kiss. She wrapped her arms around him, swaying a bit and I realized most of us, except Summer and Gemma, had a lot of wine. And for the most part, we were behaving. Until I spoke again of course.

"Umm, I had wine," I told him and giggled. "Can the one-eyed monster come out to play?"

And that was when there was silence no more. Everyone burst out laughing.

"Dude, you should know better than to not ask if you're on speaker when these women get together," Landon called out to Rowan from across the room.

"Woman, you are getting a spanking for that one," my guy said and a tingle raced up my spine.

"If it is a punishment you are trying to dish out, you better try again," I teased.

"Sweetheart, if you want the…" He paused, amusement lacing his tone. "What did you just call my cock? One-eyed monster to come out to play, I will load the boys in the car and come get you right now."

The ladies fanned their faces and dropped to the floor, holding their stomachs as they laughed uncontrollably.

"Well, I guess since we're not done here, he'll have to play tomorrow," I said and hung up.

I guessed Gyth and Lyric outside were probably getting a call right then, even though Landon was inside. Rowan was most likely asking them to check on the state of our minds. That made me smile. And I'd been spot on when the knock sounded at the door and we opened it to two muscled men with eyebrows raised.

The evening was a hell of a lot of fun.

But I knew in the morning after all the wine, I may be rethinking that.

WHEN I THOUGHT back to the evening before, the headache was worth it.

The next morning all the guys, kids, as well as Teal who had come back, were at Alley's house. They had said every time they had a sleepover that the next morning everyone congregated and had some breakfast.

I'd finished eating an amazing Danish from Capri's that I think Teal and Kace picked up. The woman could probably survive on our group's sales alone. We all seemed to frequent there a lot. Alley had also made pancakes, bacon, sausage, and eggs. Everyone was in a food coma which also seemed to happen a lot with us.

As I leaned back against Rowan who had his back to the wall and we watched the kids finishing up their grub, Teal started babbling.

"When we picked up the baked goods from Capri's, I told her how you wanted to lease the store next to her and open a new bookstore."

I heard Rowan's surprised intake of breath in my ear. It was only the day before that we'd seen the sign and I was hesitant about talking about it at all. He was probably shocked I'd even mentioned it to the girls.

"You should have seen Capri," Teal went on. "She looked so excited at the prospect of not only having a bookstore there since she loves to read but also to have you be the one right next door."

My forehead crinkled in confusion. "Me? She doesn't even know me."

She batted away my comment with her hand and I realized the ladies did that a lot. They were very expressive, not just with their mouths, but talked with their hands too.

"Capri said she instantly liked you and had a good feeling about you. Plus she said your son was adorable." Since she was close to Zander she rustled the hair on the top of his head and he laughed. "I think she's lonely. I mean she loves talking when any of us go in, but I never see her with anyone and she doesn't talk about family. I've never wanted to pry, so I'm not exactly sure. It's just a feeling I get."

"She needs a man in her life. I'd set her up with Lyric but he's taken." Teal winked at the wall of muscle that growled like a grizzly bear at her words.

"He's saving himself for Ruby. Once he pulls his head out of his a—" Alley looked over at Embry and gave her a ha-ha look. She almost owed the swear jar more money and the little girl knew it by the smile on her face.

"Wait, I only know one Ruby. Are you talking about my nurse, Ruby?" I asked.

"The one and only," Alley said. "Lyric and her have a thing."

Another growl from Lyric. He looked the part of a grizzly with his facial hair. Sometimes it was shorter, but he'd let it go a little longer right then. It actually looked good on him.

"We don't have a thing. You are all a bunch of meddlers," he said in an exasperated tone. But I could tell he truly wasn't mad by the look on his face and giving them shit right back.

"Mommy, I want to help with a new store!" Zander exclaimed, taking us back to the original conversation and saving Lyric in the process.

I'd realized then what I had missed at the hospital when everyone was carrying on.

"I miss the last one. But I am glad we are here so it worked out, right?" Zander smiled.

My little guy was a smart one. Because I was pretty sure it was all working out. And I was hoping it stayed that way. Zander had been talking nonstop about his sleepover and at one point Embry asked if she could be there the next time. It had been funny to watch the boy's faces scrunch up, but in the end, Dexter and my son had told her yes.

The thought of the three of them together reminded me of Luke, Rowan, and me. A fraction of sorrow sunk in. I missed Luke so much.

"I want to help too, Auntie Brin," Embry added.

Then Dexter said he did too and Hudson, Embry's little brother ran around yelling, "Me too, me too!"

All the adults were watching me, nodding their heads yes in a show that they wanted to help too. The girls had already told me that the evening before, but every man was doing the same.

"You guys are too much." Tears welled in my eyes.

"That's what family is for, my mama always says," Embry added with a nod of her own.

Looking around the room again, my heart fluttered with love.

"Okay, let's do it!" I said.

Cheers went up around the room and sank into my soul.

"You got this, baby," Rowan whispered in my ear. "And I am right here with you. Always."

I'd felt so lost after losing Luke, taking off with Zander on my own, and losing everything.

But I'd found my way again.

And as sad as things had been, maybe I'd been on my way back to Rowan.

Chapter Thirty-Three

ROWAN

I NEEDED IT TO BE PERFECT.

Or perfect for her.

"Do you even know what you're doing?" I asked all the guys.

The girls had their get-together a few weeks back and it had been our turn. I didn't think they knew what they were getting into when I had asked them all to lunch and told them I needed help.

I probably should have asked one of the ladies, but these guys had my back, and I wanted to do this with them.

So there we all were. Me, Braxton, Gyth, Landon, Kace, and Lyric, all standing in the jewelry store as I looked for the ring that I would give Brinley as I asked her to marry me.

"Of course we do," Kace said. "Well all except this dipshit over here." He leaned over and smacked Lyric upside the head. "He'll need our help soon enough."

Lyric had always claimed that finding a woman and settling down would not happen for him. He'd been a good sport about it but standing in the store he looked different and didn't speak a rebuttal to Kace's comment like he usually would.

We were all looking at him but he was staring down at the display case. Kace glanced over at me and frowned.

"I think this one is nice," Lyric mumbled.

I leaned over and looked into the glass case. The ring he was pointing out was in fact beautiful, and believe it or not, looked as if it would be just what I was searching for. How did he know that? All the other guys took a peek.

"Can we see that one?" Lyric asked the sales lady.

She did as he requested and started to hand it to Lyric instead of me.

"Not me, give it to him. He's the one getting married." His voice was kind of robotic and I was wondering what in the world was going on. "I almost got married once, but I won't be doing that again."

Taking the ring from the woman, I held it in my hand and stared at Lyric in shock. All the guys' mouths were hanging open.

"You never said anything," Kace said.

"It was a long time ago. I asked before I left for the military, and she said yes. I came home and found her in bed with someone else. Marriage called off. It's your typical story. She is blissfully married to someone else now."

He said it so matter-of-factly, but you could tell he was still wounded. Now it was clear why he always said he wouldn't be joining our club. Couldn't blame him either.

"I'm sorry, man," Kace said. "It doesn't matter if it happens all the time or not, when it happens to you, it's fucked up and it hurts. But believe me, there is someone out there for you. And she won't be a cheating bitch." Kace was pissed on his friend's behalf and I could understand. They had a lot in common.

"You guys found the good ones, but I'm not trusting someone like that again." Snapping out of the funk he'd gotten into, Lyric looked at me and pointed at my hand. "What do you think about that one?" Nodding at the ring, I peered down.

"It's perfect," I told him.

He'd obviously searched for rings before and had good instincts. I hoped someday he'd let go of the notion that all women would do what his ex had. We had proof right in front of us that life after that bullshit existed.

"Just don't look at the price," he joked.

When I looked anyway, I gulped. The guys laughed.

"I warned you," Lyric said.

"She's worth every penny. Let's just hope she says yes." That scared the shit out of me. What if even with the hints and talk about the future when it came right down to it, she said no?

"You got this one in the bag," Gyth reassured me.

These guys were fucking amazing men.

Chapter Thirty-Four

BRINLEY

WHAT IF NOBODY SHOWED UP?

I couldn't believe we had gotten everything ready so fast. And while I would be getting more and more inventory of books in, I had a pretty good selection to start.

Not only that, but I had my first author who was doing a signing at the grand opening. Sure, it was Alley and she was my friend, but she was also an awesome writer who had an amazing personality. On top of that, she'd also gotten some other authors she knew in and out of the area to book a private signing at my store in the future.

None of this would have happened in a month if not for all my friends and the kids too. Each of them played a part in the opening of my new store. Including Capri who was making some delicious pastries for the event. The woman was wonderful and had already become a good friend. It was clear she fit right into the mix of all us ladies, and as Teal had mentioned, it seemed like she could use us in her life as much as we enjoyed her being in ours.

So somehow we'd made it through Thanksgiving, which we all spent together, and were just a few weeks from Christmas. My store was decorated for the opening but in holiday style. Red and white twinkle lights were strung outside the door and throughout the space inside. I also had two Christmas trees that were beautifully decorated, one inside and out adding to the ambiance of it all, and there was mistletoe hung sporadically throughout so couples could get a little smooch in if their hearts desired.

Rowan had already put the mistletoe to good use as we set up. Anytime I was near it, he would sweep me into his arms and claim my lips in a passionate kiss, stating we were under the mistletoe.

Like the man needed an excuse to get me to kiss him.

I was thinking about how I could use one of those kisses from him right then as I sat at my desk going over a few last-minute things and let the nerves get to me. Rowan and I were the only ones left in the shop finishing stuff up, Zander having gone home with Summer until later this evening when she'd meet us back at the store a short time before it all started.

As if I had summoned him with my thoughts, I looked up to find Rowan leaning against the door jamb. I scanned his big, beautiful body and everything but him slipped from my mind.

Looking directly into my eyes that had swept back up to stare into his after my inspection, he said, "Penny for your thoughts, Buttercup."

I chewed on the inside of my cheek. What I was thinking right at that moment had nothing to do with my opening anymore and had everything to do with how delicious the man in front of me looked. Faded jeans, a white t-shirt stretched across his chiseled chest, hair mussed, and a light sheen of sweat that shimmered on his face and arms.

Who the hell knew sweat could be so damn sexy?

But on Rowan, it was a turn-on.

Getting up out of my chair, I rounded my desk coming to the front of it and leaned against the wood.

"I was thinking about how I'll feel if nobody shows up except our friends tonight, but then you walked in and my brain went haywire."

Rowan raised his brows, shut the door, and stalked toward me. "I'm glad my presence helped free your mind, but I can do more to make you forget your worries."

Once he reached me, he gripped my hips and with ease lifted me up and placed me on the top of the edge of the desk. He slid his slightly, rough palms up the inside of my bare thighs, and took my skirt up as he went, causing every nerve ending to tingle in anticipation.

Stopping in the vee of my legs, he leaned in and kissed the side of my neck. When his hands reached their destination, he yanked my panties to the side and his thumbs brushed against my sex. One digit slipped inside and I mewed like a kitten as the sensation had me reaching for release in a matter of seconds.

My palms hit the desktop and flattened against it to give me leverage. I pushed up into his touch. He played, bringing me to the brink of orgasm, and then backed off before starting all over again.

"You're a tease," I whined.

His deep chuckle washed over me and then his hands left my body. I was about to protest until he gripped my panties in his grasp and ripped them off. With hurried movements, he got his jeans undone and shoved them along with his boxers down in one fluid motion. Then he reached behind his head with one hand, gripping his shirt and pulled it over his head.

I watched with lust-filled eyes as he came back toward me and grabbed his cock, lining it up perfectly with my core.

A naughty, excited feeling raced through me at the fact that he was naked, while I was almost fully dressed, and I was going to get lucky in my new office. By christening the space it was bound to add some good luck to the opening.

He notched the head of his manhood at my entrance, wrapped his arms around my backside, and then grabbed my ass. In one fluid motion, he sank deep, causing all my air to leave my lungs in a quick rush. I gripped his shoulders and my head fell backward as he set a fast, merciless pace.

"Oh shit, I forgot—"

I didn't care what he had forgotten, I was too far gone, and he wasn't leaving my body. "I don't give a shit what you forgot, don't you dare stop!" I yelled, moving my hands to his ass now and holding him to me.

He didn't stop or protest.

Pounding in and out of me repeatedly, he took me on the journey of a lifetime. His bare cock was nothing like I had ever felt before and it alone with the woodsy scent, mixed with his perspiration, and the growl that rumbled from the depth of his soul had my orgasm bursting free. He kept up the frantic pace until I was coming down from my high, then he slammed home one more time and emptied his warm seed into me, sending me over the edge again.

My head hit his shoulder and my body felt like Jell-o in his embrace. I listened to his heavy breathing and the thump of his heart as we both sat motionlessly.

Once I could move, I raised my head to look at him. "That should tide me over through the opening."

"Glad I could oblige." He leaned over and nipped my lip and then gave me one of the kisses I'd been hoping for right before he'd walked in. "Should we talk about it?"

I knew what he was referring to without him coming right out and saying it. "No. I loved every second of it."

"Me too, baby."

I'd never experienced sex with anyone but Rowan and while I should be freaking out about us not using a condom, I just couldn't. The feel of him pulsing and bare as his release exploded inside me was something I didn't have words for.

My body was relaxed thanks to him.

I HAD WORRIED FOR NOTHING.

The place had been packed and the evening had gone better than I could have ever dreamed. It seemed to be a huge success and I was on cloud nine. Not only had I sold a lot of books, but people signed up for the book club I'd decided to start at the store, and Alley sold all of her books as well.

Everyone had mingled while I met some wonderful people who truly loved to read and got talking to them. Because let's face it, if someone wanted to talk about books then I was all in, they just better be prepared for a long conversation.

Once things had wound down and the only people left were our friends, I kicked off my shoes and sighed, flopping myself onto the comfortable couch in the reading nook area I'd created. Zander raced up and jumped onto my lap, then wrapped his arms around me, hugging me tightly.

"That was fun, Mommy. We got our store back!"

My son had always loved being with me in my other bookstore and helping me out. When it was always just the two of us, our bond had been stronger than Gorilla Glue. It still was, but now we were stuck with some other truly amazing people. And he and his dad had grown so close in the short time they had been together.

"Yes we did, baby," I answered with a broad smile on my face.

Clink, clink, clink.

From the front of the room, the sound grabbed my attention and I looked over to see Rowan standing with a glass of sparkling cider in the air, tapping it with a spoon. We'd used cider so everyone was safe and the kids could join in. But the ladies had already made a toast, making me and everyone else laugh as well as shed a few tears, so I was confused about what he was doing.

"I said yes, Mommy," Zander whispered in my ear and then turned to look at his dad.

What in the world did he say yes to?

"Brin, I'm so damn proud of you." He'd been looking at me but glanced in Embry's direction and pointed at her, addressing her specifically. "And I know I owe your jar, so put it on my tab." Embry giggled and then Rowan's gaze swung back to me. "You did an amazing job here tonight, and I know you will keep doing a fabulous job. Let's all toast and take a drink to Brinley."

I hadn't realized everyone had glasses in their hand and Summer was pushing one in mine as everyone sent up a cheer.

Tears pooled in my eyes and threatened to spill over.

Rowan turned and set his glass on the front counter and kept talking. "Losing someone you love breaks a person's heart. I should know it happened to me." He took a deep breath and I couldn't believe he was bringing this up in front of everyone we knew. "When I lost my sister, that was the ultimate loss. I let the fear of caring for someone just to lose them or hurt them consume me and I walked away from you. From *love*. Losing you ruined me, but I did that to myself. I hurt us both."

I saw liquid gather in his eyes and seeing the big, strong man I loved with all my heart struggle and cry, killed me. I took a peek around and everyone else was feeling him too.

"Baby, somehow I got lucky and you found your way back to me. And not only that but you gave me a second chance I didn't deserve. Which I'm so thankful for. I am honored to be here with you as you set off on your new journey and I am praying you will let me be there every step of the way."

"Here it comes," Zander said, softly.

I didn't have time to contemplate what the heck was going on with my son because Rowan pulled something from the pocket of his black slacks that he changed into when we got ready for the event and dropped to one knee right there in front of me, our son, and our friends.

"I already asked our son and he said yes." Rowan looked at Zander, giving him a big smile that melted my heart.

Our son knew. That's what he'd been hinting at and Rowan had asked his permission first. I felt dizzy as so many emotions swam in my head at once. But love was front and center.

Rowan brought his gaze back to mine. "I will never walk away from you again. I promise to love you and our son for the rest of your lives as well as any other children we might have. And you will always be able to count on me." He took another deep breath. "I love you, Buttercup. Will you marry me and make me the luckiest man in the world?"

As he finished both mine and his tears spilled over at once. I didn't have to tell my son to move so I could go to his father because he jumped off my lap screaming yes as he raced over to his dad and launched himself at him at full speed.

"You did so good, Daddy!" Zander yelled and everyone burst out in laughter.

Rowan hugged his son tight and then got to his feet as I moved off the couch and mimicked my son. I ran and threw myself into his arms, screaming, "Yes, yes, yes!"

Everyone cheered and when I pulled back Rowan kissed me senseless.

"Not again."

I thought that came from Dexter but wasn't unlocking my lips from my soon-to-be-husband to double check.

Then I heard Embry say, "This always happens. *All of* them like to kiss, but one day I will too when I get married."

More laughter rang out when her father, Braxton told her, "That will not be until you're thirty, young lady."

And since I knew Embry was always saying she was going to marry Dexter, I knew it was him that commented next.

"Thank gosh."

Nobody could hold it together. They laughed so hard they were in stitches.

All of this went on as we stayed in our lip lock. When Zander wrapped his little arms around us, we finally broke apart, and Rowan scooped him up into his arms.

"Hang on to me little man, there is something I have to do," he told Zander.

With our son hanging onto him like a monkey, he grabbed my left hand and slid the most perfect ring onto my finger.

"When's the wedding?" Kace called out.

Gyth smacked him upside the head. "Shut up, knuckle-head, he just asked her."

I didn't care if he'd just asked me or not. I couldn't wait.

"As soon as possible," I told everyone.

Rowan gave me a sexy smirk. "Name your place and time, sweetheart, and I'll make you my wife."

Another round of cheers went up around the room.

"Is tomorrow too soon?" I whispered to Rowan. "I've been waiting all my life for you."

He laid his palm on the side of my face and caressed it softly. "Anything you want, Buttercup."

I was only half kidding and teasing him, but I'd marry him in a heartbeat. I'd been scared for nothing. Rowan wasn't going anywhere.

We had the rest of our lives.

Chapter Thirty-Five

ROWAN

SHE SAID YES.

The fabulous fucking sex as I took Brinley in her office earlier not only helped her but me too. We'd been talking like there was a future for us, but I still worried she would decide that saying yes to my proposal was risky after I'd left before.

I'd contemplated whether to pop the question in front of everyone, but it truly had been great having them all there to witness one of the best days of my life.

With our son spending the night at Dexter's and after getting everything cleaned up, the two of us headed home to celebrate.

She had said our earlier lovemaking would hold her over until after the opening and since it was over, I was ready to take my future wife to bed.

Little did I know, when we walked out of the bookstore life had other plans for us.

And they weren't good at all.

Chapter Thirty-Six

BRINLEY

"Somebody help me!"

The teasing plea flew from my mouth after Rowan pinned me against the closed bookstore's glass, gripped my butt firmly in his hands, and kissed me breathless. I was pretty sure the man had a butt fetish. But since it was my butt he worshiped and I reaped the benefits from it, I was okay with that.

We'd just finished locking up Brinley's Books—the same name I originally had for my first store that I'd lost—and I was looking forward to getting home so I could have my way with my fiancé.

My desire was amplified tenfold when he pulled back from the kiss we'd just shared and nipped my earlobe, shooting tingles straight to my honeypot, as the girls liked to call it, when joking around.

"Can we go home so the one-eyed monster can come out to play?" I teased.

Rowan growled and grabbed my hand pulling me toward the lot his truck was parked in at the side of all the buildings. Someone was in a hurry. I giggled, but the laughter died when we got to the front of Capri's place and her light was still on. Everything else was closed and she was still at it.

I yanked on Rowan's hand to stop him and knocked on the window to get her attention. When she walked out of the back with an unsure look on her face, I felt awful. I probably scared the poor woman. When she noticed it was us, she walked over and flipped the lock, then opened her door.

"Hey," she said.

"We can help you finish up," I told her.

She motioned us with her hand to keep moving. "No way. You two get out of here and celebrate, I'm just about finished. Scoot."

"You sure?" Rowan asked her.

"Positive." She smiled sweetly. "Congrats and I'll see you on Monday."

After dropping Rowan's hand, I walked the few feet that separated us and embraced her in a big hug. "Thank you for all your help again tonight, I couldn't have done it without you."

She squeezed me back. "You're welcome. Have a good night." She released me and winked before shutting the door and locking it again.

Rowan picked my hand back up in his when I returned to his side and we started walking again. We'd just reached the edge of the lot closest to the main street when everything went to hell.

Quickly.

My free hand flew to my forehead to shield my eyes from a pair of high beams that flicked on from a vehicle parked up ahead making it difficult to see. An engine roared to life and when the driver revved it, my blood ran cold. The sound took me back to the evening I wished had never happened. The night my son and I were ran off the road.

A truck shot forward coming straight toward us as Rowan simultaneously released my hand and pushed me behind him. He yelled for me to get down as shots rang out. Without thought and doing as I was told, I dropped to the ground. My hands and knees hit the concrete with a brutal impact, gravel digging into my tender skin before I was flat on my stomach.

Pop! Pop! Pop!

Rowan followed me down and landed right on top of me, the weight of him heavy against my body. Was he trying to shield me?

"Don't move," he commanded in a strained voice.

What was wrong?

He didn't sound right. Scared to death, that time I didn't do as I was told as I pushed with all my might to move his solid frame off me and rolled him to his back. Rowan groaned in response. My hand was wet and I squinted as I moved it closer to my face.

Oh my God.

"Somebody help me!" I screamed, my words a repeat of the half-hearted plea I'd spoken earlier. But this time, there was nothing playful about my desperate cry for help.

Blood! There was so much blood!

I can't lose him like I lost Luke.

"Where are you hit?" I wanted to run my hands over every inch of him, but I didn't want to hurt him.

He took a couple deep breaths. "Leg and arm."

I was yelling again, my frantic mind spinning, when Capri burst from the door at the front of the bakery and started running toward us, the sound of squealing tires echoing in the distance of the cold December air.

"Get back inside now and call 911!" Rowan yelled at her as the sound of the engine grew louder and my fear spiked.

Oh God. Was he coming back?

"Baby, are you hurt anywhere?" he asked.

Wide-eyed, I shook my head. "No, I'm okay." The scrapes on my hands and knees didn't count when he was lying there with gunshot wounds.

"I want to keep it that way." Beginning to sweat, he nodded toward Capri. "Go with her."

He'd lost his mind. "Not on your life." I jumped to my feet. "I am *not leaving* without you."

Capri hadn't listened well either. When she reached us, both of us bent and grabbed under one of Rowan's arms. He winced and cursed in pain as we got him to his feet, which wasn't easy. He was built like a brick: hard, heavy, and tough.

I heard him mumble as we worked our way toward Capri's open door. "Stubborn women."

The sounds of wailing sirens grew closer as the roar of the truck engine disappeared. He must have gotten scared off knowing that help was on its way.

"I called them when I heard the shots," Capri said, answering my unspoken question.

The woman was getting hugs for a lifetime from me.

We reached the door and Rowan told us to sit him down on the pavement as multiple cop cars and an ambulance screeched to a halt in front of us.

I dropped to my knees beside him as people swarmed around us and took in the blood dripping from not only his leg, but his arm too.

He'd protected me and got shot in return.

Sucking in a breath, I tried to control the shaking that started at the thought of losing him. But he was strong and he was holding his own. However, when he winced in pain trying to pull his phone from his pants pocket, the trembling got worse.

Seeing him hurt was killing me.

I frowned. "What are you doing, give me that." Lips set in a firm line, I took the phone from his grasp as the paramedics started assessing him and getting ready to put him on a gurney.

"Call Braxton," he told me. "Tell him what happened and to meet us at the hospital. I need someone to catch the son-of-a-bitch!" Rowan was mad and with it some strength in his voice grew which gave me more hope that he'd be perfectly okay.

I didn't want to take my eyes from Rowan for a second to do anything but help him, yet I knew that if I didn't make the call he'd do it himself and he was in no shape. With shaky hands, I dialed Braxton's number.

"Baby, tell him to call Gyth right away too so he is being vigilant. I don't know what this jackass knows or where he might go next."

What if my son would have been with us? The thought had me panicking and I couldn't think straight. Thank God he wasn't but what if this crazy man went after him anyway?

Everything seemed to happen at once. Capri was talking to the police, the phone was ringing in my ear, and they were loading Rowan on a stretcher when Braxton answered the phone.

Thinking it was Rowan, he addressed him and that was when I burst into tears.

I faintly heard Braxton calling out, but I couldn't speak.

"Here, honey, let me have the phone." Capri put her palm out. "You go with Rowan and I'll follow you to the hospital and bring the phone with me."

Mechanically, I placed the cell phone in her hand and hustled to the ambulance. I jumped in and sat beside my fiancé. When his hand reached up and touched my face, his thumb brushing over my cheek and wiping my tears away, more instantly fell.

"It's going to be okay, Buttercup. I promise. Nobody is going to take me out when I am about to marry the love of my life." Despite being shot he gave me a sweet smile and winked.

He was going to be okay, but was I?

For a while, which felt like an eternity, I wasn't sure if Rowan would be okay. Earlier I'd thought we would be together for the rest of our lives and an hour later I was wondering if that time had already come to an end.

Luke didn't get to live out his life as he should have and I missed him so much. I wouldn't have been able to fully catch my breath again if I'd lost Rowan too.

"I love you so much," I whispered, resting my head on his stomach.

"Ma'am, I'm sorry, but you can't lay on him like that," the paramedic said.

A low growl vibrated against my head and erupted in the small, closed space. I'd heard Rowan growl before but it was usually a sexy one. This time it said, 'back off' and the man bit his tongue and didn't say another word. And that was damn sexy. My man was a beast.

He brushed his hand softly through my hair. "Where were we? Oh, yeah, hearing you say I love you is always music to my ears."

I promised right then to tell him from that day forward how much I loved him.

And the second I could, I was going to make him my husband.

~

THERE WAS STANDING room only in the hospital emergency waiting room and very little of it.

That worked for me because I couldn't sit if I wanted to. I'd been pacing the floor like a caged tiger going out of my mind waiting until the moment I could lay eyes on Rowan again. I just needed a glimpse to be a hundred percent sure that he was going to be completely fine.

I glanced over at Zander and was thankful he'd finally fallen asleep. Summer gave me a soft smile as she held my son in her arms. He looked peaceful. Something he wasn't when he'd come into the hospital looking for his daddy. Gyth had already explained that Rowan was hurt in a gentle, easy way, assuring him that he was going to be okay, but Zander was beside himself.

The feeling was mutual.

I could only imagine how frightened he was after what had happened to us and me having just been in the hospital recently, then having his father wind up there too.

Alley came up beside me and laid her hand on my arm. "Hey, sweets, can I go grab you some coffee, water, or anything else?"

Shaking my head, I took a deep breath. I couldn't drink or eat anything, my stomach was twisted in knots. "No thank you."

It seemed as if we'd been waiting forever. "Why is it taking so long?"

Deep down I knew he was going to be okay. Everyone from the paramedics on the way, to the nurses we'd talked to so far had said he was, but the more time that went by, the more I started to panic again that they were wrong. Summer, being not only a nurse herself, but also my friend, had also reassured me that he was going to be just fine. And it was her that seemed to settle my nerves more than anyone else. She was bright, maternal, and had a way about her that set people at ease.

Hand still on my arm she rubbed it up and down soothingly. "It shouldn't be too much longer."

All of our friends were waiting too. Hence why there was no room. We were a big group. Everyone was there but Lyric and Kace who'd had a hunch they wanted to check out, along with checking on Stella, crazy Michael's wife.

Rowan had been a big part of helping to make her feel safe, which is why this stuff was happening, but we didn't blame her at all. Rowan would be glad to know she was alright and I would too.

The poor woman had felt horrible when she'd heard about her husband—who she was divorcing—hurting Zander and me. But she'd been through hell and she deserved to be free of it.

Of the monster.

My breath caught in my chest when I turned and saw Braxton walking toward us with purpose. I hadn't even seen him get up.

"I was in the hall and ran into the doctor. Poor guy, I practically pounced on him asking for information. But it's good news. Rowan is all stitched up and heading to his own room. Both the bullets, the one that hit his arm and the other that hit his leg, went straight through and missed everything vital."

All the air swooshed out of my lungs.

"The doctor said he was demanding to see you and Zander. He is as ornery as ever from the sounds of it. Once they get him settled, a nurse will come get you," Braxton said, walking up and pulling me into a big hug. "He's okay, Brin. You can rest easy now."

Letting him take my weight, I leaned in soaking up the

hug and the relief of the news. But then I pulled back, wide-eyed. "What if it happens again?"

Just as my pulse started to race, Lyric and Kace walked through the automatic doors that led to the emergency waiting room and saved me from the panic attack about to take place. Lyric gave Braxton a nod and then looked at me.

"We got him, the shooter is in custody. Michael won't be hurting any of you or Stella again."

I almost sunk to the floor in relief. Braxton grabbed on tighter, holding me up. Needing to show them my thanks, I pulled myself from his arms and rushed over to hug Kace, then wrapped my arms around Lyric. Pulling back, I looked up at him. "Thank you."

Lyric nodded and then his eyes widened as he took in someone behind me. I turned to see the nurse Ruby standing there watching us. Or it may have been only Lyric she had eyes on. She seemed to snap out of it and looked at me.

"Hey, Brinley. You guys sure all seem to make your way through this hospital a lot. I'm just glad you are all doing okay." She snuck another peek in Lyric's direction before bringing her gaze back to mine. "If you'd like, you can see Rowan now. But only a couple back at a time for now, okay?"

I wanted to find out how they caught Michael, but I wanted to see Rowan more. He was in custody so my mind was at ease and someone would tell me the details later.

"I can show you to his room," Ruby said.

"Let me just grab our son." It may have been awful to wake the little guy up when it was so late, but he would want to see his father and know he was okay. I rushed over and gently took Zander from Summer's arms. Her smile was bigger now that we knew all was well with Rowan.

Everyone was so close and I was glad each of our friends could rest easy now.

Zander's body wrapped around me and his head lay on my shoulder. "Is Daddy okay?" he mumbled. "I want to see my daddy."

"That's where we're going, baby. You can see him right now." I hugged him tightly and walked back over to the nurse.

"We're ready."

The pretty redhead's gaze roamed over the rest of the group. "I'll do what I can to get you all back to see him shortly. Follow me," she told Zander and me.

"Sounds like they are keeping him twenty-four hours to monitor him and then he should be set to go home," Ruby said as we walked down the hall.

That wasn't very long but I just wanted our family together in our own space. It had been a long night and we'd been through a lot.

"So, what do you guys all do that brings trouble to your doorstep so often?" she asked, keeping the conversation going. When I glanced over, she scrunched up her face. "Sorry, it's none of my business, and I didn't do that very well."

She'd been wonderful when I'd been in the hospital and if the ladies were match-making her with Lyric it was obvious they liked her as well.

"It's okay." I turned back to watch where I was walking as I told her about the guys working for *No Surrender,* what they did there and for people in their homes, venues, etc. I realized when I got done that she hadn't said a word and was incredibly quiet.

Looking back in her direction, she looked lost in thought. I wasn't sure what that was about but I didn't ask because we'd come to a stop outside Rowan's room. My heart picked up and I was almost nervous to see him.

Silly, I know.

Once I walked in I didn't want to spend another minute without him again even though I knew that wasn't possible. We both had lives and work outside each other. But at least we'd be married soon.

"What are you waiting for?" Ruby asked. "Go on in."

I looked down at the stunning, diamond ring on my left hand, that sparkled with love. And an idea formed.

"Ruby, do you think you could help me with something?"

"I'll surely do my best. What did you need?"

A big smile split my face.

I had asked Rowan if tomorrow was too soon.

Chapter Thirty-Seven

ROWAN

GOD, THEY WERE A SIGHT FOR SORE EYES.

When Brinley walked in with our son in her arms, I had sunk into the bed and my body finally relaxed. I'd been so full of tension that it had almost hurt worse than the bullets that had penetrated my skin.

Not knowing what had been going on while I got checked out and stitched up had me full of nervous energy that was so charged it could have lit up a hundred city blocks. I didn't know if my family was okay. The shooter was still at large when I'd been brought in and I'd had no clue where he might go next.

"Hey, Buttercup," I said softly, as I extended my hand to get her to come closer. "Are you okay? Did someone check you over?"

"I'm fine, I wasn't hurt." Brin's face held a layer of hesitation as if she was assessing me to see if I was really okay though. I just wanted her by my side. Zander must have heard me call out to her because his head popped off her shoulder and he turned his head quickly in my direction.

"Daddy." His sweet voice calling out to me settled my frayed heart and soothed my soul. My family was okay.

My girl and my son came closer and all I wanted to do was yank them down on the bed with me, hold them, and never let go.

I patted the space beside me and Brinley shook her head. "We need to be careful of your injuries, are you crazy?"

"I'm crazy about you. Now both of you get down here closer and let me feel you." I smiled. "It wasn't so long ago you were saying something similar and how you wanted to feel alive. Now it's my turn, but we'll save the good stuff for later." I winked.

"What good stuff?" Zander asked.

Brinley gave me a sharp look to silence me and I chuckled. "He's talking about the amazing treats from Capri's."

"Oh, I want some of those, they are awesome."

With another stern look from my girl, she gently set Zander on the bed next to me without saying anything else. Zander scooted up into the crook of my arm and nestled his head on my shoulder, stretching out his legs.

A look of panic swept across Brin's face. "Honey, be careful of your father."

"I'll be okay." I needed to assure her. "It's my other side, so get down here and kiss me before I lose my mind."

Without hesitation, she leaned over and sealed her lips to mine. Everything inside me felt right the moment her mouth hit mine. I closed my eyes and sighed.

Zander made a silly gagging sound. "Not this again."

Brinley and I pulled apart and burst into laughter. Zander followed along. I tried to hold in the curse and the wince that it caused, making my injuries a bit painful. I managed to keep the cursing at bay, but not the look that crossed my face.

Jumping back she scowled at me. "I told you we needed to be careful."

I stretched out my good arm and lightly grasped her wrist. I wouldn't let them give me any more hard-hitting pain meds when I got into my room because I wanted to be awake for when I finally got to see my family. I was hurting some, but I wasn't going to let on and make her worry. "Baby, come back here before I lose my mind."

Zander hadn't moved. I looked down and realized he fell asleep in a second flat after commenting on our kissing. My boy was tired. Brinley's gaze followed mine and her face softened at seeing our son. When she looked back up at me I saw tears shimmering in her eyes.

"They caught him," she whispered. "I don't know how yet because Lyric and Kace walked in right before I was told I could see you. I realized I didn't care how, just that they had. My only concern at the time was getting back here to you."

I still had a hold of her wrist and I pulled her in close to the bed again. "Sit please?"

She didn't argue this time and sat down just below where Zander's feet stopped. It wasn't close enough for me, but we weren't moving our son right then, he was exhausted.

"I'm sure Lyric or Kace will fill us in. I was sick with worry about you guys and I'm so fucking glad the bastard is in custody. I knew the guys would come through, but I didn't know what might happen in the in-between time." I took a deep breath and tried to calm my rapidly beating heart. "I'm so sorry he ruined your night."

Brin was back off the bed. But she didn't go far. She was just getting in a better position to grab the sides of my face in both her hands, and with her beautiful blue eyes staring into mine, she said, "He didn't ruin anything. We won't let him." Then she leaned in and kissed me once again.

Pulling back just a smudge, she whispered, "I love you. Now and forever."

I felt a tear hit one of my cheeks. "Don't cry, sweetheart. It kills me, you know that."

"These are happy tears. I'm so thankful you are okay and we don't have to worry anymore." She stood tall and bit her lip. It was endearing and sexy. I loved watching her do it. She did it when she was thinking hard or unsure about something.

"What's going on?" I asked her.

"I have a surprise for you tomorrow." She glanced at the clock on the wall. "Well, technically it will be later today." More lip biting was going on. "Remember how you said for me to name my time and place? And you also said that I could have anything I want?"

My already hammering pulse picked up further because I knew exactly what I had said and what she was referring to. "I did say those things and I meant them."

She smiled. "Good. Because we're getting married right here in a few hours."

I felt my eyes go wide.

"How is that possible?" Confusion set in. "And what about a dress, cake, and planning all the fun stuff?" I'd give her anything she wanted, but I didn't want her to regret it later. "I don't want you to miss out on that and resent me for it later."

She shook her head side to side. "Rowan, all I want is to not wait another minute to be Mrs. Brinley Caddel."

It was my turn to smile. "Damn, that sounds amazing."

"So, is that a yes?" Anxiety rolled off her in waves. "You will marry me today?"

"I want nothing more. And I will do anything you want, Buttercup. I told you that."

She squealed a little and Zander stirred once more. "What happened?"

Brin moved her hands from me and rubbed our son's back. "Nothing, baby. Daddy and I are getting married today."

"Yay," he said sleepily and then was sound asleep again.

"So we are doing this. Are you sure?" Brin asked.

"Don't make me spank your ass right here in the hospital, woman. I've never been surer of anything in my life."

She sat back down on the edge of the bed. "How did we get here?"

I chuckled. "You gave my stupid ass another chance, that's how. And we're meant to be."

"Yeah, we are." She grabbed my hand and held it in hers. "Which also means I know your stubborn self well. Don't think I don't know you're in pain." The look she gave me was pointed. "You're going to take something for that and get some sleep."

She left no room for argument so I would do as she asked. But only for a few hours.

"Fine, but only this once because I'm going to be fully awake when I make you my wife."

"Can't wait," she said. A dreamy, excited look crossed her face and it was adorable.

"I have one question though," I added after something important dawned on me. Battered with the events of the past hours, my brain was a little foggy so I hadn't thought of it at first. "How did you manage to get the hospital to let us get married here? And what about our friends?"

Lord knows our group would be bent and pouting for

months if they were not there when we said, 'I do.' Especially Kace and Gyth, they were big babies.

Her face lit up. Bright and more beautiful than ever. "They'll all be here." She winked at me just as I'd done her minutes before. "And I have my inside sources to make it happen."

Damn she was amazing.

∾

THIS WAS REALLY HAPPENING.

I looked around the room that was packed like sardines and shook my head in amazement.

My girl and her inside source, which I found out was none other than nurse Ruby, had actually pulled it all off. They, however, did have some help since I saw some of Capri's goodies on the counter under the window along with a bunch of flowers someone brought in. There was even a big plush, brown teddy bear.

"When we fall, we fall," Gyth said, patting my shoulder, a smile on his big mug. "And I get to do the honors and hitch the two of you."

I gave him a stern look. "No funny business, you hear?"

He slapped his hand to his chest over his heart. "You wound me. Would I do something like that?"

"Shithead," I mumbled.

"I'll leave the good stuff to Kace. He has a knack for that kind of thing," he replied.

A deep chuckle rumbled from deep inside me. These guys were a pain in my ass. But when your friends were as close to you as brothers, that was the way it worked. Thinking of family brought on a bit of sadness and it settled heavily in my heart. I decided to not hide my feelings.

Something I'd been working on since Brinley walked back into my life.

"I wish Luke and Jelena were here."

Gyth gave me a look that was both sympathetic and sorrowful. I knew he wished Luke was here too. "They are watching, so marry your woman, and live the best life you can with your family. That is what they both would want."

"Thanks, man." I gave Gyth a chin lift and he returned the gesture.

Gyth smiled then and clapped his hands together hard. "What do you all say we get these nuptials going?"

Everyone's eyes snapped to him and cheers went up around the room. A little loudly for the small space, but who the hell cared? Nobody by the looks of it. And besides...

I was getting married.

It didn't matter that it was nine in the morning and we were in a shoebox-sized hospital room. Or the fact that Gyth had to help me stand and I was wearing a pair of loose, black sweats and a white, short-sleeved t-shirt so the clothes didn't rub against my bandages. The pink tie dressed it all up.

A laugh rumbled, silently inside me.

Where the tie came from was anyone's guess. Embry probably had something to do with it. Maybe she made her mom help her get it for her dad at one time. The girl was crazy about pink, it was her favorite color just like it was Brin's. So pink it was.

Everything was coming together. The fact we didn't have to look over our shoulders anymore as we started a new life with each other was amazing. After the shooting, Lyric wanted to check on Stella and he also had a feeling that Michael would go to her home after the attack on Brin and me because that was what he'd done after he caused the accident, sending my woman and son off the road.

His instincts were right. Him and Kace together caught the fucker in his truck outside Stella's home and that was the end for him. For all he'd done, the guy was going to prison for a long time.

It was time to put him out of our minds and our lives.

Ruby had helped put this together and was monitoring things so I watched her walk in from the hall and stand back by the door to the side. Everyone else, but Brin, Zander and Summer were already in the room. All our friends, old and new. As we waited I watched Lyric looking out of the corner of his eye at Ruby. I also saw Kace notice the same thing.

When Gyth had said he'd leave the good stuff to Kace, he wasn't wrong. I was just glad it was directed at someone other than me when I saw him bump Lyric's shoulder and say, "You know I officiate weddings too. Want to make it a double?"

The look on Lyric's face was priceless and I couldn't help the laughter that escaped when he told Kace very quietly, "Fuck off."

They happened to be right by me so I heard it all and from the chuckle that came from Gyth, he had too. It was a good thing Embry didn't. She had enough money as it was and Lyric would have gotten a good reprimanding from her mother over that one.

Summer walked in and went to stand across the room next to her son. Music started to play from someone's phone and the song, *From This Moment On* by Shania Twain and Bryan White started to play. The words were so right and every beat, every lyric of the song swept through me.

The door slowly swung open and my breath caught in my throat. The sight of Brinley walking in wearing a simple, but beautiful silk, white dress, with a sparkling, elegant diamond necklace around her neck, and a small pink bouquet of flowers in her hands, as our son led her toward me was almost too much to handle.

Tears gathered in my eyes.

She was stunning.

My son was proud.

And when they stopped in front of me, the tears fell down my face.

It was Zander who spoke first as he handed me a piece of paper he'd held in his free hand, which I hadn't even noticed. To only be five, he was mature beyond his years.

"I have a gift for you, Daddy." He held the piece of paper out for me to take and then kept talking. "Since you and mommy are getting married I wanted to ask you if I could have your last name like mommy will. So you can fill this out and then we will all be a Caddel."

Sniffles could be heard all around the room.

I looked down at the official papers that would allow me to be added to Zander's birth certificate and change his last name. God, these two were killing me in the best possible way.

Not able to squat down with my leg yet, I motioned for Gyth to pick Zander up and stand him on the bed. Once done, I wrapped my arms around him and hugged him close. "That is the best gift ever and I can't wait. We'll fill these out together as soon as we get home, okay?"

"Okay. Now can you marry mommy?" He pulled back and looked at me, then attempted to whisper, but it still came out loud enough everyone heard. "She said she has been waiting a long time for you and is a nervous wreck. So I think that means we need to hurry."

Laughter replaced the sniffles and I smiled like a loon, turning to wink at my girl. "We better get a move on then, right?"

Zander nodded vigorously and Gyth put him back on the ground where he stood next to his mother as she and I faced each other.

I grabbed both her hands in mine as Gyth started the ceremony.

"It wasn't that long ago that I told Rowan things had a way of working out. And here we are." He looked at me and smirked. "I told you so by the way."

I shook my head. He just couldn't pass up the chance to throw in a jab.

"Both Brinley and Rowan told me they wanted to say a few things to each other so I am turning the floor over to them. Brinley, ladies first," Gyth told her.

Brin took a deep breath to get her emotions under control.

"I have to make this quick because I've been waiting for you for so long. I never imagined you would ever feel the same or I would become your wife but I had always dreamed of it." She swallowed and her voice shook. Everything about her was beautiful.

She collected herself a bit and then continued. "You were one of my best friends, but also so much more, and while I wish Luke could be here with us, I know he would be happy that the two of us found each other again. You gave me the most precious gift in the world. Our son. And now you're giving me yourself for the rest of our lives." Tears trickled down her cheeks. "I love you, Rowan. Always have and always will."

How was I supposed to follow that? I would say what was in my heart.

"For your benefit and mine, I will also make this short and sweet because I want nothing more than to make you my wife. I'm not as good with words as you are so bear with me." Shit, I was nervous. This gorgeous woman did that to me. "I was an idiot."

I didn't get any more out because everyone laughed and Kace yelled, "We already know that, now get on with it!" That just caused more laughter. I glared at him and he just chuckled. I don't know who was worse sometimes, him or Gyth.

Once the noise died down, I started again.

"I always had feelings for you, Brin. I was just too scared to admit it and ran. You also were my best friend, and while you always will be, you are also the only woman I have ever loved. Our son and you are the best gifts you can ever give me. I don't need anything else." Like Brin had done, I took a deep breath. "I love you, Buttercup. I don't even have the right words to express how much."

The smile she gave me lit up the room. She glanced down at the ring already on her finger.

"I didn't want to take it off and we don't have one for you yet with all of this done so spontaneously," she said, "but I promise we will get one."

Without hesitation, she pounced. And although she was careful not to hurt me, she was quick. Closing the space and going up on her toes, she wrapped her arms around my neck and locked her lips with mine. The tip of my tongue licked the seam of her mouth and she opened as I took the kiss deeper.

"Let's keep this PG, there are kids present," Kace called out.

We broke apart as everyone cheered. Then Gyth's booming voice echoed around the room.

"I guess since the kiss is out of the way already, I now pronounce you Mr. and Mrs. Rowan Caddel. If you want, you may kiss the bride again."

And I did just that.

When we broke apart, Zander was hugging our legs and Brin whispered, "We made it."

"Yeah we did, Buttercup." I winked at her and she smiled.

Everyone gathered around, congratulating us. The feeling of my wife next to me and my son by my side was the most amazing thing in the world.

My heart was complete.

EPILOGUE

Brinley

TWO MONTHS LATER

I HAD THE MOST AMAZING VALENTINE'S GIFT.

Who knew we could fit so much in just a few months.

Rowan had healed, we had our first Christmas and New Year's together as a family, which we celebrated with all our friends. Brinley's Books was doing amazing and I was still helping Alley. Capri had become one of my closest friends and was close with all the other ladies as well. And another change was that Ruby and I kept in touch. It was only here and there, but I owed her so much and told her that when we talked.

On top of all that, we had taken Zander with us and went back to our hometown to visit my mom, Rowan's mom, Luke, and Jelena's grave sites. It was hard but therapeutic at the same time. They were all such a huge part of us and always would be.

We did manage to stay clear from Luke's parents which was a blessing. And we had been house hunting and just put an offer in on the house all three of us fell in love with.

Zander especially liked it because it happened to be right down the street from Gyth, Summer, and Dexter's house. I wasn't sure what would happen to the condos but Rowan and Gyth owned them so for now they weren't being sold. There was a rumor that another one of Braxton's military guys may be coming to work for him so someone would probably be using it again before long.

I sighed and looked in the mirror.

Zander was with all the kids at Braxton and Jurnee's house with Jurnee's parents who were babysitting, along with another teenage girl they used sometimes. With that many kids they needed an army. All the adults were meeting at *No Surrender* and going out for Valentine's Day.

Glancing at my slim, pink dress I wore for the occasion I decided I better cherish it while I could.

"Hey, baby, are you—"

Rowan's words died as he stared at me from behind in the mirror.

"I was going to ask if you were ready, but please say no." He gave me a sexy smile and wrapped his arms around me. With a sigh, I sunk back into him. "I think I need to examine this outfit thoroughly and it may take a while."

I giggled.

We truly didn't have much time, but there was something I needed to do. "I have a gift for you."

"Is it under this sexy dress?" Rowan asked hopefully while wiggling his eyebrows.

I turned in his embrace. "Umm," I hesitated. It kind of was. A giggle escaped. "In a way I guess it is."

He looked confused.

"Remember when we said our vows and you told me that our son and I were the best gifts you could ever get and we were all that you needed?"

Biting my bottom lip, I waited for his response.

He nodded once. "I do remember and I meant it."

"Well, I hope this next gift will be another of the best you ever get. And I guess in a way we are giving each other a gift, technically."

He waited quietly as I took a big, deep breath.

"I'm pregnant." I blurted. "So see, I guess it is kind of a gift under my dress right now." For a second time, I nervously waited for him to respond.

His eyes widened, mouth dropped open, and then he picked me up and spun me around. "We're having a baby?"

He placed me on my feet. "Oh shit, baby." Panic contorted his features. "Did I hurt the baby?"

I busted out in amused, happy laughter. This time he got to go through it all with me and if he was worried about me now from just a little spin, I could only imagine what he was going to be like later.

"It's fine," I reassured him.

"We're really having a baby?" He whispered the question like he could hardly believe it. It was endearing and my heart beat with so much love.

"Yeah. We are really having a baby. And if it is a boy, I'd like to name him Luke. If it is a girl, I would love to name her Jelena. What do you think?"

He blew out a breath and I could see the emotions swirling in his dark eyes. "I think you have a way with gifts. You have made me so damn happy, baby. I also think the names are perfect, whichever way it turns out."

My heart was so full it nearly burst. "I love you, Mr. Caddel."

He leaned over and gave me a sweet kiss, then took a small step back.

"I love you too, Mrs. Caddel."

A beaming smile split my face.

This was my life and I loved every second of it.

Then it got even better.

"I have a gift for you too," he said. He'd already given me so much, including a gift certificate for a girl's day at the spa that cost a fortune so I could take all my friends.

"You already gave me a gift."

Without another word, he dropped to his knees, lifted my dress up my thighs and when he leaned in, his warm breath floating over my sensitive lady parts, I decided another gift sounded pretty damn good.

I also decided being late was worth it, when his lips pressed against the front of my pink, lace panties.

Damn I was a lucky girl. Or should I say a lucky wife.

"Sorry we're late," I announced as we hurried to meet everyone in the lobby.

While it was Valentine's Day, there was no way we were letting anyone get out of coming that night. All the couples were there and Lyric was chaperoning Capri and Gemma both. I smiled at everyone and waited for someone to remark at any second. My money was on Alley or Kace.

I should have actually bet someone because I nailed it.

"You couldn't wait for a little nookie until after the date," Alley called out, causing my cheeks to heat.

"We were celebrating," I told her.

She raised her eyebrows in question.

I looked at Rowan to see if he wanted to tell them or me.

"Go ahead," he encouraged.

I smiled brightly. "We're having a baby."

All the ladies rushed me, squealing and wrapping me up

in hugs. The guys surrounded Rowan, clapping him on the back. Congratulations were given out and it was such a tremendous feeling.

Bliss washed through me and my heart beat with a tidal wave of love. I looked over at Rowan and we exchanged smiles, mouthing *I love you* to each other.

Then the door burst open and everyone jumped to attention.

We'd had our fair share of scares, each and every one of us, so the way the person rushed in when we were not expecting anyone alarmed us all.

My gaze took in the woman standing just inside the door, looking unsure, and if I'm being honest, more than a little petrified.

"Ruby?" I said aloud.

She looked like Ruby, but also completely different. Gone was the sweet, makeup free, girl next door, red headed nurse. The woman in front of us was all dolled up with makeup, sexy clothes, and looked like a model.

Her eyes scanned the whole group and I could tell she was about to run. It hadn't escaped someone else in the group either.

Lyric walked over to where she stood.

"Ruby, what's going on?"

A note of fear crossed her features.

She glanced over at me. "Remember at the hospital you told me where all the guys worked and what they did?"

I nodded my head to confirm I did in fact remember telling her that. "Yes."

Her eyes left mine and they went back to Lyric who was standing only a foot away from her.

"I need some security cameras and an alarm system put in at my house. I have to protect my family."

A deep, intimidating growl erupted from Lyric, and Ruby took a step back. I could see from where I stood he felt bad that he'd scared her. He closed the distance again. "You don't ever have to be afraid of me," he told her.

They stared at one another, both breathing hard and he said in a softer voice, "Nobody is going to hurt you and your family."

"Talk about déjà vu. This reminds me of when I walked into this place. I hate what is happening to Ruby, but she is in good hands," Teal whispered.

"I thought we were going to have to work a lot harder, but she came right to him," Alley said.

Turning to look at the ladies, it dawned on me what they were talking about.

"Here we go again," Summer said.

"You think?" I asked.

"Oh yeah," Alley said.

I looked back at Lyric and Ruby.

And I had to agree.

It's not the last you have seen of this amazing family of friends. Join the group again as they watch Lyric fight his undeniable feelings for the spectacular red headed nurse in, Ruby's Savior, coming December 2022.

ACKNOWLEDGMENTS

To my best friend, Jaimee Parker...I am at a loss for words. Good thing I finished the book before that happened, lol. No really, there are not enough ways to say thank you for everything you do for me. This is book five and none of them would have been possible without you. You are a beautiful soul, the best friend anyone could ask for, and you are a saint for putting up with me. Love you to pieces.

A special thanks to everyone who helped me with this book: My awesome cover designer Avery Kingston, my beta readers, Crystal and Leslee, my editor Angel Nyx, my arc group and all the amazing readers supporting me through each and every book. And to my family who has faith in my writing journey.

ALSO BY C.M. YOUNGREN

SOUL SISTERS SERIES

Entwined Souls

Unlikely Souls

Forbidden Souls

NO SURRENDER SERIES

Teal's Savior

Brinley's Savior

ABOUT C.M.

C.M. Youngren is an author of swoon-worthy contemporary romance whose dream in life is to own a bookstore slash coffee shop.

She lives in Oregon with her husband, two daughters, son-in-law, a precious granddaughter, and her fur babies. She loves 80's music, movies, reading, and adores singing regardless of if she can hold a tune or not.

Hopelessly addicted to watching The Voice, driving her best friend crazy, and eating tacos are some of her favorite things.

Made in the USA
Columbia, SC
29 September 2022